August '16

#ABP

ISBN-13: 978-1514790205

ISBN-10: 1514790203

Published by Thomas Bartlett

Copyright 2015 Thomas Bartlett

All rights reserved.

Cover Art and Design Claire Giles

Website: http://thomasbartlettbooks.com/

Twitter: @TomAlicante

Facebook: https://www.facebook.com/tom.alicante

Americans Bombing Paris

by Thomas Bartlett

This book is dedicated to Michael Lydon 31st January 1976 – 23rd May 2011

Peace and Love my Friend.

"Let us not pretend any of us care one jot for the other. Let us not continue with that conceit. Let them not stand there and say they noticed the blood on my sleeves."

Johnny

Chapter 1

Saturday November 9 2002

I stood on the balcony as the first planes came screeching and screaming in. Flying lower than they needed, to get a better look. The view must have been amazing. Plunging low, then high, undulating at something around the speed of sound. Even American Air Force pilots were unable to resist the allure of Paris. Le Top Gun.

My vista was the Bibliothèque François Mitterrand, The National Library and blue vapoured sky. I peered into clunky, sad and lonely apartments normally filled with small furtive people. People who went to bed understandably early once sated by the nightly variety shows. The buildings were all empty now. Only a few of us had chosen to remain in the city. Fewer again had managed to elude Le Thermo-Nuclear Imagination Facilité, like for fuck sake? This device had scanned buildings inside the Périphérique, the ring road, for two days before the bombing looking for people like us. People who had stayed behind.

Watching the news on her poxy little Parisian television earlier, pictures of the Paris Périphérique, full of people as they all flocked to watch Le Spectacle American d'Horreur Militaire. Dignitaries had managed to have a stand built, where they could sit placidly and view turgidly the planes; or sit turgidly and view placidly the planes. The scene reminded me, and them, of Formula 1.

The French military had also shown up, just in case things got out of hand. Although I struggle to see how they could have got much further out of hand. But then again, since the beginning of this whole thing, nay my whole life, my credulity meter has been unable to establish a zero point.

I suppose if anyone was to blame for the resulting debacle you could start with Osama and the whole planes into the building thing. Or failing that we could go back a bit further and blame the CIA for teaching Osama so well. Indeed one could be forgiven for admiring the level he'd reached. Osama was the Luke Skywalker of passive aggression or peaceful violence or some other such thing. The Soviets of course shouldered some of the blame for invading Afghanistan or maybe we should flick back one more page and blame the Americans and the Soviets for using small poor countries as geopolitical gladiatorial arenas. That would probably cover it until we went back to blaming Hitler, followed by Versailles which of course leads us to the French. Creating a beautiful shiny gold cercle vicious. Whatever about any of it, American fighter bombers/washer dryers were flying over Paris about to release their cache, a French word if my memory serves me well, to release their cache of death.

These bombings were what in recent days had come to be known as punishment bombings. In fairness to the Yanks and Prez Bush, they had given us an un-coded warning and allowed the French authorities five days to clear the city. Negotiations had been continuing at a high level, and over the week certain bombing rules had been laid down both sides seemed happy enough about. Obviously the Eiffel Tower was out of bounds, a monument popular with both Republicans and Democrats. Try as the French left did, and wow wee did they, they were unable to have Euro Disney nominated as one of the "Five Targets". We had not been told which five targets were chosen, as the Yanks claimed this would provide an unnecessary risk to their service men and women. Never before in the history of risk has an army so well armed been so easy to put at risk.

The missing piece in this tragic bloodied jigsaw was Iraq, a country America had already been at war with not so long ago, you might remember. Well, they decided that all that ordinance sitting in Fort Worthless, Fort Apache and Fort Bravado and all those other bloody forts needed a destination, or as they say, a customer. The geniuses behind the arms trade, and believe me there are many, have figured out that war is their customer. So naturally they must spend their marketing and advertising budgets on creating new customers, or as we would call them, targets. Iraq had long been a good customer to these companies, for that is all they are. Saddam, as everyone now knows, was once a friend to the Yanks and fought against the evil Persians next door. Mr Hussein was, in terms we might understand, a Yankee military franchise, up until he decided to expand into areas already owned by other franchisees, in this case the humble Kuwaitis. In the Middle East it is hard to discern what is meant by normal words but humble seems to mean on our side, sneaky and/or rural.

There is no need to dwell on what has passed, or as some left wing scholars call it, history, the Americans have taught us that at least.

Ignore everything relevant for relevance can kill a war and ruin a market quicker than anything 'cept education. Flash forward and as the clouds of dust settled in New York, as the strategists spun everything they could from the whole thing, Iraqis once again heard their name being bandied about. Naturally for the average Iraqi this was bewildering and, might I suggest, terrifying. Most Iraqis have not had the benefit of a Harvard MBA in instantaneous strategic decision making. These MBA courses have a long and storied list of illuminated alumni and aggressive academics, many of whom work for think tanks. Think tanks, I understand, are places for people whose thoughts are more dangerous than tanks.

Well so far so de rigueur right? The French got the memo about Iraq and the weapons. The French and their own Prez, Chirac, had been grooming Mr Saddam for a franchise or two of their own. France decided to continue, or as they lyingly claimed, to begin trading with Iraq.

This put a whole lot of people in a bad position right? McDonald's for one, as they made more money in France than any other country in Europe, so you could hardly expect them to boycott France, sacre fucking blue. Bordeaux wine makers, they could not reasonably be expected to stop selling wine to the Yanks now could they?

America went crying to the UN about France not abiding by the UN resolution regarding sanctions on Iraq. The French then used what is fast becoming known as the Israel defence i.e. if they don't have to do it why should we. In my day that was called the Jimmy Muppet defence, as he was the only one using it on the playground. But I digress. The playground is a veritable bastion of maturity, pragmatism and humanity compared to the world of geopolitics.

All this toing and froing had been happening over the last few months. How these cretins had cajoled us into this situation was still unfathomable, safe to say it had not been for lack of MBAs. If only all the MBAs and Grandes Écoles (French Ivy league slash MBA equivalents) were made to fight naked to the death instead, live on television. This is absolutely the best solution to all of these problems; hence it shall never ever receive any credence whatsoever.

So Bush and Chirac squared off and Bush came up with an ultimatum at the end of October. Or, if you know Bush, somebody else came up with an ultimatum and he delivered it. Many people who understood little except the limitlessness of their own glibness would often say Bush was the biggest victim in the whole sorry episode. They would then sigh and maybe shake their empty heads. Of course the children who were about to die in Iraq might have had something to say about that, but then they did not grow up as the President's son and all the pressure that entails. Bush announced if France did not cease trading with Iraq the United States of America would be forced to take action.

Chapter 2

Saturday November 9 2002

Sitting in her old green armchair long eroded into someone's lumpy shape, I lit one more stinking cigarette. The planes' noise was now all there was. As the little black death sticks dropped from the planes, the juxtaposition, the awkwardness, strained my visual comprehension.

I was frightened.

They were carpeting the Bibliothèque François Mitterrand with bombs. It was a wonderful idea the whole carpeting with bombs instead of annihilating or destroying. The military must have been up all night thinking of that one. Bravo. The Library held a copy of every book ever published in France.

As the first black stick gently fell against the reflecting windows it seemed at first, to press the glass, then all at once...............pause, softly poof, something inside the library pulsed forth once like a cartoon heart, reversed inside and rippled out through the suddenly four dimensional image.

BOOM.

CHAOS.

The noise caught up and the sartorial elegance of the whole thing, the goddamness of it, whooshed away out of me. I stood suddenly *surprising myself and fell down as hell yanked my marionette strings. Somewhere inside the throbbing echo chamber of my brain I understood the building had been hit, the floor dropped away from me. I screamed noiselessly into a deafening drum. But of course nobody could hear me. Half crying I felt the heat on myself, firstly on my arms. I saw my arm hair sizzle down to nothing. The noise. I cannot describe the noise because I could not hear, I could feel vibrations but I didn't understand them. As more and more of the planes unloaded all that shiny black ordinance, or product, or death; the ground destabilised and no longer was something I could trust. I was holding onto the railing on the terrace as I slipped down the horizontal plane. The rumbling rolling earth made standing or thinking or shouting impossible.*

Briefly. For are not all thoughts brief? And are machines not just our own attempts to emulate the animals? I hark back to why I ended up in Paris. Maybe to prove something to myself? More than anything, I had wanted to have a look before I was too late. And no, I do not mean I foresaw any of the horror I saw and caused, I mean before I was too old. I'd been twenty five, almost unaware I'd missed out. Twenty five had become old as I approached it. Twenty was now considered to be the new twenty five. So that made me thirty.

"How exactly had that happened?" I would often reflect as I made a few decisions.

Paris, when I arrived, was a hotbed of DIY and loneliness. It was shocking how people could really be that into DIY.

The strange thing about it was the general level of common or garden misery in Paris. Working and walking amongst Parisians was bliss. I felt like a god of laughter and mirth, a giant too amongst those petit Galois. The first hint of trouble came six months after the planes went into the buildings. The world still shook. Paris was not going against the Yanks yet. McDonalds was full and the two Presidents were doing deals with one tyrant or another. I understand the French see themselves as the European Yanks. They talk about it all the time. The French have their own culture in a death grip, of love apparently. Obviously they need some gentle help from the ghettos, suburbs or whatever the hell you want to call them? Districts perhaps? But for some reason they refuse to ask for or accept it. France refuses to believe in cultural evolution, thus Paris gets older and nobody is sure if this is OK or not?

I can't say I was unaffected either. I had been disappointed by Paris at first, but then like anyone you grow to know and then love, it becomes your reason and your heart. Once you start having sex in Paris it makes more sense. Grubby beauty. Armpits and sweat parallel its structural memories of smoke and ruin.

I was watching along with the world as the Yanks made ready to wreak revenge on the poor Iraqis who, whilst I am sure deserved it, could surely have been cut a little bit more slack. I felt for those guys.

I was melting, I was inside the final moment and the dimensional sides themselves were folding out and flattening; boom boom boom. Folding out, as, all at once, I saw everything again, no clearer now, that would be a lie, just again.

I remember the night Bush told the United Nations he was going in to Iraq no matter what happened. We were in a drinking club of our own creation. We'd discovered our bodies' reserves and had set about using them. So whilst we drank, the world decided to go to war. Or not war, it was something else these days, one couldn't call it war. But then war was always one step ahead and one step behind one never knew, so war it is, and it was that we called it.

We went to restaurants which only served duck and chips. Girls more beautiful than each other, walking around knowing full well their beauty was their only hope if it really was war. I had restarted smoking twenty five minutes after arriving in Paris for the first time. The war gave us all an excuse. We drank in Paris like Musketeers on leave. The day jobs we ghosted through paid us enough, and the rest, well, we were known men. Bar owners wanted us. They paid for the privilege. Bought us, like booze eye candy. We provided authenticity, falling around arguing, low grade menace, all taken well. We were a motley crew, one given to easy stereotyping. There was me Johnny, one American named Dean, two English called James and Peter and a couple of international extras we tolerated because we were nice people.

The French had been ignoring the sanctions for a few months. France had already said there were no weapons of mass destruction and that America was lying. The Americans were very sore about that.

"Matter o' fact that's 'bout the most sore I don ever seen them 'bout anything" as Huck Finn would say.

The news seemed to suggest that Bush had said if France did not cease trading with the Iraqis then the US would be forced to take action. If a million geese laid a million golden eggs, the media could not have been happier.

Chapter 3

Wednesday October 2 2002

That particular Parisian Wednesday evening was a typical one, the trains full of people who couldn't quite grasp why they'd bothered to go to work that morning. Many knowing full well nobody would have noticed, understanding nothing they'd done had made a damn bit of difference. Months 'til the next holiday. Just the beginning of scarf season really. People would wear scarfs in Paris until the first of May irrespective.

I used to love the trains, the Métro, legging it around. Racing the anonymity. I bannister slid my way down to the La Défense trains, wincing at the chicken and egg sandwiches spot-lit along the way. What's the story with them eating the flesh and the egg? There were also lots and lots of shops selling tat. Selling umbrellas, selling earrings, selling ties.

I surfed the escalator down to the beginning of Ligne 1, the best line for all its crap. I got a seat and sat down pulling out one of the many books I read to shut out the voices. The trip was sexy all the way. One never knew who'd get in, that day my book was not numbing enough to prevent me from looking up every stop. I watched the feminine silk softnesses all doe eyed board the train slightly frightened, slightly irritated at not yet having found a beau and a house in the suburbs to hide from the eyes.

The lovely rocking rigour of the train aided my transition into sultry evening. I was the first arrival into the bar, my hips caressing each zinc corner, skidding onto the seat. The bar man an English guy, but not Peter, a guy with a pronounced skill for talking about serious things which mattered not a jot, offered me his hand that I shook. We foreigners quite liked some of the French traditions. The handshake amongst ourselves an obvious one. Kissing every girl we meet, another favourite. The bar was an island bar with the staff as the show. We were the audience. I sat on a stool looking at a mirror, watching behind me, as was my wont. There was nobody but me and the English, the TV blurting away in the background, coming up to the six o'clock news. I had decided on Guinness, probably the best all round drink in the world. A brilliant starter drink. Reasonably heady, soft on the stomach, at least at the beginning. Full of iron, yeah right! I had three newspapers under my arm. I was determined to get to the bottom of the day's news. I raq, E raq, A raq.

"Had we really only ever been talking about oil" I wondered, as oil poured down from the skies in some kind of cruel practical joke. But of course it was not the oil that was falling and burning, it was everything else. All around, everyday products dripped down on me, foetal but on my knees. The first real drop glooped onto the back of my neck, made me spasm as another drop burnt a fist sized patch of some synthetic material from my jumper exuding more oil.

"Has everything in the previous ten years been made from oil?"

Yes.

Yes it has." I thought through the wincing pain.

I had of course known this would happen. It's not as if we hadn't been warned. But I, like a few other burning fools, was still there acting the maggot. I needed to get out of the building. I turned, scorching surfaces at all plains. I began to choke again and twisted towards the floor, lifted and fell; ruining my knee. I groaned.

Wednesday evening in the bar there'd been none of that. I'd been into my second Guinness my shoulders lower now, loosened by the over ripe alcohol. I was smoking a delicious cancerous cigarette, knee deep in current affairs, stuff that really had nothing to do with me. Did I hope to stop it? Did me knowing about it matter one single bit? Did it fucking fuck. But still I learnt as much as I could. Scanning and harvesting, dividing the whole by the number of newspapers read, and flipping it on its central axis spinning like a globe in my head.

The television news was beginning in slow motion. Shapes flinging through the air; bang, boom, wham, then landing for no apparent reason. All the while the inane panicking music score, typical dumb ass television news opening, another thing the French are the same as us on. Boring. But then tonight was not that boring. The first image was American planes on a previous bombing mission. The headline reader spoke with all the haughty dignity expected of a member of the aristocracy. "Tonight President Bush has warned France to cease all trade with Iraq or the United States will be forced to take action."

Outside her door, the central atrium of her apartment block was not yet burning, but opening the door had encouraged the flames to reach long, hard and orange up above me slapping and licking the ceiling, yet only pretty stellar sparks of dust sprinkled down at first. I swung myself up and then down, forward as I half scampered down the stairs. I lurched forward almost too quickly nearly blinded by the grey smoke billowing biliously from all the vents. I needed to get out immediately. I had two more floors to go when the second loud explosion blew. I looked up, all I could see was beautiful fire, strong and unfriendly. I made it to the front door as the staircase started to crumble, rupture then avalanche. Solid wave like whooshes propelled me out the hall to the front door, rammed me against it, the glass held.

There was apparently no other news that Wednesday night. The English lent back slouched up against the wall, he might as well have been chewing a barley stalk as he watched along with me. Bush was angry that Chirac was continuing to ignore his demands. Bush may have thought something else but we could not tell. He said he was angry. The Americans seemed to be alluding to Chirac trying to curry favour with his Muslim voters. Laughable as a motive, but not admittedly as a by-product. There was also some suggestion of anti-Americanism. Also laughable.

Chirac had much more time for Americans than for Arabs would be an OK thing to say. Not controversial. The crux was that sanctions would hurt American business, whereas bombing is America's business. That crux was nowhere to be seen in any of the reports that night. It hadn't really occurred to me yet either. The whole story was making me feel a little sick. My mouth filled with bile but it passed as I swallowed and used the cigarette smoke to damp down the sick.

I pushed the door quickly, surprised I was now running as fast as my scorched legs would allow. The building in front vibrating and rippling, boom, boom, thwack. I had to get away. Right was where I was going, but things were slanted against me. I fell left and worried about myself and thought of life being over and how I felt like a fool, a trivial fool; the worst kind. I thought of the Stonethrowers and how we had aided and abetted this stupidity, but then I thought of her and my heart squeezed acute and tight. My twisted gut wrenched inside for 30 years of nothing, one month of something. I could hear the next wave of planes coming; I had no idea from where. I had to move. One of my legs was more painful than the other. It depended on something I could not fathom. I thought of all the slight silly stupid things I had ever eaten or done or said. At least I'd had a good time, I think. But that didn't give me any solace, just then, none.

I needed a purpose and I'd had a purpose all along. My only purpose was to find her and bring her away. She'd have stayed, she did things she understood straddled the confliction of good or right or nice or bad or dark. She understood, I think always, that standing watching them bomb was important. Standing to the side of the fray was not something which could be excused any longer. She'd have avoided the evacuation searches.

Where she should have been was her apartment, my lookout, but the squat was closer to the Bibliothèque. But but but. But nothing. No more buts. In my defence I had not allowed buts to stop me. History had overtaken me. And the Americans may have saved me. My beautiful precious irrelevance once threatened had been reimagined once again. The times had changed to catch up with me and leave me behind.

I needed her then. I thought of hope and what that would mean. I couldn't quite have hope, not yet, not as I hunkered on the corner once again remembering something I'd nearly grasped before: in war everything is war. Nothing is exempt. I lay against a wall which due to its slight curve protected me from the falling debris. That wall was war; the road was war, the noise war, all war. Not one thing, everything.

Not beautiful, not even close, just smoke, ash and destruction, mainstays of the human experience. Although it had been a while for us all round these parts. My grandparents would have recognised the scene from when they were young, which is probably why they died. Old people have more sense than to go on living. They get to the stage where they can no longer bear to watch us wreck the place, off they sidle. Good luck to them, they were right, but it's too late now. They'd made the same mistakes we made, learnt too late the same truths we now felt jolting against our confusion and our epoch making bullshit; truths demanding to be let in.

Chapter 4

Wednesday October 2 2002

Wednesday night in the bar we argued and decided to do something. We wanted to form a club within a club, call it the Stonethrowers. It was going to be an action group rather than a drinking group. I feel the same way as you do about movies within movies, or worst of all plays within plays, but this was more of an offshoot, a tributary. I wanted us to cause some problems for corrupt rich people in powerful positions. What kind of problems? Well, stone-based problems. They are going about their business while their company exports arms to blah blah blah and they get hit by a stone in the head or the back. The great thing about using stones as a weapon is that they are untraceable. Untraceable and sore.

Lo-fi is the way to put these venal fuckers under pressure. Obviously the head is a bit dangerous, god forbid they might actually feel one iota of pain, one single electrical jolt of discomfort. Floating on gilded lilies getting stones lofted onto them in their well-guarded little ponds. What could be better than that? We were goading idiot right wing media to write beyond inane articles about how the Stonethrowers wanted to stone the world right back to the Stone Age. They of course obliged. Right wingers on the whole are statistically more fun to go drinking with, but when you sober up with them beside you in the bed, you need to kill them unless they have repented.

The way to look at all this is of course simply. The Stonethrowers grew out of the exasperation of a group of guys in Paris who got fed up drinking and wanted to give something back. Namely stones. Namely stones thrown with accuracy at the guilty, rich and powerful, thrown at men. Innocent poor people get fucked all the time. In most countries getting fucked is seen as an acceptable by-product of being poor, an in-built motivation to work harder. This of course is millionaires' drivel. The Nasdaqians and the Footsies of this world need to feel the cold breath on their neck like the rest of us. The cold wispy breath of a stone cold projectile. In this case a projectile even older than Coca Cola. Frightening.

We were to have no other agenda. In the modern world agendas drag you down or back. No matter what you do someone will always ascribe an agenda to you. Tack one on. We decided to try to hit a good mix of people from the right and left. We put together a list of targets with final refusal being given to the Stonethrower himself on each target. Next we needed to train and that was when the fun began, as well as when I met her.

From what I can discern journalists now have become unwitting, for they are without wit, mouthpieces for corporations, governments, power, and general evil. Corporations say it, they resay it. Maybe I am missing something; so corporations only have our best interests at heart? No they are actually pissing in our rivers. Or the other argument, which seems to be while allowing corporations to do whatever the living fuck they want, we benefit through some magical capitalist process. Hmmmmm.

Journalists' chief enemies seem to be bloggers, principles, the environment and anything which even slightly suggests socialism. They have been so utterly co-opted and embedded, henceforth they need not be included in anything other than firing squad lists, first against the wall etc. Sports journalists are not included, although they need to watch themselves. I am of course referring only to Western journalists as their counterparts throughout the rest of the world, while technically the same, do not have anything in common with them. Honourable exceptions yada yada yada.

Drink had been taken. Me Irish. Two English guys; James and Peter, one yin one yang both good lads. They embodied all the great things about England. James a rough lad from the city, patriotic every day, liked a brawl, enjoyed being racist, and strangely was the only one of us with black friends, which sums something up about the English contradiction. He worked in the French stock exchange, the Bourse.

Pete, a southern public school boy with beautiful dark skin, when drunk he could be described as affable, at any other time he could be described as diffident and affable, he was given to understatement and pink, he ran the bar, the Bug. Our American guy Dean was totally up for it. East coast hairdo with a west coast morality, he looked like an Italian sitcom actor of no repute. He worried about the environment and worked as a salesman for something or other dot com. We had our share of hangers on, but all in all we were a bunch of people whose masks had slipped off one night talking. Without our masks we admitted to each other deep down that we did, contrary to what we said and how we acted, we did care.

Chapter 5

Saturday October 5 2002

Our care was to manifest itself in stone throwing, not pelting. Carefully aimed projectiles, formed by the earth from its own angst and distress, then thrown at fat white men's heads. Yeah what about it? Tough is all I can say. We needed to learn how to throw properly. We met that Saturday down by the tree, outside the cool squat in the 13th arrondisement. The squat people watched us avec trepidation at first. Mostly kids from vertical mirror lands, unable yet to see their own reflection in their actions.

She watched down from the tall window, stood in it, pretend coy to the side. Looked down at me like I was going to rescue her, rather than doom her. I knew half her face first, the left side. I knew it just by looking at her. She watched us from start to finish as we set up targets thirty metres away and then threw. I didn't speak to her that first day so I'll leave her out of our story until I do. I find if I think of her at all, I can't keep hold of any other thought. She blurs then scythes my mind through. My eyes try to water now as I write this, not weep, water. I have no emotion left with which to weep, just infinite celestial tears.

For us the whole process was about trying to find some real traction. The smooth sided world made us want the action. Want something tangible. We'd all grown up on war, been fed it every day, safe war, TV war. War was guys on holiday. The book, The Guns of Navarone does not have a single woman in it. We tried to understand why the world had to be like it was. Either overly feminized or overly macho. Designed with the loser and the winner in mind.

We worked jobs, with the exception of Peter, that had no worth. James was pretty wealthy and wasn't ashamed but he knew his posting was horse shit of the highest order. Spend one day looking at any TV business station and it is obvious we're mocking ourselves. Economists abound. Economists are really only financial historians. But unlike normal historians who by and large know their place, Economists purport to know what is going to happen. They have graphs. Don't make me laugh. Worm tongues the lot of them. Courtiers for the financial aristocracy. Whatever happens there is always one predicted it. Base covering lizards.

But I tangent until I am horizontal. I remember the whole thing. That first day none of us could hit shit. But we spent four hours hitting it anyway. We shuffled and scuffled around kicking up the dust looking embarrassed but we didn't quit. The trust fund orphans peered at us from behind the pressed finger putty windows. The squat was a beautiful building, once a mill, I think. In Ireland it would have been described as a castle. Towers on either side, decent graffiti, suitably baroque maybe?

The four of us lived in montage, for we were the bastard children of television. My mum was a TV, my Dad a VCR. These future kids, they were made of silicon and understood tech like I can program a video recorder. We were the television generation, most of us sired in its useless garish glow. Fat lot of use television was. It was useful for about an hour then along came computers. Good bloody luck.

The day was October. Is this shit really important? It was dry, not crisp, more damp, although not soggy. The sky was water spilt charcoal and vague as dragged cotton whisps. We were to a man, from countries where the weather was worse. So you will understand the weather was never that important to us.

I am Irish. Relevant in many ways later on, as it explains my stupidity. I was the only Irish person in our crew, still nearly too much Irish. Statistically one point one Irish person per group is a surfeit. But being the only Irish person in a group, incredible. You could draw on your whole Irish life up 'til then as a joke reserve. I was also the leader. Although the only reason I was the leader, far as I could figure, was that I was. Everything I did back then; I always ended up being in charge. I've had a kind of loose manipulation thing going on my whole life. I strive at the beginning of any relationship, sprinting towards the winning podium of friendship. Once there I allow it to disintegrate and trickle down between my fingers.

The ill-informed say Freud reckoned Irish people were un-psychoanalysable. My understanding would be, it's not a depth with us, it's a circle. There is always somewhere else to go. Even when I'm talking to my best friend, I am lying to him and to myself, he is doing the same. I have a natural distrust of anyone who likes me, or of anything I say being overheard; I worry it will be used against me. In Ireland people do not rat, or whistleblow when they should.

There is a skew in our national character. Exactly half of the country conforms to the stereotype of the feckless circular speaking Irish. Of the other half, well around half have left. Figure that one out.

When the light began to fade and everyone was tired and the sugar had mostly gone, we felt resolute, we'd begun our adventure. Pete stood there and looked into the middle distance. He was always doing that. The middle distance was his Mecca. He'd thrown poorly.

"I will do better next time, gentlemen. Rest assured."

James laughed and slapped him on the back of his pink shirt. "We need to talk code names and the only place I think we can have that conversation is the fucking boozer. One thing this stone throwing malarkey has managed to do is keep us off the sauce for a Saturday afternoon."

When he said this I mildly panicked. Calculating how much drinking time I had left 'til Monday. Not enough.

"Come on lads let's leg it. I'm gagging." I insisted, no longer pretend supine.

Dusk now amongst us, I couldn't really see her anymore, but could. I asked her later how long she'd stayed there, but she never answered questions like that, looking at me as one does a perplexing oaf. That time she rolled over on top of me and we somehow managed to fuck again, although I was not really hard. She was good like that. She needed to be. She was, after all, going out with a functional retiring alcoholic who threw stones and worked in a magazine for expats. Lucky we both had a sense of humour.

James, Peter, Dean and I went to our favourite bar out of the thirty three thousand bars in the greater Paris area. Saturday was a quiet day there. We knew the place and had carte blanche. Besides the odd wayward tourist nobody was likely to bother us. It was called the Bug. Normally Peter hated going there; people always wanted to talk to him, expected him to greet them like a thirties club owner pressing the flesh played by Mickey Rooney or Sinatra, loose ties to the mob.

"Alright lads we need to talk targets. Targets and logistics"

This was Saturday October 5 2002. I remember those days as the best of my life. Often people let their youth pass them by. Not us. For we were engaged. We drank and we fought and we got angry and we fucked and ate duck. The gentle suffocation of suburbia awaited two of us. James craved it even then. He secretly yearned to go back to yob England, to lie down on some fresh towels and drift off into the world of cold wet concrete and fabric softener, of tarmac smells rising with the fresh rain, sharp jagged window frames cutting your finger. Kids? What the hell are they? None of us ever ended up having any.

Dean was already married. Americans and their early marriages. He was happy then, I suppose, but not for much longer. I'd always imagined the French marital leash he yearned for would gradually tighten around his bull neck, snap and he'd fall forward once more. But that Saturday when we walked our limbs hung loose. We were formidable enough. The French youths would not deal with us because, although we were mostly white, we were tall and obviously foreign. Yeah so we felt free.

"Targets, I am going to hit the head of SocGen." Peter spoke first with a gregarious smiling head tilt.

"I think I am going for someone from Novartis," James all default defiance.

"Me, someone to do with petrol. Probably Totale." Dean nonchalant and maybe the coolest one out of all of us, at first glance another shiny faced American, at second an outsider slumming it with the Euros.

I laughed "Jeez lads, difficult, fuck sake. They'll not be easy. Each has his own security detail."

Peter was not to be deterred by things like difficulty, especially as he was going after the banks. "I want that plague so bad. My bank account's with them, I think it's past time they paid. Every emotion banks make me feel makes me want to kill someone. But I'll refrain from that as yet, settle for hitting some twat with a stone. We think at least two of these guys will attend the OECD conference next week. James says he can get us in."

So that was how it went. Rivers of pints flowed through us. And on we talked. We were sore and wanted something done. Peer revolution perhaps; though no grand idea like that occurred to us. By that stage in their lives most people have realised that nothing they do makes a damn bit of difference, the only thing available to do is get yourself a slice of revenge or settle and shut up.

As the night wore on, we drifted into the nickname, codename thing. Sure there was a military aspect to our mission. Most of all we wanted to assume new identities, to disappear away from ourselves. We were not sure we liked ourselves anymore. Like how much can a man like himself if he works with paper and phone calls? That's a job for a robot really. We were not proud and the stone throwing was the manifestation of that. The pointlessisation of the world continued apace. And we were at the vanguard. I wrote and sold little ads in a classified mag. James phoned up rich people to ask them to let him bet money on the corporate ponies. Dean worked in a virtual office that allowed people to access their files from anywhere in the world.

Like if breathing was not so easy, I would have stopped. It had become required to regard moaning or dissatisfaction as a form of weakness, so out of deference I will not moan much longer. But they are jobs for weaklings. The rise of the weak was something I couldn't quite fathom, but which I also viewed with total fear. The weak controlled all computers now and were always complaining and crying, getting married and declaring they were gay when they weren't. Anything to fit into the weak niche that so ruled these days. Life was becoming a musical and no matter how good a musical is, it's still a musical.

We were kind of out of it by the end of the night, slurred sentences punctuating each sip; I'd never tell the others, but I viewed what we were doing as culture war. I was a drama queen myself and a closet weakling. We each had our reasons. Boredom was the single thread that ran between and bound around us. Allegorical paper cuts bled us, printer ink seeping from us. Reading the Economist, then talking about it like we gave two fucks about mining in Burundi. This was what we had become. Info fools.

Pete served ponces drinks for a living and was the better for it. Maybe. He claimed to feel like a whore. But only if he let the voices in. He was a great bar man. Strong. Wouldn't always give you the drink you asked for if he knew better. To the French he was a miracle man. Panache they used to call him. Pissed him off. Pete secretly loved to fight. Panache was his given codename. Easy that one.

As the night wore on we began to weave in and out of meaning. There are a couple of landmarks in any night in Paris, the last Métro perhaps the most important; if you miss that then your best bet is to either stay 'til first Métro or maybe hoof it. Taxis are an unbelievable pain in the ass, no matter where you are or where you are going the taxi driver looks completely aghast when you state your destination,

"Tour Eiffel, s'il vous plaît?"

"Je connais pas, c'est où ça?"

Chapter 6

Sunday October 6 2002

The end meshed into the beginning of the next day. Prison was where we were all heading, sure as shooting. So be it. I didn't care for my life any more than I cared for my bed. Sunday morning I got up, went round to the rotisserie and bought four drumsticks and a rack of ribs, some roast potatoes and a baguette. Living in Paris was alright. The hangover was lurking in the background pretending to be disinterested. I also bought a 1970s thriller long enough to keep the voices at bay. I'd discovered if I read quickly, finished the book as I was going to sleep, the story and the characters wandered on into my dreams. Sunday, and maybe Monday, were the only two nights I ever slept. As I mentioned, we were using up our marrow, having figured out this was the only thing we had left that was ours to use.

I was not content that day, discontent. So I reefed on some beloved rags and shambled down to the squat to get in some practice. I'd not been much better than Lord Pete. I set up some dead bottles and cans from last night's squat festivities. The way I figured it, we'd have one shot at hitting our targets and we had to hit them from as far away as possible. All angles, if possible moving away from the target, body shaped to mask the throw. Then wrist flick, with as little movement as possible, physics our co-conspirator. Silence was a given. The less we looked like we were throwing something, the more chance we had of escaping. Cowards we were called. Ha fucking ha. The Yanks have taught us all that cowardly is the way of the powerful. They wanted people to meet them in open warfare, while they sat on deck twenty miles away and bombed people in huts. Or, even better, using supersonic jets to kill people who didn't even have electricity. Flag fluttering bullshit. Then they complained about car bombs. Bad show. There was no honour in any of this, we had the sense to realise this early on. We never worried. I was steadfast in my fuck them attitude. Once you realise the whole thing is a Mexican throw in, there is really no need to worry.

I wanted the stones to be about the size of a golf ball, light grey so as to not be seen against the sky. I toyed with the idea of shaping them like small birds but then discarded it as folly. I could feel eyes on me as I walked and threw. Walked and threw. It was going to be quite difficult. I smiled to myself with one eye closed as I glimpsed something I had never known.

She gingerly tip toed out of the squat. Or, as I discovered later, the trendy artists' retreat. She had a camera hanging from her neck. A bit grubby, wearing weary jeans, no shoes and a blue vest, dark hair, I hesitate to say any further south than the Med. I didn't want my picture taken. She didn't try to take it. I went over and introduced myself. I was thin back then. Real thin. Thin like a child or a rent boy. I wore a stolen T-shirt nobody else in the whole of Europe had, that was just fine.

She said her name was Naya. I was taken aback briefly by her perfect name, but outwardly I was calm. Inwardly I was at a ninety degree angle. We spoke in English; hers was perfect. I asked her what she did, or something stupid and irrelevant. It wasn't going to be that type of relationship; no shopping and no owning. She liked me already, had decided. She understood I was learning to throw stones at somebody or something that deserved it. She never asked that day and I never told her.

I asked her "Would you like to come for a drink?"

She replied "I'd like a coffee."

I may have exhaled slightly, she smiled and then said,

"OK a drink."

She had a flip flop in each jean back pocket and put them on. Nothing in my life had really prepared me for how those little things made me feel. Like the protector and the parent, the subject and the slave. We both scuffed our way away from the squat, hands in our pockets swaying. I was conscious of holding my breath. I was trying not to try too hard. I thought about how cigarettes could punctuate the pauses and the drifts.

There was a table free outside the expensive glass and purple neon bar in front of the squat and we sat there. I looked off, pretending, or grasping, at depth. My mind was totally blank, worse than blank, it was full of blank.

"Where are you from?"

"The south."

"Are you a photographer?"

"No."

"Do you have any brothers and sisters?"

"I was an orphan."

"Was?"

"Yes"

The eejit waiter came over to mis-take our order. I was not in the humour and met his jaded coal eyes with vigour and granite.

"This is not my first time in a bar." I told her.

"Obviously"

She ordered a brouilly. Me a demi. We sat there and I pulled out my smokes. Offered her one. Like all French people she didn't say no. She didn't say anything.

She smoked, I smoked. It was sweet. Her lips were suitably pouty, but she smiled when I looked at her, turning her head to meet my eyes each time. Her mother was Spanish hence the name. I let that one go. I let them all go. What, did I really mind? Even at that early stage, being with her made it hard for my mind to focus. She had something about her, she was smouldering on a slab. All over her body her clothes gave glimpses of skin, made me kind of crazed. Always did. I ordered some pâté and some bread, we ate small sandwiches without talking. She associated with me happily. She was like a sexy urchin. I dug it. I really did.

She asked me some pretend questions.

What did I do? Where was I from?

Like most people from the South, she couldn't give a toss about Ireland. Was not even sure where it was. Suited me fine. I'd left there, was happy not to talk about it.

I was very conscious of her body. I moved my chair around the table to sit facing her and beside her, brushing against her each time one of us moved. She liked it too, going to the bar to get something, sitting back down into our entangled bodies. The darkness making the lights shine brighter. Paris is nice in the day, but at night it is breathless. Flashed thighs along with the whites of beautiful eyes, monuments worthy of the name and most of all lights, so many lights.

She went somewhere for ten minutes. Returning in boots, with two helmets. Slick. The best way to get around Paris.

"Where do you want to go?" she asked. Smiling. Always smiling, never met a French girl who smiled before.

"You're in charge" I said.

Off we went. The only way to do the city. Bareback. On horse power. The traffic was nuts; hoi polloi returning from their weekend bolt holes. She was brilliant. I gripped behind as instructed. We headed north. North towards Oberkampf.

Oberkampf's a dirty cool street that scrolls off above you as you walk the slight gradient. We walked into a place called Café Charbon, I think, and sat. They brought us menus. I ignored them, she ordered two steaks, one bottle of red and then some Badoit. Badoit was, is and always will be the greatest of all sparkling waters. Small bubbles.

After what should have been too long, we started talking. Mostly about what we thought about things, revolving records, flickering movies. She was still in college studying art. I knew nothing about art. But I listened like it was instructions for life. She talked about movements and trends, the difference between up and blue, six and smooth. I could never really fathom the nuance. But my mind rippled and shook anyway listening to her soundtrack.

I went to the jacks returning to see her being chatted up by some blue shirted Galois. Nah, not this time. I stood tall beside him. She was not really speaking. He was giving it socks. He looked at me; I told him to jog on. I'm not ashamed. I understand politeness is a virtue, but there must be a limit, and this was the only time I was really impolite, but she made me covet her. All he'd needed to do was engage, to introduce himself to me. But he wanted to measure wallets and I was going to knock his face in. She, by now, was ignoring him. I sat, looked at the barman behind me, shrugged and opened my hand towards the cadre cad, the barman did not bat nor flutter, nonchalance totale.

The guy jogged on muttering something as he went. I never mentioned it again. I was not the jealous type, but why should wankers rule the world?

The meal was kind of brilliant. The candle flickering making us both seem interesting and alive; secrets perpetually revealed and unrevealed. I understood then; this was what everybody was always going on about. Infinite ephemeral reflections, hard to know where the smiles originated, each of us igniting the spark in the other. Our grins felt like lifetime culminations of each other. At one stage I leaned over the table and gave her a kiss on the lips. Like I had been doing it all my life. She met my lips with hers, so very perfect, my hand touched the top of her shoulder, slid up her neck, smoothing into her hair behind her ear. Everyone in the bar may or may not have stopped while that happened. The clinking certainly seemed to fall silent. After that my mind refused to hold onto a single thought. Nothing would stick. I felt a glow behind my eyes, another nascent burning smile. Work the next day, was the only bad news. But in reality that was mere detail. This was it. Was all of it.

"Let's go."

"I'll drop you home. Have things to do tonight."

Normally this would have had me spitting being the spoilt child I was. But with her, "No worries. Cool."

We sat on her bike for ages necking like in the fifties. I think at one stage I was trying to drink the saliva out of her mouth. She gripped my head, her fingers tight into my hair. On and on it went, delicious tongues. We nearly toppled the bike and that awoke us. I had her number already and I went back for three more warm sopping kisses before leaping up to my flat.

All thoughts of stones and Iraq and work far from my head. The fucking buzz, Christ.

I went to bed, it was still early. I wasn't going to text her. I was going to wait. But for what? We'd set in place a chain of events that in some way or another would change me, her, the world, the political landscape? Tolstoy would argue, if he could be bothered, one does not set events in motion, due to a confluence of a million other things they are already going to happen. So maybe what happened was not my fault? And everything that happened was not bad. I'd always tried to stay out of other people's lives. Advice was as close as I ever wanted to get. That although we may be the star of our own life, we are not its director. I texted her.

"Every thought I have turns into you. I thought it was only a rumour. Goodnight. Millions of kisses."

And she replied.

Chapter 7

Monday October 7 2002

The stone throwing was personal score settling. Revenge. All without explanation. I thought briefly of that stupid, exciting television show, 24. How they tortured every character on the show. How everybody was guilty until tortured. Even then they were probably still guilty. People who'd been in the CIA for years suddenly became activated enemy sleepers. It was the beginning of the dumbest run of shows ever known to man. 9/11 ruined many things, least of all was television. It made everything into a terrorist show. The most powerful country that has ever existed. Always remember that. I did, but we were not after the Americans. They were too far away. Or so I thought at the time. Little did I know they would come to us.

We didn't have grandiose ideas, like we were after the "good men who did nothing" from that exhausted quote. The head of an international bank, in this day and age, is not a good man who did nothing. Not by a long shot. Other than that, I went to bed happy. My mind refused to sleep, I thought of all the problems that were to come. How maybe I'd just take Naya away with me. Never going to happen. Where would I take her anyway?

When I woke up the next morning the news again was all Iraq. How on Thursday the US Senate and Congress would vote to authorize the use of force in Iraq. Such a great shame, I thought to myself, as I listened and watched one fool after another, lemming their way up to spout platitudes of death.

"They don't get the death thing, they don't understand it. Their words kill people." I reasoned into the mirror.

One more thing to blame Hitler for. Hitler was the bulletproof argument trotted out by those simian fools every time someone piped up to question the need for war. "Imagine if we could have stopped Hitler." Nobody mentioning of course they could have stopped Hitler if they'd been bothered. Most of those gobshites had been to Yale or another Ivy League palace. And what do they learn there? They learn that the most important thing is the sale. Say whatever you like, as long as you get the sale. Always be closing. Once sold, the war was going to make a lot of people a lot of money. People didn't want to hear it then and they don't want to hear it now.

The whole thing made me feel ill, as I stepped into the queue on my way to Rue de Rivoli. Rivoli beside the Louvre, Tuileries, Place Vendôme, an extremely sexy street, with maybe a few too many well-dressed old people. I worked just off it in an office with computers and static carpet and much grey. Everything was metal so you could hang up a printed note with a magnet. God those notes. "Please refrain from putting paper towel down the toilet." Could they not just make the toilets more powerful? A French toilet has about the same power as a child's cough.

In work that day I was distracted and flitty, but my job was so very easy. I'd been doing it for years, besides I was sober, and un hungover which made me akin to a superman. The rest of the people in the office were French. Lovely people, oh so very dull. Gliding from one petit café to the next. They all had hobbies. A sure sign of a boring life. One guy climbed mountains every weekend. He had two kids. What? Why have the kids? He lived in Paris all week then went home every weekend to Grenoble to climb mountains. I have not walked in his crampons, so I will not judge him. But why have kids?

"Must have kids. Must continue procreation. Have never liked kids, going to have them anyway. Kids now born, going to climb mountains. See you when they turn twenty one." I imagined his life chant.

Monday lunch I stayed in, finished all the ads, rang some clients in England and the States as was my remit, couple of German ones too. Good work.

The Stonethrowers needed to be ready in two weeks. The OECD conference was to take place on 21 October at the OECD HQ out in the 16th. Swanky and secure, as would befit the home of the info office for the elite. On the other hand a lot of open space nearby. Could go either way? Nice park close by to serve as a rendezvous point. The streets alongside were not great escape-wise. The drop off area for dignitaries seemed to be in the open. I need to go down and have a look for myself.

I called James, told him not to bother with tickets for the conference. We wouldn't be throwing stones inside, the less we were associated with the event the better. As television had taught us, the less connection one had with the crime, the less chance of detection.

"No worries mate. Any other news? Did you see the latest increase in the war drums? Is it just us? Does no one give a damn?"

"People care. They don't think they can do anything about it. They believe they're powerless. They're probably right."

"A little bit like 1905 the whole thing. Gap widens. Global elite do whatever they want. Inevitable war."

"I don't want to think about it. Makes bile come up into my mouth. You on for a pint Tuesday? The Bug?"

"Course, a plus. Peace."

"Peace."

I rang Naya, she answered very normally and yet my throat started to swell up. I'd kind of half expected some game or other, but that was not how it was going to go. Thoughts fled my head on hearing her voice. I kept hearing the words "olive skinned" like someone was whispering it to me. I was totalled. All in, only the second day. Deep breath. Explanation not necessary, not going to be like I was. Speak straight, speak true, no nuance, like fictional Johnny.

"How long have we known each other? Feels like twenty thousand light years, since before the stars were born. Dinner tonight?" I did not want to leave things unsaid as I had done my whole life.

"I can't honey, meeting friends." Pause of milliseconds. "Or maybe I can. Give me five minutes?"

As she hung up I tried to tell her it was OK, for some reason it was cool. Deep down I was engaging in some form of emotional manipulation, not wanting to establish a precedent of separate social engagement cancellation. Jesus, what kind of a person had I become? I was like a male woman's magazine. Like a committee deciding on how best to date. Really needed to stop watching television box sets. The box sets I watched had become my own experiences and memories, they were creating alternate fictional neural pathways.

"Allo. Oui, ce soir. Ça marche. Où?"

"Marais, Métro Saint Paul?"

"Bon. 19 heures."

"Cool"

Then she hung up. And that's how it went. Smooth. All along the horizontal. Beautifully balanced spirit level. The second half of the day unpeeled itself like any other French afternoon. The rest of the office came back in dribs and drabs. The work punctuating the little coffees. They all lived in the suburbs. Going home was what they all lived for; despite the fact they'd be in bed by ten at the latest. I'd recently asked one thousand French people how they were. Ninety five per cent replied they were a little tired. Gutting. But I loved my colleagues; their loyalty to me was astonishing. At the beginning they'd regarded me with suspicion, but after a year or so, they now were embarrassingly nice to me. Generous people. Presents of food and invitations flowed my way. Telling me to use the 'tu' form of the verb. Trying to fix me up with errant nieces or cousins. My foreignness suggested errantness to them; hence they felt the need to look after me. Good people.

To be clear, a lot of what gets you through the day in Paris is the beauty and the opulence. The beauty could be the scarf Genie, the pictures editor, tied around her shoulder to offset the shock of a full bare arm in October. It made me picture her naked, every single time I looked at her. Around the corner was the Ritz, I only had to close my charlatan eyes to imagine the slightly shimmering suits, the glinting uber watches, the dashing men; industrialists most. Shiny bright things.

Like all facades, it enabled us to imagine we were part of it. If the American dream is wealth then the French dream is beauty. I probably read that quote in the Economist. All canned and packaged beauty of course, but the non-stop seduction sometimes was OK.

Due to my not taking a lunch, I nearly completed two days' work. I told my boss I wouldn't be in the following morning. She was happy about that. She often worried I didn't take enough personal time. So a hopeful Tuesday morning off was not the end of the world.

Chapter 8

Monday October 7 2002

Percolation. The percolation of ideas was my new thing. I gave myself an hour on my own while I waited for her. I sat smoking cancer sticks. Resolutely minging. Sipping a few demis. Sketching and winnowing away at the various problems. Drawing pictures of arcs.

We had exactly fourteen days to get ready. Not even close to enough. Work expanded into time and vice versa. We needed practice and we needed to do it slightly less in the open. The front of the squat, while not exactly the Champs Élysée, was still no good. Bois de Boulogne would be better. I sent out a text to the other three suggesting we make a day of it Saturday and to bring their own stones.

At seven exactly she arrived. Stood feet together heels a-clicked. I stood up, nearly knocking over the table. Was I supposed to pretend not to be eager? I wondered somewhat pointlessly as I'd resolved never to be anything other than eager. I easily lifted her with my hand on the small of her back. She arched her back up into the kiss, her thigh coming up the outside of mine. Wow. What a kiss, warm and wet. It was difficult not to feel elated. I could feel people watching us, I liked it.

"Let's wander?" I suggested as I grinned, speaking into her still kiss opened mouth.

"I have somewhere in mind for about eight? Thoughts?"

"Parfait." She whispered.

It was light romantic drizzle, just enough so that every ten minutes I had to stop to clean my glasses and to kiss more. I was starving for her. She met me half way each time, crashing into me. We tripped and slipped around on the cobblestones, feigning consternation when it was perfection. The Marais area was putting away its shopping face and putting on its night make up. The Marais, the gay area, was a perfect place to bring a girl. We arrived at the restaurant; our table was ready.

The bistro was hap hazard, big and airy; they were burning old window frames in the large open fireplace. There was a big ass St Bernard slumped half dead on the ground from the irony of the whole thing. A country looking woman ordered everybody around, conducting. She beckoned to me as I entered; I half knew her so went over and presented Naya. She delighted at the name. They chatted while I looked around. I'd been there first a year or so ago with my father; liked it then; food was good, uncouth, meat frayed and bloody; like it always should be. There wasn't much choice either, the way I liked it. Big menu restaurants make me want to kill myself.

We sat and once again the spiral began our own zoetrope. Lights blurred and merged into food, into fire, into wine. Glimpses of her flashed white teeth. Of my laughing at the mystery. The smiling, stupid smiling. And round. The owner, Rita was her name, if that is possible, sent over the odd flourish. A few samples to start, a shared dessert at the end, the strange phenomenon of a village raising us, global approval. The wine tasted like blood and we went for the second bottle. It was going to be messy. By the time we were leaving, Naya was sitting on my knee. What was one to do but dance on and out, not deny any of it, least of all the rhythmic murmurous twists round and round? We paid and moved towards her bike, which was bad, neither of us in any state.

The trip to mine was teleportation. I lived in the badlands in the north of Paris, we went into my local, a Berber bar. They too were charmed. They wanted to ask was she one of them, but didn't out of some deference to me. Who knows why these things play like they do? But the main man was happy I had brought her. I was too. I liked the guy. Myself and James amongst the only non-Berber guys ever in there. Honorary due to us being foreign, I think.

Five wooden flights up to the flimsiest door you ever saw. A duck could have kicked it in. We stumbled into my room. And before the whole thing kicked off, before I ravaged her, and she mangled me, just before, we lay right up beside each other on the bed, noses touching for a long lost minute. Then boom. You know how it goes. Sweat dripping. Rutting would be polite. Strange how it began so very, very dirty. And we never settled for anything less.

During the night we kept fucking. Hard to know what the hell was going on half the time. Glorious really. The morning was so naked, the light shot through the window illuminating the mildly displeased dust, everything distilled and a beat slower. I made her a cup of Irish tea. A slight nod to the Emerald Pile. She loved that. I had made it sweet as hell. My mate used to call it butcher's tea. When you've both been fucked ragged and raw, when the booze has left you giddy and very orientated towards lowness, sweet tea is the business. We sat up drinking it but also lying down. Like, I don't mean to go on about it, but physically, I was exerted, maybe even exhausted. After we'd placed our cups on the bedside table with that really old sound, we both dozed off clasped together right at the soul.

"What's the stone throwing for?" she ultimately and eventually asked.

We weren't having a quick conversational type moment, so I could've thought up a lie. But most of my life was a lie. Soft lies like snowflakes and mostly to myself and the people I care about, de rigueur and overlooked. Why lie?

"I'm not sure it is a good idea that you know. Nor am I going to lie to you. So I am dans une predicament."

We both were limbering up for it. Loosening out our respective egos. Cracking our personal ids.

"Hmmmmm. I'm not going to like this am I?"

"No. Whatever happens you are not going to like it. How about I say we're going to cause some trouble. And then I can tell you more. Or you can ask questions?"

"Trouble, like at a football match? Hooligan trouble?"

Two years ago that's exactly what I would've been doing. What had happened to that happy go lucky hooligan? Where had he gone? I know where. He went the way of the weapons inspectors and everybody else who'd tried to talk sense. That sweet toothy hooligan knew it was time. How could I explain it to her without us sounding like the idiots we undoubtedly were. I couldn't.

"No, not football trouble. More like anarchist/political trouble."

"But you are not an anarchist."

Fucking French. Say that to any Irish girl and they'd roll their eyes, turn over and fall asleep. Naya had probably dated an anarchist, slept with a Maoist but preferred Dadaists.

"True, but I want trouble. I want to do something. Nobody is going to be badly hurt."

I don't have a religion, nor any belief in anything unscientific, but I do believe that to tempt fate is a bad thing to do. Inwardly I cringed at my own stupidity. She pondered this as she put on her jeans. She continued to ponder this as she put on her top. I too was pondering it, but this was not an argument over something I was about to change. I wasn't about to alter my plan. Even for her. Not yet anyway.

She paused briefly like all pauses and spoke, "OK. This isn't the end of this matter. But nor is it the end of the other matter. Kiss me quick before I go. Last night was a film epic let's not ruin it with the concerns of mortals. Call me." Like I said, perfect English.

"Cool." I jumped to walk her to the door, already she was out of it and flying down the stairs with daring and agility. Fit girl. I lit a smoke and walked over to the balcony overlooking the scrawny road. Living in the badlands meant my apartment was brilliant. She looked up as she got on her bike, she gave me a vigorous wave and a smile which resonated through the minds of every single person on the street who witnessed it.

Was this all an act? Was she an enemy agent? Who was the enemy? The OECD? They did have a lot of pretty girls working there? Jesus though, must have been a long assignment? Always knowing where I was and what I was doing. Not before I did, but whilst I did, nearly as worrying.

I tried to think of the whole thing in a series of Venn diagrams, but since the day and hour I was taught Venn diagrams, I have struggled to find an actual use for them, beyond my own amusement.

Chapter 9

Saturday November 9 2002

I lay there not dying. Jesus, if rivulets of pathos and disgust could have run out of my tear ducts to wash away my weakling tears, they would have. Instead I stood, demi-crouching, hunkered and deciding.

The squat.

By my non-military reckoning the Americans had bombed from where I was toward the Bibliothèque, around five hundred metres. They had flown up the vapours through South Paris. The squat was quite close to the Bibliothèque. It was over to the east, not far from the Périphérique. So this meant, well? I had no idea what it meant. The planes sounded absent and the explosions more muted.

My normal hearing had not returned but I could hear some things around me. One solid icy scream came from the tower block to the front of me.

"Not this time" I mumbled to my own damn self.

I could not afford to be side-tracked towards that magnetic terrified scream. What other time was there? But "Not this time" was what came into my head. I was going to the squat. I took off, firstly zig zagging. Inside I was clinging on, my fingers white, but then it was my first bombing campaign. The skies now silent, no more planes clapping the sound barrier.

"What did I expect to find in the squat?"

I could not close my mind to that thought. The answer beyond any comprehension I could handle; without my grasp.

I took off down the road. Some fires; but mostly smoke and dust. Some rumbling like a low hum or gravellous gargle, difficult to know from where.

I was in the 13th. There was a text message on my phone. I didn't have the psychological faculty to deal with anything non-movement, survival related just yet.

It was not from her. I managed to know that as my focus slipped from the text and back to my new immediacy, borne of danger and peril.

"Should I walk down the middle of the street, out in the open? Little chance the French army would be out already? They would wait until all the bombings had been completed, right?" Walking alongside the decapitated smoking buildings seemed to be asking for trouble, half were perfect and untouched although it would be wrong to say they were indifferent, everything was worried, all things had been undermined. There was an eerie smoke everywhere, lingering as if only it remained alive, the smoke clouds the only discernible movement, confusing me, lazy drifting swarms of dust.

I walked down the middle of the road finally having decided, determined to at least bring symmetry to the auspicious occasion. My clothes were wrecked. My hair had been singed. My knee bled, well *maybe more seeped, into my shoe. My eyes and ears hurt and a viscous puss leaked down my face. I was alive and well.*

The concentration was hard to keep, to hold, I kept blinking as if incredulous. I think I sat for a minute then realised what I was doing. Did I sleep? No, maybe not. Nearly.

"Go. Go." My mind was arguing with my body directly, I did not seem to be involved. I was not between them as usual; maybe they could make the decisions from now on?

I struggled again inside and out, indecision and blurriness wavering me. All at once I released myself from explanation and hared rabidly from left to right up the road.

Why was I going to anywhere? I was not. I was endeavouring to look back into a mistake I had made and fix it. Reach behind me into the past. Plunge my long sorry arms through the reality yoke, and gasping, grab her into the present with me. So I ran.

I got to the Rue Tolbiac. It was not as bad up there. I finally read the text. The Americans had said there would be no more bombings, that two was enough. High level negotiations. Ongoing. The usual.

"Where was the second bombing?" I said out loud.

Pete had texted me. He was around, although I assumed he was outside the Périphérique. Wherever he was, he had a phone. He'd used a different number. I would reply. But not yet. I knelt. I could hear a vehicle as well as smell burning bread; something ironic like that.

Yeah a vehicle was coming. I was twisted inside out. But I knew this was still war. I was a known face and now that things were going to be getting back to normal. NORMAL. The word sounded both gemütlich and terrifying. The strength of the sombre smooth 'N' followed by the dull powerful 'L' awful. It may have meant it, but it was not it.

I lay in along a wall out of sight. Two troop carriers rumbled garrulously down towards the Bibliothèque.

"Bollix." I said aloud.

Time, as usually happens, had returned from its hiding place inside the explosions. Time had re-staked its claim as the most strange and compelling human construct.

"What was I doing?" I asked myself.

I got up again; nothing around. I listened, then trembled slightly. My mind had internalised all my screams.

What had I expected? This. I'd expected this, I'd wanted it. I thought I'd not be around to have to understand my decision. To understand stupid and death mixed, to see the bodies caused by it.

I walked down the hill listening. There was another rumbling explosion, sudden then languid. I beat down to the corner, before the bridge over the train tracks. Why was I there?

Naya.

Fucking Naya.

Naya.

What

had

I

been

thinking

?

I did a shimmy down the hill. I could now see the Bibliothèque. Fire crews were arriving from everywhere. I'd never believed that bullshit about Bush liking reading. He never once acted like he had read anything except condiment instructions. Bet you he picked the BNF, as it was properly known, himself.

Punishment was right.

The Bibliothèque's four towers burnt like four books opened on their end, exactly as they were designed. Perfect and sad.

Books, what harm have they ever done? Bush was always the anti-intellectual. The anti-learning.

I leant into where I was going and pushed on. Pushed on. I was at the wall outside the squat and I flogged my extremely sorry ass over the wall and into the grounds.

Was someone standing at the window?

Chapter 10

Tuesday October 8 2002

Worry began to prise its way into my head as Naya sped off on her rocket, I blocked it. I did not believe this was me losing her. I had two hours to kill. I had a shower. Scrubbed myself raw and clean holding the shower head as one comes to expect and prefer in Paris. Put on my civvies. I felt light and clean. I bustled onto a mid-morning Métro, as the screeching wheels pulled off my head swam with stone thoughts, sex flashbacks and general under the skin heat. I headed over to have a surreptitious look at the OECD HQ. I had once taught a guy up there. So I knew the way.

The 16th arrondisement is a residential area. Mexican ambassador's children can be seen walking from their limos into white-walled palaces. The place is very staid, not much action down the OECD end, up the other end there are the sports grounds et al. Museums and embassies and parks and rich people. I liked it well enough, although perhaps a touch quiet on a Tuesday morning.

I walked through the little park down onto Rue André Pascal, on which, as far as I could figure, the delegates would be dropped off.

"Jesus it's tight." I said out loud.

Embassies and delegations everywhere. Short of throwing a stone at the Élysée one could not find a much more guarded area.

Better alone or together? One, two or three of us?

Questions that needed to be answered. Other than that, shit, it would be difficult to escape.

"Maybe we should wait for a more opportune moment?" I thought idly while I smoked towards my death.

"Would the heads of these companies go to this conference themselves? And, if so, would they have the area totally cordoned off? No, not totally. Also, we had our disguise. My whiteness would render me next to invisible to the French security forces. Throw in some decent suits and we might just get away with it." I mouthed my thoughts as I strolled, contentment in action.

I was considering doing the first one myself. Better that way. Lead by example. Back to work for the rest of the afternoon, much to contemplate. I did the next day's work. I also made a run at helping some of my co-workers, as they were so very, very slow. In their defence they were a lot more thorough than me. But they wallowed in their thoroughness, as if bathing in milk. I'd worked hard when I first got that job, very hard, but got the hang of it quickly. Out of deference to my morning off, I stayed to six thirty. I still felt guilty, some things you cannot rationalise. After work I reckoned a walk would be best, so off I strolled rolling my shoulders to unfurl some of the little knots.

"The Stonethrowers needed to get their act together", was my main thought as I strode along.

In Paris absolutely nobody gives a shit about you. If you were queuing for the last baguette in France, people could not be any ruder.

But that was cool. When I first arrived I was super polite, trying to kill them with kindness. This policy of appeasement in a city of 15 million, did not make even the tiniest dent. And why would it? This was their city and their culture. A culture of total rudeness, impolitesse totale. So I walked straight through every single one of them, bar the infirm, pregnant and child. Who knew the answer could be so easy?

Cursing and spluttering in my wake, I really was a good bit bigger than the average Parisian, I'd come to realise this was much better, I was adding to l'expérience culturelle. Umbrellas I swatted away like flies once they came close. My walk was eventful and energetic. It also allowed me to contemplate the nexus of Naya, the Stonethrowers and me.

Astonishing. I had lived thousands of days on earth and most of them could have easily slipped inside the other like Russian dolls. I remember individual days only if time stamped by drink or sex or some difference. So now 2002, having finally decided settling was not an option and that I was too much askew. Having accepted I could not do it, could not master the steps set out for me. Following dance steps laid out by someone else was not something I could countenance. I had met someone in Paris, the epicentre of world cheating. A place where it is difficult to believe in any kind of relationship except a shallow, venal, destructive one. You can say with certainty when you meet a French guy of any age in Paris, "He is cheating." They do not even hide it. Never knew I was such a prude until I arrived in Paris.

The final few yards into the Bug is my favourite approach on earth. After you cross Faubourg Saint-Honoré, lots of soft bends, boutiques offering tantalising glimpses of magazine lives, worn corners guiding you to your seat, the bar demanding to be worshipped. The two bar men similar in appeal to rock stars. Pete was working that night; otherwise we would have met somewhere else. I sat on the elbow of the middle. There was a midpoint walk through for the staff and regulars to avoid walking around. The place came alive midweek evenings. The suited and booted of the local financial working French. All wearing their uniform, blue shirts, blue suits, the odd crazee guy with brown shoes. The girls all slightly subservient to the guys, something which was prevalent in most French offices at the time. Even when not the case, a seventies style, secretary boss type relationship was the norm not the exception.

Dean arrived in, looking suitably dashing and harried as was his way. He wore it well, a little old fashioned but that's OK. He had a kind of corporate hippie thing going on. His was a sweaty allure girls loved, that along with his Lord of the Rings style wedding band, ensured he got a lot of attention. He hip slid through the middle gap, calmly and expertly shaking hands all round as he sat down.

Pete ran his place like a gentlemen's club, eagerness or rudeness were not tolerated. He raised an eyebrow at Dean, looking back at him, as he stood pint glass under the tap, finger on the trigger.

Dean, our American, was singlehandedly bringing politeness and enthusiasm back to France. He claimed that these "traits had long been lost, ever since the decimation of the Grande Armée under Napoleon."

Dean nodded solemnly at Pete, shook the outstretched hand wearing a smile you could put on a coat hanger. I gave Dean a hug as was our way. We existed in a world of Woodstock and weed, pretend yes, but pretensions like these enabled us both to navigate the inner drains of city dwelling.

"Well what has you so loose man? Like hugging a fucking rag doll?" he astutely astuted.

I thought about lying. Jesus, I always thought about lying. I was a liar.

"I met a girl, yer one from the squat. Went down on Sunday to get in some throwing time. She came down to me and we went for a drink, then dinner last night."

"You shagged her the first night, first date? Nah come on? Don't lie to me." Dean.

"No. I never said I shagged her any fucking night. I slept alone on Sunday."

This kind of frat boy laddishness annoyed me no end, as he well knew.

"She rides a motorbike. A slick beat up Ducati."

"Does she now? Does she indeed. You tell it like I know who "yer one" is? I don't. Who is she? Pray tell? O lord of love."

His flouncing around doing a half decent Irish accent made what he was saying sound funnier than it might otherwise have been. His sense of humour was decent.

"Her name's Naya. She's from the south. She's absolutely gorgeous. She's in college studying art mothafucker. Studying in the École nationale supérieure des beaux-arts." I kind of grinned, truth is I could not stop myself.

"The fucking where? Christ on a stick. Nice job. So go on. Did you see her last night?"

"I did and I brought her to that place in the Marais I used to go on about"

"The sexy place?" He was referring to a cavernous basement boozer in the Marais pocked with nooks and crannies for chancing one's arm.

"No, well I was going to go there, afterwards. But figured I would just bring her on home, after the two bottles of wine."

"Did you bring her in to meet Zinedine?"

"I did. He approved. Had a coffee and a calva there, after we went back to mine, she stayed over. Was great. Had the morning off. So got to do the whole morning cat yawning dusty sunlight thing."

"Wow. High five. High ten. OK. Alright. Everyone relax. Put the gun down. Step away from the weapon."

We both smiled and did a laconic cheers. Pete who had listened to everything, standing just out of eye line, where he lived. Kind of a butler's position, if there is such a thing. He lined up four glasses as James walked in, grinning, dark, beautiful, French looking, all that glitters is gold. Gay good looking. We all had a Sambuca. I love Sambuca.

"Occasion?" James asked all bovver boy business, as he let his immense shoulders rock from side to side settling into them.

"I met a girl" I volunteered in order to stave off the avalanche of abuse I was undoubtedly going to receive.

"Alright then, to?"

"Naya" they all looked at me double take mouths mock agape.

"To Naya."

We then inhaled the shot. Gorgeous poisonous medicine. Warms the chest.

"Three pints Pete please mate. When you get a sec."

Pete hated it when we ordered. He preferred to have anticipated.

"I went down to check out the OECD yesterday."

This got their attention. Pete had to serve the chosen people, he wandered down the bar but he kind of kept tabs anyway. I would fill him in.

"Well what do you think?" James asked sculling half his pint, using it to stop anyone from lip reading him, then looking guilefully over the rim at me and Dean.

I continued into the more logistical issues. "Well, we have thirteen days to get ready, point one. Point two, it is in one of the most heavily guarded areas of the city. Point three, we need to put together a feasible escape plan."

"Any good news?" Dean asked. He was the least in of any of us. His missus and him were having trouble. We'd given him an out on many occasions. But he remained inside. He was all for it at the beginning, in fact I'd always felt he and I were the project's parents. I reminded myself I would need to take him aside and deal with his reticence once and for all.

"There is some good news my fellow fuckheads. I am going to do the first throw." I said with a salesman grin, hoping to lighten the mood.

"Bollix, you going to be the hero?" James was not a man to let anyone else be first. But when it came down to it, I was in charge and he understood this. But I was only the boss with everyone's blessing, before you think I am better, for I am not.

"Well, if you think about it, the first throw is the one they will least expect. After that it will get progressively more difficult. The first is the least heroic."

"Other things that have occurred to me are: we'll only need to carry one stone. There'll be no evidence left once we throw it. We use plastic gloves, a quick wash of the hands should ensure no residue. I picked up some stones earlier today from a garden around the corner. If the cops get so far as to analysing or tracing the stone they'll hopefully discover it's used in gardens all over Paris. This might enable us to fool them into believing this was just an opportunistic troublemaker, until we strike for the second time." Our eyes glazed and feral. Both mute and understanding.

"I am not sure if I need anyone with me, maybe one other person, right beside the target who can keep in contact with me? Security cameras are a different matter. Not sure where they are and who has them. But I also don't want to go back there. None of us should is that clear? Any other reconnaissance will have to be done by internet. No one is to go back there? Agreed?"

"Agreed" Dean.

"Yeah maybe" James.

"No maybe mate. Direct order. You want to be in charge, I'll gladly step aside. Otherwise...."

"Alright, alright. Fucking Irish prick." James.

"Cool. Back here tomorrow night. I want ideas for targets. I want pictures to ensure we don't smack the head of UNICEF on the head. They all look alike to me."

"They do all look alike." Dean said, happy to move away now from prison cells.

We laughed. Serious and steadfast feelings activated deep down. Face skin pulled taut as we clinked glasses. Pete right there as he always was. Posh people, wow when you get a good one. They are pretty great. Soon we would be beyond the point of no return and I for one was gagging for it. Anything not to have to pretend that photocopying was a legitimate pursuit for man. Like I don't have any truck with hunting or any of that shit, but let's not pretend phones and computers and grey plastic don't give you cancer.

"Meeting adjourned until tomorrow. Think on all of it. Think it over and get back with potential problems. No writing shit down. No telling anybody else about this. OK? Good."

I choked a touch at this last bit and James looked at me quickly, like a bird noticing an insect rustle a leaf, metres away. Smart, smart guy; way too in tune. Bootstrap smart, all that crap, but kind of true.

There was a match on and we all loved football.

But we were nearly done with football as well. Fed up as we were with the distance. Comparison is the thief of joy.

So I will not compare.

But suffice to say footballers would want to watch themselves too.

The rest of the night passed off without incident. James tried to get into some French lady, she at first was having none of it. But in the end she relented. He was bowler hat charming and ladies could never get enough of it.

Chapter 11

Tuesday October 8 2002

Does it matter how much we drank? Way too much. But we were not caught yet, and we were about to go up against the machine. That, as any real soldier will tell you, is thirsty work. I got home last Métro. Weirdoes trying to threaten me in my local Métro station, me drunk, laughing, telling them to fuck off. I have not been in a fight for ten years, and the fuck off, as usual, did the trick. I arrived home and Naya pulled up.

I was pleased. She stood there with the helmet and shook her hair out. Heck Mossad? Really? Really? Way too beautiful, I was slightly suspicious then. But then I relaxed into the idea that has given me solace my whole life: my own irrelevance. Say it.

"Who the (and you must over bite your bottom lip when you say it) fuck am I?"

I constantly beat against the boundaries of my psyche, thin as a fly's wing. I was borderline all day. But I was also moving forward so don't mock me, I am made of sensitive cells like anybody else is.

"Alright beautiful. You local?"

She smiled at that.

"Alright beautiful. You drunk?" Was she spying on me?

"Yip. Is that OK with you?"

"Fine. Will make it easier to get you into bed"

"I was going to bed anyway. You are welcome to come with me to the land of the dancing shadows." I kind of flounced that last bit out. Drunk is right.

"Let's go Tupac." She may have had remarkable English but she seemed to know fuck all about hip hop. I took her hand and kissed her and then said hi again. Every single new couple in the world does it while they are learning to kiss. And yet, it's still great.

My stairs was an experience, the only way to deal with the five flights was to sprint, or else you could lose hope half way up. So we sprinted. She nearly beat me. Lucky, I kind of, sort of, knocked into her nearing the top. But it was stair running, not like normal running, full contact. We both laughed and coughed when we got to the top. I was weirdly rejuvenated. Moving industrial silhouettes on the four walls encouraging the fantastic. She made it seem like I was brilliant. I slept heavy waking once in the night, arms wrapped around her like my sub conscious expected her to escape. She was in on it as well holding my arm like a life raft.

In Ireland I would have considered the two of us saps. But here in the 18th arrondissement in Paris, Tuesday 8 October 2002 it was OK. I would squeeze her and she would squeeze me back. Do girls ever really sleep? I have no clue for I know next to nothing about girls, save what they look like, and how I like their taste so very much.

I woke first. I was a morning person. I got up earlier than any normal French person. French babies slept later than I did. Naya slept on. I got ready. Dappered up. I opened up my computer and thought about my life in the three or four minutes it took to start up. Not much to think about. This was the obvious peak. Between her and the Stonethrowers everything was pretty great.

Pity I was going to wreck it. But I was going to wreck it. Fuck it all up. Like my heroes; I built things only to destroy them, demonstrate my ownership of them.

I left her until the last moment then I woke her up. Nothing drives a girl sex crazier than a guy trying to leave them in bed when he is dressed, nothing. She took it real personal too. Basically grabbing my tie to asphyxiate me back into the bed. I am not saying we were like porn stars and that she was some exaggerated woman and all that stuff. But we were like porn stars and if I could have imagined someone out of thin air, she would have been pretty close. Pretty close, what a shitty thing to say. That is me though; hedging my bets even as my horse is romping home.

She gave me a lift to work. Weaving through the traffic and the beautiful people. James had a motorbike was what occurred to me. That and the fact that I had my hands up her jacket. Maybe I should throw a stone at myself. I seemed to be the one ruining it for everyone. Whatever about it I held her tight, my hands inside her clothes intermittently giving her body a squeeze to let her know something I could not quite voice yet.

Work was exactly the same luxurious piece of piss it always had been. I spoke to the same advertisers I always did and got two new ones off a lead from Pete. He should have got the weekly commission. This made me seem like a man in control.

And ye know, I was as in control as anyone in this story. The Military Industrial Complex was the only one really in control in this tale.

Work stretched out in front, then accordioned back. I left at five thirty, my normal time. My colleagues would all be there until seven doing god knows what? I had been there at eight, they started arriving at nine thirty. They seemed to think they worked in the fashion industry.

Chapter 12

Wednesday October 9 2002

The walk to the Bug was the usual NFL game. I let my thoughts wash and swish around. My head was full, I hesitate to say of shit, but that is the word that kept coming up. A motorbike escape was definitely a runner.

We all did this thing like skiers as we came into the Bug. Looking back now, I can only imagine what we looked like. Idiots. Yeah idiots. But today I was first and there was no one else. Only Pete and his fellow rock star, a new bar man who served the grunts. The chefs were in the back, a little piece of Sri Lanka. I had to shake hands with every single person in the bar and that was grand.

Pete checked the mirrors and stood facing me. Reflections kept us safe. I related last night's conversation to him. He listened properly like he always did.

"What do you think?" I asked.

"I think that we are on the right track. Clearly the two main problems are practice and escape. We need to quickly start hitting targets. With each stone thrown in anger the heat will increase exponentially. Each one will be more dangerous. I am not sure what a good result will look like? All of us in prison? That is surely a loss?"

He did not expect me to answer, if anyone else was going to be in charge it would be him. So I listened and someone else walked in and I went back to smoking stinking chokers, my bronchial nodes heaving.

Next in was Dean. I remembered thinking to myself that he was supposed to be married. But it was not my affair. There were more things to think about than why he had turned up. Sometimes Dean acted like another Dean and I would see a little glimpse of why it would be so easy for me not to like him. He grooved around the bar making friends and enemies of girls and boys alike. We greeted each other and the night sprung forth with us as its source.

Dean's job was something that, maybe, had come between us. I'd known him for years, when we first met we worked together in an employment agency, chasing tail. Now I couldn't always remember what it was I liked about him. I sometimes wondered did he think we were different to him, less dedicated. I normally like Americans. For all my guff I like the way they do not apologise for every last darn thing, they are normally up for all manner of shenanigans. Also I was born in Ireland which is the fifty sixth state. My childhood was mostly A-Team and crisps. Those dusty lots above Hollywood where they shot M*A*S*H and the A-Team were my memories and my dreamscapes. The last time I was in the States I was struck by how they were in the process of ruining their own country. That is a lie, I was not struck at all, I'd heard the rumours.

When James came in we reconvened the meeting. They all had done their assignments. Impressive.

"I was on the motorbike with Naya today." I ventured. James interrupted me vigorously.

"I thought the same thing, I can pick you up? Sounds great. I had a gawk at a map, I'd venture I'd have you back in your office in fifteen minutes."

"Sounds good. Let's talk about it one more time. Want to give my mind a chance to spot any problems. Thanks though, for the offer, and not allowing me to ask and interrupting me and....."

"Alright mate get the picture, settle." James smiled, a rare sight as he was normally pretending to be gruff. Doing his normal my body is too big for me shuffle that he loved, shifting his weight from one foot to the next.

I decided to go home early that night. Not sure why, had a feeling I needed to not be so drink sodden. I slept alone that night. Naya had a thing.

I called her anyway. I liked the phone and I lay in the dark talking to her as she made ready to get into bed. I suppose I could have asked her over. But there is something to be said for pace or tempo, I had never quite mastered it. That night though, I feel we got it right. The last ten minutes of the conversation one or other of us dozed off; I opened my eyes into darkness and wished her more kisses than stars. Corny as hell.

"Goodnight Johnny. Goodnight."

Chapter 13

Thursday October 10 2002

Naya invited me to some soiree the next night at her college. I was tempted to bring a few stones. Joking apart, I went because she asked me, and I might already have fallen for her, note the dishonest use of might.

The do was in her college on the Left Bank. École nationale supérieure des beaux-arts. I even like writing it. The place was seriously old school class. D'Artagnan greeted us. There was Hugo eating leopards and drinking Châteauneuf-du-Pape. There was El Greco, or some other show off, handing out canapés made from tiny birds that had been caught by the students that day, in nets made from moustache hair. I was a Philistine from the old school. So I went around trying to establish which alumni I knew. Matisse was the most famous I could find. Most people wore brand new leather biker jackets.

But Naya was the main event. She and two others had an exhibition. They had won the best of year award and this was their prize. So I looked around at the art. Were the people at the exhibition faking it? Did they know what they were looking at? Naya's pictures were made with Henna, on what seemed to be thick fibrous wall paper, they sat out from the frame, like they were three dimensional. They were cool and I could not have created them. So that was OK? But art? I was really only interested in art as a means to antagonise the right wing press. I was just as happy when a guy put on an exhibition of all his train tickets laid out around a room. The guy winning an award and getting paid, the press having a micky fit.

There were little canapés being handed out by servers wearing masks designed by one of the other winners; clever too, the face part cut out, only masking the rest of the head, unnerving but very cool. I love food more than art and I love canapés the most. The only criticism of French food I can think of is they do not really do cocktail sausages or garlic bread, two glaring omissions in a delicious catalogue. The canapés were great. I had around thirty. I was a competitive eater at receptions, nobody except me knew, noticed or cared. I was competing against famine, scarcity, running out. I was still Irish underneath the veneer, and we are at heart starving savages.

I wandered around and did not speak to, I think, anyone at all. I was apart. Was I bored? Bored sounds like I was a child. I was elsewhere. There were speeches and then there was the college building itself which was splendid. Old Paris. Perfect. Back when those shapes and sizes made sense. Paris could never agree on anything architectural anymore. The Pyramid, the Pompidou, the Tour Montparnasse all derided. Me? I like them all, I suppose I could take or leave the Pyramide, but the other two always surprised my visual. And what was this sudden idea that people were supposed to agree? Agreement between people usually resulted in mediocrity.

I went and stood beside Naya for the last hour, having given her enough space previously. She understood I was not trying to get her to leave. I made that clear. She was the centre of the room. The human pressure of the coming war made everyone, including us, fall quicker. She had started to look into my eyes, preparing to jump into them it seemed. But my eyes worked like anybody else's, I was all there for her if she wanted me.

I was not afraid of her. I was afraid for her though, entering a period of turmoil I was courting. But I heard the celestial music just like she did. I walked with a smile. We had first spoken Sunday and this was Thursday. I was standing holding her hand, as she spoke to someone around on her other side, faced away. 'We' suggests, there were two separate people. It felt like there was only really one of us already. I imagined a disco ball above us as we slowly spun.

I liked to do this thing of letting my eyes fall back into their sockets, force the blood to pump quicker around my body, pretend I am observing everything at the same time as repairing all my damaged cells. I did this then. She was looking at me as I did it. I probably looked like someone with a bomb inside me. I was the bomb. I was the guy the papers talked about, but you wouldn't have known it. In years to come my neighbours would talk about borrowing sugar off the Stonethrower and how I had always appeared so normal, perhaps even banal.

I used to be obsessed with having one more drink. So after everyone had gone home, pretending to themselves this was what real people did. After they had worried their way home. Yeah after all that, I found myself looking at Naya, wondering whether I was in the wrong, was she better off without me. Too late already, was my only thought of note. Thinking when she was looking at me was not really an option. I could not handle the duality. Being with her was the only thing I could do at that moment. Both of us loved to slide our hand round the back of the other's neck, find the place where our hand fit, to pull the other in for the languorous kiss. That week, that was our thing.

We took a left and the river was right there in front of us, and past buildings remained where they had been all along. This is the view. The same view people saw three hundred years ago. That is important even if absolutely nothing else is. Let your mind absorb that, then garner experience from it and remember you are but an ant. A big big ant. Irrelevance is a cloak and a shield and a sword. In times to come nobody would remember us and that too was grand.

I asked her what she saw.

"I see the city, tunnels and history, establishment on top and underneath. I see structures' shadows and lights, I see a gaping mouth, the river as the tongue, buildings as teeth and always the lights. You see it too Johnny don't pretend to be the industrial Anglo. Let's ride the river?" We got on the bike, headed first towards Bercy then switched sides and did the Diana run.

We winnowed through the many paths and slides, there is some modernity but it always looks a little like the imposter. Paris of the mind can only look like the past, and the modernity only looks like the pesky suburbs creeping in. The suburbs where all the new people live. Thrilling and bleary we came up Boulevard Barbès to my place. Tramps fighting on the street tramp fighting. Not too serious. Drunk tramp couple. Loud faces slathered with spit and fury. They looked at us angrily.

Seeing god knows fucking what.

I wheeled the bike into the courtyard. The tramps with their minds of floating boozy landseas. There definitely seemed to be something OK about being homeless in Paris. They were everywhere. In the 13th, where I once lived, there was a group of homeless carnival people who slept on mattresses, with their dogs, underneath the raised Métro line. Grubby yes, bonecold definitely. In the morning, when I walked past them, they would be sitting up in bed watching us eejits traipsing our sorry asses to work. Watching us like we were the homeless, the different. Pointing.

Yeah I know being outside sucked, and yet outside was my overall favourite place in the world. They would be unscrewing the cap on a two litre of diesel wine as we walked past, smacking their lips at us. If I was to make a call; they were happier than us, the human bots. None of us surprised anymore at how bad it was. Expectancy of disappointment, de rigueur and mounting. The weight of wearing a suit to a job that paid you in restaurant tickets could not be measured in gravitational units. It was smooth denial and acceptance all at once.

I followed her gorgeous ass up the stairs. Marvelling at my ownership of it. Let us not be fooled. I wanted it as my own. She had no real use of it anyway. In my apartment I stood right there in front of her, letting her open my fly. Being anywhere near her I was almost ready. We were in the kitchen though. I could be seen out two windows. I gripped her shoulders, the shudder already unlocking down deep in my centre ready to roar ripple out. Then she stopped and smiled.

Prison rules.

I lifted her up and out of the chair, slightly using my strength to overcome. A little cheat maybe, she laughed and nestled into me.

Things zinged against my mental arousal but I remained strong into the bed. The epochal delectable rise of a girl allowing you to pull her jeans off. I nearly got the pants off too, but had been vaguely woozy and mesmerised by the fish flip.

Heels off.

There was only us there and the light was on. I was not that drunk and she wasn't at all, but that never mattered. She was more into sex than me. Always was.

We grappled, I photographed everything with my mind, storing and living it. Trying not to cheat it. I thought later, as we finished all over, she was seducing me into something I did not understand. I was not in control. I was only glimpsing things as they were revealed to me and then re-covered. I lay there momentarily perfectly positioned in the seam of her and me and satisfaction of future and past. Me with her there right up aside me. Yeah sleep. Fuck sleep. Stay tuned, you might not be awake for much longer.

Sleep was all around us.

Sleep kills.

Never found it that enjoyable. We both sucked and licked our way through the next infinite space. What was that taste, us? Tasted like I imagine a honeysuckle would taste like, if I had created the plant myself from memory. So much honeysuckle.

Naya and I must have talked in that first week, but besides the few things I have mentioned, besides them, I can only remember what being with her felt like. It all felt like fear and drowning, but drowning inside my own body. Dropping down inside my skin. My eyes looking out my chest and sometimes being almost unable to come up for air. I was afraid, or more accurately, I had a constant pit-of-my-stomach punched feeling.

Best time of my life.

Every day I wanted to call the stones off more. But then what would that make me? It would take me back. Would I have ever met her without them?

No.

Always remember that. The first thing it brought me was the best thing I've ever had. So I had a duty. A male duty, something that women think is stupid about us. But sometimes the wrong follows the right; you need to establish something that was necessary for the right thing to return. Right Wrong Right. Up 4 yellow.

Chapter 14

Friday October 11 2002

Friday the battle bloodied king of days. Swollen oceans of time in front. Thank you for the hope. Thank you for your beautiful daughter Saturday and your pious sullen son Sunday.

My mag came out Friday so there was always an added frisson in the office. No other day did I get electrostatic shocks from the doors like Friday. I could not go near a door without getting a jolt. The office loved it. French people's love of slapstick physical comedy has remained undimmed by immigration or two world wars. I will say that for them.

That Friday was our largest ever print run. Someone somewhere was making money. My boss Clarinet was delighted. That Friday's edition was crammed full of advertising. I was proud. O so proud. I walked out into the cold air streaming down like rain. The city felt strong that Friday evening, fortified. I turned left and walked towards Place Vendome. Napoleon stood cold and tall; ignored on top of his column. I still liked him, even if now he is seen as a monster by the bien pensant.

The practice weekend was to be planned. The night glittered and sparkled through and against the yellow wet windows, falsely expectant of what we might achieve. There was no confidence in the group then.

Suddenly our idea seemed very small. Slight and untroubling was what I had always liked about it; representative of us. The very act of us talking about it seemed to be weakening our resolve. I felt like I could let it slide. The momentum, sand through our fingers.

The pithy drizzle enabled all us walkers to pretend we were hidden and alone, that was fine. My ego dampened down. I was not sure, which made me more nervous. The gentleness and the softness of Naya mind and body, meant that for me I was finding the tug of those soporific suburban dreams strong. I'd nearly not got out of bed that morning. I'd nearly quit. My job, my duties, my upbringing. She was a bit like a revolutionary. I was pendulous now. No longer moored to my own solid harbour. I had been cut adrift.

I was going to have to get rid of her, in the non-Mafia sense. I stopped walking at Madeleine and thought for a minute. I had no notion of getting rid of her. But that was what I needed to do. My usual ambiguity was wreaking havoc on my innards. I stopped breathing to stop myself over breathing. I could see eejits looking at me as I stood there, leaning up against green artful scaffold.

The thought occurred to me that I could always kill myself. What harm? Was that not what I wanted to do anyway? Was that not what I was doing? Shaking my life as a red flag, asking them to recognise I am not them. And the price for this normally was absolute. There was nothing I wanted more than to go back to when I had not considered the Stonethrowers. I had worked towards this for years. I had allowed myself. I had become obsessed with myself. There was not enough room in my life for Naya and me. There was barely room for me. Crammed so chock full of furious vagaries of soul and sense was I.

I started breathing again through an unlit cigarette. The Irish inside of me spoke, told me I was only pretending to panic. Told me none of these emotions or feelings were anything other than false idols, borne from years of imagined experiences and lessons taken from falsified events that never meant anything and sometimes had never even happened. Reading signs as mine when they had no context. I had no context, except one I put around myself. Depth of nothing, circular depth. Inside the tube of the eternal tire of life.

When all this passed, when I was back, I lit the smoke, and walked on. In Paris nobody 'cared. So very relaxing. Within five steps I was surrounded again by people whose mind had never touched upon me, and never would. They thought about a shed roof in Marne La Vallée they had seen that morning they'd liked. They thought of an interesting piece of furniture that spoke to them. They thought of all these things together at once. I could not hear them. But I looked where they looked, and I was not afraid to leave myself behind, if only for a few minutes of respite from the me me me. March march march. All of us together creating the dreary flow.

The rarefied air of business around Madeleine on the way to the Bug made for distraction. I was early enough and the millionaires were still ensconced in their Potemkin pressures. Kerchiefs of industry. Fair play to them. Being born into it must make it normal.

Dean was there already. This was a glitch on the phrenic plane. I went to give him a hug like a champion. It was like hugging a used human tea bag. He was troubled. Peter was over stage right conversing with a lady with Swiss eyes. She lived in a house around the Bug, hundreds of years old. Innocuous doors leading to palaces, protecting the occupants from everyone else; from modernity, from progress, from time, inverted icebergs. My pint arrived, as if I myself was a member of the privileged class, I knew I was, but sometimes I forgot, bleating about some bullshit, the colour of my Ferrari, servants stealing, the cost of jet fuel. I was trying to make myself rotten, best as I could, to spoil the whole barrel.

"Well motherfucker what's the story? Why do you feel like wet bread lying on a pavement? Everything OK with Geneviève?"

She was his blue blood French wife. Strangely sound. Strangely enticing. Strangely married to that schizo. She seemed no longer to care what he did. Dean needed her to care. He needed to have a rein; she point blank refused to put one on him. This led to him lurching between being a madman and a stay at home husband. I did not like having to act like I was the kid convincing him to come out. But I loved him enough to do it the odd time. We all had ankles and this was his.

"Yeah everything is great. Better than great. She booked us a holiday away without telling me."

This was the usual thing they both indulged in. Neither listened, so everything was misunderstood or unheard. Two strangers married as children. Now adults, they looked across the table at each other wondering if they wanted to bother with the effort of falling in love or walking away. Either choice seemed to act as a double negative. Both feigning fatigue on a level of ennui unachievable anywhere else on earth except Paris, or perhaps Vienna.

Geneviève's family had them living in some preposterous and fantastic apartment in Montparnasse. So they both went from sofa, to cupboard, to bed, to toilet leaving behind little murmured breadcrumbs of self-pity slash scorn for the other to press with their finger and lick off. Either on their own was great, together they dismantled the atmosphere on a chemical level, nullifying evenings out or nights in.

This was probably another fresh start or new leaf in a forest of them. Judge thee not, though, was right. There was no future in pedestal standing. You always eventually fall off, so narrow is the space.

"So I am going to Canada, Friday." Dean.

Chapter 15

Friday October 11 2002

Betrayal at absolutely any level releases a toxin into the blood that cannot be denied before it is absorbed. Its absorption causes a reaction along a chain until it can be destroyed by electricity and air. I felt my veins contract at the sudden shock of venom. I could hear Peter pause as he sensed the air flatten then inflate. Peter continued to chat with the eyes but he now was upright and preparing himself for the next thing.

I lit a choker. I used it as a pausing device. Dean understood and continued.

"I know this is not good. I understand I've made commitments to our group."

At this stage just after the end of the Twentieth Century, language, and particularly assertion or pre statement assertions, had changed from lonely obsoletion to inversion. Thus I could assert from his assertion that he did not really 'know' or 'understand'. For if he did, there would not have been a conversation, for to know and understand would have prevented it. He understood and knew something other than what I knew and understood.

Dean was our family so there was really nothing I could do. Can you love a brother less? Folly though this was, loyalty to the family an obvious societal and familial inculcation. At that moment, as he sat there speaking to me in the language of pure undriven excuse and whimper, I wanted to strangle him with a length of cord.

Why?

Strength was unity and he had removed a corner of the square. He also knew without responsibility. This was trouble. It had been as much his idea as it had been mine.

"OK" I spoke. "OK, you will be away for how long?" French question structure a bane of all our lives.

"Two and a half weeks."

"So you're out?"

"I am out."

At least he gave me that. At least he didn't start up again with panting meaninglessness. Forcing me to chase him. He quit.

Mostly, nearly, almost, always, things that go wrong have a shadow you step onto first before you hit their origin. I had been feeling the chill for a few days now and ignoring it. Would he have asked Geneviève to book the holiday to get him out of the throwing? Would he have needed to? Was he lying I wondered, so I asked him.

"Are you lying? You are going right?"

I think he considered playing hurt. If he had gone through with it maybe things would have been different. The hindsight prism never allows for clarity, removing context and causality despite what the experts say.

"Course I am fucking going. I have not and will not ever tell anyone. No matter what. On pain of death. Promise, swear; the whole gamut."

"Alright then. Another pint?" I glanced at Peter, now reappeared in front of the tap.

"No have to go. Will be in touch."

And like that he was gone. I considered developing a twitch as a conversational diversion. I considered following him out and kicking him, from behind, in the balls, just to make him really understand and know. Taste the bile of it. I considered lots of things then. I'd watched my friend take his name off our list. I knew he was right to go. Geneviève was worth the whole thing. He was clearly a weak link I thought. But he was a bloody brilliant throw, all state baseball brilliant. He had seemed so keen.

Peter brought over my pint. And Dean's bill. The bill he had left unpaid. We both looked at each other.

"Out?"

"Out."

"Talk tomorrow. He won't be there?"

"No, probably won't be around for a while."

James bounded in nearly killing some tiny trader who was trying to gets Peter's attention. The trader tried to speak, tried to get some point across, gesturing with his twig arms. Peter turned into him, guided him around a column away from James. He had breathed in the toxicity and was now fully alert to danger.

"Sit down you fucking maniac. Bigger and taller fish to fry." I was in no mood.

"Shake my hand you Irish cunt. Shake it unless you want to kick off right now."

I smiled, despite the whole thing it was only life after all, I stood up and shook his hand, he was a strong fucker but I was seething inside and he got the picture. I waited as Peter got him his life blood, lager. Piss if you ask me. OK out of a bottle when you can't see it. But in a pint, it really was piss in a glass.

"Give it to me, no, wait. Dean, right? Dean is getting married again? They are renewing their vows? Dean is, insert fucking first world problem right there. Go on hit me with it?"

"He is going to Canada with the missus, so is out of the group."

"The fucking prick. I am going to fucking break his face."

"Relax, you're not going to do anything. Maybe we're better off? He was already the weak link. He was wavering. I should have spoken to him. My fault."

"His fault. And only his. Yeah Pete thanks. Two whiskeys ice also. Serious drinking needed."

I told him the story from the beginning. There was not much to tell. We knew the ending. It was fair enough and if it had been anything else, we would not have minded as much. With the stones there was an issue of security. Mission integrity. What were we going to do, kill him? Probably not.

James, "I think we need to speak to him. Impress upon him the importance of keeping his mouth shut."

"How are we going to impress that upon him? He's not a fucking goose. He's not afraid of either of us. Pushing him away is probably worse. Let's sleep on it right? Nine o'clock tomorrow at the entrance to the Bois. Bring supplies. Just the three of us. Bring stones. You can make us a target."

"Yeah I know. Last thing I am going to say about it. But I am fucking pissed off. That septic prick. Leaving us in the lurch like that. And what a throw. Fucking angry. Ye know, if you'd asked me, I'd have said it had been his idea in the first place. Gutless wanker."

Pausing then thinking anew, James continued straightening out his skin, his suit and his id.

"Nine tomorrow is a little ambitious, n'est pas? We'll be wrecked. Busted flush. But I'll be there."

"Have you got a target? Time and place?" I asked.

"I do. You?"

"Yeah, have done some research. And I think I can get the head of the European Central Bank early doors on the first day of the conference. First will be the easiest. The first and the second anyway. Not sure they will understand what is going on initially."

"Yeah are we really not going to release a statement? Anything claiming responsibility? I am sort of thinking we should. Or else our message will be lost."

"The message will be lost anyway. The media will fuckin spin that shit whatever way they fuckin please. Reminds me, we should think of hitting someone in the media, non?" Wishful thinking on my part.

"Anyone in particular? Surely there are better targets. Not as if that shape shifter Murdoch is going to suddenly appear in our sights." James sat facing the bar, supping, neither of us facing the other, like tarnished and varnished old men, each sank into our own problems and skins.

"Jesus that would be sweet. The moron's mogul. Magnifique. You're right. Leave the media alone. Although I sometimes think they are the true villain of the piece. So utterly cowed." I could feel my default rant bubbling away ready to overflow.

James felt the same, "Sing it brother. What else have you got? Seems to me that it is so true, so inherent, so obvious, it's lost its power. I feel upside down. I feel transparent. I feel fuck all except my little pet rage. I forgot I had it. All these years. Making money. Pretending I did not care, that nothing mattered. More. More. Now I have more. So much fucking stuff, I own antiques you know, how the fuck did that happen? Even listening to myself. I am the teenage adult. I am that person. I need nothing." James looked stiff, took a long pull on his pint.

I pondered and watched the rest of the world treadmill past. James and I speaking low like we had arrived at a point of profundity when we hadn't.

"It's all being done in our name. There's nothing we can do about it. Except throw stones. They'll not make a difference. All we're doing is alleviating our own guilt. Strange how when you say that, it sounds bad. Negative. Churlish." I was feeling more and more that it was going to happen and that made me strong.

"Churlish. Nice. Word of the week. I want to call ourselves something. I want to give ourselves a name."

Peter had moseyed over to us.

I asked him, "Couple more pints please, you up for nine tomorrow morning? At the entrance to the Bois? Supplies, stones, nickname ideas and who, where, when, of your first target."

A surly nod. Surly only in look. Surliness was more James. Peter was more prepared, ready, diffident. Hugh Grant always comes to mind. Being Irish any posh English comes across as Hugh Grant.

James had a couple of his co-workers coming for a pint. They came around the bar. Young eagles. Why did we hang around with these people? We were undercover.

"Bertrand, Céline, Arnaut and Stéphane this is Whiskey Chief."

They loved that, as did I. So just let your mind imagine, expound it all from there. The place slowly boiling us all alive, marinating our brains. The girl was pretty and French and pretending. Pretending to be interested in what we were all saying. As if we mattered. She knew about the future, as some girls seemed to. Knew we were all fake, knew she was supposed to be the audience as we jousted for her feigned attention. What else was there for her to do? The other traders were somehow worse. Two married, one engaged. But they were all single tonight and our group attracted more girls and boys. By 11 o'clock we were the dominant group in the bar. I was more than half cut.

I could feel myself luxuriating in the comfortable plushness of drunkenness. I thought about the words Whiskey Chief and The Stonethrowers and I was mildly happy.

Chapter 16

Friday October 11 2002

A finger brushed my elbow pressing firmly enough to get my attention. I looked up, discreet like, and Naya was at the door grinning. She was watching me. Peter had seen her, and being the gracious host, had given me the heads up. He always just knew. He ushered her through the middle. Introducing himself and giving her the bisous. James was also now on full alert. She sparkle-smiled into our zone and allowed herself to be kissed by James. I was looking around but she came up behind me, putting her arms around me, kissing me on the back of the jaw and then around into the face. French girls understand their men live in a jungle of their own making. She may as well have pissed on me to mark her territory. She was wearing a red mini skirt with her leather jacket. I had her waist. Of such sweet things make up our destiny and heavens.

"Hello mister popular. Thought I would surprise you." A lot of girls go on about things. They want to have a conversation about things. Pound them out. Break them down. Naya never did. She was a bit like a guy. Let a lot of things go. Not that I was necking with Céline but she had been in my area. Slightly having breached the line between my knees as I sat. Céline now gone to be bored by somebody else.

"Nice surprise honey child. Where've you been?"

"I was at a friend's house doing a potluck. Bit boring. Thought about you, so hopped on my bike then came down here to taste you. Cool?" and she opened her mouth onto mine, she was giving me a fucking fever with her hot tongue.

"Very, always." I prised her off and spun her round to face the bar. I nodded to Peter who stood aside us, ready. She ordered a Mojito and he made it to stun. I had warned her about the strength of the drinks. I had also told Peter he did not need to stun her. But he was his own man.

I offered her a seat. But the music was not to be denied. Peter had the place drunk and dancing now. There was a slight madness to that bar I never found anywhere else in Paris. A collectiveness of purpose. A promise between all there to forget or never remember. To remember and never forget. So James took her off me, the two of them did some ear whispering, some close contact dance stuff that made me think about things. But I know the voice of booze when I hear it. It sounds just like your own voice, but next thing you know it is carnage, you have punched a mirror, staring at yourself sucking down the blood from your fist wondering who broke the mirror. On day six of my relationship with Naya I knew it was not that type of thing. I knew we were different. But whatever about all that, I went and took her back to me. She kissed James bye and I suggested we go back to her place. She was not too drunk to notice it was her place and not mine I had mentioned. She was not that drunk. Close but no cigar.

"I prefer your place." She said simply and turned pulling me behind her. I do not really let anyone be in charge of me, I bristled, so she was going to have to do better than that. I wanted her to convince me.

"Convince me. Why not your place? I've never seen the inside of a squat."

"It is not a squat Johnny. As you know it's an artist's retreat. I also have another place. Where I live most of the time. But not tonight."

"In the 13th. Hardly a retreat."

One would have to ask oneself what it was we were talking about. Location of bed? It suited me better to go to my place. But on I went. I was chosen by natural selection to fight the wind. I have to have my say. If I can't speak and let the words out they still form but they enter my blood in little invective filled bubbles similar to what happens to divers when they come up too quickly. Only for me it is a very, very slow build up. I've always felt I will die from it. I am relatively certain keeping my opinions to myself will be the end of me.

But I was not going to die that day. Important not to lose sight of where it was we were going.

"OK what then? What do you think it is? Anyway I don't really live there. I have my own place. I have my own apartment. I'm not a clochard." She was still stuck to her guns.

"Agreed. OK let's go to my place. Fuck it. Fuck it all. You got the bike?"

"Nope, too drunk."

Peter was already ringing a cab for us as we arrived at the end of the pointless discussion.

The cab driver was typically sullen. A lot of people in France, particularly Paris, hate their jobs. They derive a deep loathing from what they are doing, they seem to think they are pawns in the Capitalists' game. They are probably right. I let Naya deal with him. She was a charmer and I was not.

Come to think about it, what exactly did she see in me? Purpose is the only decent answer I could ever come up with. A man of purpose. That purpose was to throw stones. But a purpose is a purpose right? And I was admittedly more steely, steelier? And I was funny. Real funny, I thought about jokes most of the day. Imagined conversations, so if approximations ever occurred I was ready. I paid the sulk in money, small tip. I could never quite allow myself to not tip as was deserved.

I think that evening if I had wanted, or if she had wanted, we could have had an argument. About the stones namely, using the apartment argument as a Trojan horse.

I was pissed, angry, and as we sat down on my bed she lifted her top straight up. And there was no arguing with breasts like that. She was wearing a bra the likes of which I had never seen. Designed by some scandalous Italian millionaire designer. Grazia. Other than that I attacked her as she had her arms trapped above her head, I held her down and she laughed so much I thought she was going to get sick. Sick like a sexy, delicious pig. I twisted the top tight, negating her arms ability to escape anywhere.

I used the other hand to slide her skirt up. Her leg skin looked glossy and orange in the street light peering through the window. I put my face down right into her middle and I breathed in like a man dying then I breathed out really warm and up against it. She bucked then, half killing me. I had to take evasive manoeuvres. I enjoyed that, she was now on top of me laughing and looking determined. Her skirt now a belt, her underwear dark red like her bra. Lacy, very feminine, very alluring, some gothic thrown in. I was not laughing though. I needed to do something with her. I was drunk but hard and her wanton, exquisite. She had my shirt off now, my tie still on me, she held it like a choke chain and choked me, looking into my eyes as she did. She got me harder and harder until I was ready to finish way too early. This was her aim. Games she loved; she was choking me now and pretending, I think, that she was in some kind of rodeo. I was losing oxygen, I was losing full stop. With a weighty growl I got up, her still straddling me asphyxiating me, I cheated a little by tickling her to drop the tie, then collapsing on top of her as a means of keeping her arms semi immobile.

I was knackered as the air came back into my lungs. I wanted her so bad though. So very bad. We were wrestling at this stage like wolves, me white, her brown. She had her legs wrapped around me pulling me into her even more. I still had my trousers on so I suddenly put my hands on her shoulders pushing her away from me and slipping my trousers down to my knees. Then I re-joined the fight. My hand tore her underwear clean off her. I knew this was risky but I figured the ligature marks around my neck would be a good rebuttal.

I put her underwear into her mouth. She was momentarily delighted stroke surprised. Her bra was next but she muffle screamed no. Quickly unclipping it at the front. I would have gone to war for her breasts so indignant were they. So completely cold, smooth and choice. I nuzzled them, then lightly licked them, then really, really slowly sucked them deeply and gently into my mouth. She moaned and settled for a long stretched moment then reached down and put the panties into my mouth. I could not have given a damn. We were both panting. She smiled at me. Her creature. Her thing. Hers.

She politely asked me to get up for a sec as if she was now suddenly sore. Then she rolled around onto her front and slightly raised her beautiful beautiful ass. Raised it as recognition of what it was we were doing. My mind transfixed, my brain charged and empty. I licked deep into her wanting more and more. I licked both and she arched back into me. She said please in a voice so sexy, my brain tipped into and out of its cup and I shuddered. I put my arm under her and arched her slightly into me allowing myself easier entry into her. I played at the entrance dragging the whole thing out. Dragging it out and then in. One of us whimpered. I was no genius but she was and this made me seem like one.

I was never afraid to do what she wanted in bed and she always brought me with her. Brought me right along to where I wanted to be. She urged me on, contrasting the request of harder with the little French accented whisper. "Faster, harder". I was fucking her by the end, no longer sensual or sensitive just plain old-fashioned good fucking. Making her forget something, maybe somebody? Fucking something out of her. I was able to manage another precarious five minutes. She increased the pressure until I was battling against her and with her. Then in long strong fortified strokes I came, plunging myself into her, she screamed slowly and softly. Her head right up into the pillow as it shook through her. Her elbows stopping her from folding. I rolled onto my back bringing her with me. Now her lying on me with her back on my front shaking. My breathing sounding like I had been running for hours. I hugged her into me. She slid round onto her front and kissed me, hand on my forehead. She thanked me. For what I have no real clue. But she thanked me anyhow. She smirked into my eyes. I was experiencing a slow whispering wave of pleasure through my body, up along my skull, my hair static and on end.

She made me want her. She made me begrudge everything around her. I was not really prepared to let her walk around without me. I know, I know, if you love someone truly, set them free. That is total bullshit. But, but I don't think I loved her yet, I just was not prepared to let her walk around amongst other men. Maybe the Muslims have a point, I found myself thinking. The moment passed and we lay there with a new moment. I knew what she was thinking. She was thinking about the stones and the two lads tonight, James and Peter.

Chapter 17

Saturday November 9 2002

I could not tell. I had nearly killed myself anew going over that wall. The drop was much further when you have only one real knee and you look like a scorched soft toy. I could hear shouting from above me. Someone had seen me. I thought about thinking, about thinking about doing something. But that was not really on. Move or hide, the two options I was still allowed. I hid.

One of the squat people came down the stairs screaming the loudest screeches I have ever heard. The guy, was his name Tom? Well Tom, was carrying a body, he was screaming for help. Could this be Naya? I stepped out of the shadows like a lurking maniac. A cancer of worry gripped me. I felt I was going to cough up my lung and then hack up pieces of my heart. The body confronted me with certainty and half sprung me out of my cheap torpor. Like some shitty cologne, my torpor clung on to me but I could feel the miasma lifting. The body looked too long. Tom lay the body on the ground like a ceremonial presentation. And that was what it was. He knelt down and sobbed briefly, putting his hands onto the body. It was the body of a young man. Tom wailed that he was dead. He was dead. Lying on the white dusty ground, the dead guy looked like he was about to move. But he never did again.

Nothing made sense. A massive explosion came from inside the squat. The outline of the world rumbled and shook as if everything was fake. It'd never occurred to me that the squat had been hit. Never once. Tom turned and shouted something. I ran over with him to the squat's front door. It was down a slope, then up again and the explosion seemed to be at the back of the building. We both went to enter. Smoke was coming out.

"Naya" I looked at him. "Is Naya inside?"

"No. Yes. I don't know. But, but there are others. Are you coming?" He finished speaking.

Was he asking me something? Did he know me, recognise me? Tom paused, looked at me, thought about what my appearance meant, let it all flow through him and then sprinted into the burning building. I suspected I was expected to follow. Could life not just leave me the fuck alone I gurned into the ether.

Bollix.

What else was I supposed to do? This was what I'd wanted wasn't it; real life? Danger?

We entered and immediately I had to exit again unprepared for the amount of smoke. I took off my outer shirt and wrapped it round my face, à la Palestine. It made a slight difference, initially at least. Tom had disappeared further up the spiralling staircase in front of us. It was dark and really smoky. There was a window halfway up the staircase. I kicked it through. Slight difference. Momentarily filled my lungs again with some real air. Tom called my name. He did know me.

"Johnny come, viens ici. Come on putain Stonethrower."

I followed where his voice led, the heat began to rise. What kind of a sap enters a burning squat stroke artists' retreat? My kind is the only answer I can give you. I knew not what I was doing. I was strangely beginning to feel better, more thawed. I locked my shoulders back and started to regain control over still slightly flailing limbs. I ran ducked, down a corridor on what I would say was the first floor. I was making it all up. There was screaming down the end. There was screaming falling from the ceiling and emerging from the smoke, it was next to impossible to understand anything of space or location or sound. I nearly knocked Tom over; he stood looking at me as if I was a madman, hand on the door waiting impatiently. Standing aside to let me in. There was a room of evil in front of us. The last level of some eighties arcade game.

The roof was open up through another floor to the sky. Two people lay outstretched on the ground one uncovered and unmoving. A girl with blond hair, wearing jeans and a massive chest trauma. She looked beautiful and dead. The dirty blood on her face looked like haute couture make up. Her hair matted and piled on top of her crown. Tom pointed towards the two legs sticking out from under the debris, cartoon style. There was a sound from there, maybe. Where had the scream come from? But this was not logic this was its nemesis, death and war. The battleground slightly different, the fight the same, always. There was constant stereo screaming. Was I screaming? Was that my voice screaming her name?

"Stéphane, Chris." Tom mouthed his eyes pleading with me. I think my hearing was beginning to come back. There was a lot less smoke in

there due to the gaping bomb made chimney. No fire on that floor although if I looked up, flames were flagging out and up.

I opened my hands with exasperation to Tom.

"What are we waiting for?"

We scrambled like men trying to rescue someone from a burning building. Essentially standing over the legs, bent over at the waist and throwing the rocks behind us, careful not to hit Chris.

We worked crazed, there was no other option. I could feel my own fear rising and falling. Tom seemed to have a dark stain on his back that was growing. I stopped for a sec and reefed back his shirt, his back was a bloody mess. Something small and long was jutting out of it, awkward like. I had no idea whether or not to take it out or not. So I took it out. It was almost too hot to touch. The wound did not bleed out. Not sure that all of the blood was his. He thanked me. And we went back at it. I was again almost un-terrified at this stage, I could hear crackling above us. Pieces of burning material were tumbling down onto us. Despite all this we nearly had Stéphane uncovered. Towards the end I took a chance and dragged him out. The showers of rocks, wood and cinders were getting steadily worse.

Possibly he moaned. Reckon he did. I gestured to Tom to grab Chris that I would take Stéphane out. He was not a big guy but he was dead weight. I could not see any outward signs of injury. He was not responding. I picked him up and put him on his front over my shoulder. That way I made it to the door not trying. I thought about putting him down, how great that would be. As if I had a choice. You don't have a choice, it is not bravery, it's normality. I let myself stand at the door *waiting for Tom. He had Chris in his arms like a bride over the threshold.*

Visibility was nothing in the hall to the stairs. But we knew the way, one last gulp, to my rear a huge clump of stone fell from above, crashing through the floor where we'd been. This encouraged us to move and our small ambulance ran. As Tom disappeared ahead, I followed. I allowed I would know when I was at the stairs. I was half running but more bounding, small bounds. There was only smoke and noise, so much noise flying up and down.

The stairs came two steps before I expected, and we were momentarily in the air, aloft but falling, I managed to ferociously grab the bannister with my free left hand behind me, putting all our weight on the bannister, which was not too happy about it. I jerked my leg down and spun on the stairs into the outer spiral. So we swung and flew, the bannister saved us then.

We were more than halfway down when a whoosh of flames flashed either side of my head. I leapt, and using terror as my motivation, I was out and up the bank and right over to where Tom had the other two bodies. Tom ran towards me, smacking my head and my back, patting down the flames. I could feel a light fuzzy burning on my crown. A haircut was the least of my worries at this late stage. Tom handed me a hard hat. I nearly laughed, but there was nothing funny about it.

I lay Stéphane on the ground; his jeans were black but hardly smouldering. There were now three bodies on the ground. Sirens and dumb, dull explosions were the sounds that slowly eased their way back inside me. Helicopters flew from everywhere, pouring water on to the giant burning books around three hundred metres in front of us. The cinema in front of the Bibliothèque was completely obliterated, along with the overpriced bars running from where I was towards the library. The one I'd first had a drink in with Naya, rubble and memory.

I looked down at Stéphane, he looked fucked. Trampled by rock. Although Chris looked even worse. She seemed inanimate. Her blood looked brown. She looked like a bum. Her mouth had foam in the corners and dirt. I touched her hand. Which was grubby and damaged. I gave it a squeeze. I had no idea what dead felt like, but she felt better than I imagined dead would. I hoped for her. There was nothing else I could do. I have no gods.

Naya Naya Naya

Chapter 18

Saturday October 12 2002

So there I was knee deep in life, wading along, loving and fighting the current. Naya lay asleep beside me breathing. Not doing anything unusual or quirky, but still I was entranced. What was I supposed to be doing with the alien in my bed? Who was she in all this? It was early. I moved up alongside her. Trying to nudge her into some act or other. I reckoned she was awake. I hadn't mentioned to her I needed to be out of the house so early. I was not worried about the time. I was worried she'd want to come with me. Come along for the ride.

"Naya, Naya wake up honey. Naya wake up, I have to go."

"I am awake you dope. I can feel you sticking me. Lie back down beside me and wake me up like a normal person, not, like my dad." I laughed as she smirked, eyes closed.

You never can tell with some people. Walking along minding your own business then, boom, you meet a really funny, sound girl, who loves having sex with you. I moved in and down and woke her up the way she seemed to want. I woke her up like that for a good ten, fifteen minutes. Then she woke me up, then we woke each other up. And then we went into the shower and cleaned each other like nit picking monkeys.

Dressed and pressed we sauntered out the door holding hands. Christ, it kept getting worse. I'd thought I'd already left behind that area of life, thought I'd already missed out on all those things, and I'd accepted that it was too late. I'd presumed I was already on the slag heap.

My inner monologue struggled. OK onwards. Let's move. Let's do something. We cannot go on like this. Does it keep getting better? I whispered encouragement to myself.

In the street, she asked me for the first time where it was we were going. I told her

"I am going to see my friends and spend the day in the park. I am getting us a picnic, we are going to practice stone throwing."

"Seriously? Well am I invited? I've nothing on today? James and Peter mind?" she was not messing about.

I wondered, was this the down side? Wanting to do things with you outside of the house? Was this a play of power, a power play?

She went on, looking at the Paris autumn sky, both clear and focussed.

Rolling her head she went on, "Suppose I could go home and do some work? Yeah you're right. Fuck it as you say."

I had not spoken. I maybe wished I had spoken. My silence allowing her to continue further into the conversation.

Besides the lads thinking I'd taken leave of my senses, besides all that, I, personally, all on my own, in my own mind, did not want her involved. Motivation? Difficult to differentiate between what I thought and what I didn't want to think.

"OK let's think about this?"

There was the element of security breach. We'd lost Dean. So that was one strand blowing in the wind, one loose strand we no longer had control over.

But then I was hardly going to tell her no. I should have obviously told her no. I needed to speak to someone about this. This was coming down to an element of trust. Coming down to whether or not we could trust her. Was the situation as tenuous as all that?

Make a decision.

"Alright let's go. We need to get stuff for a picnic."

And then we went, Métro, got the bike. She knew some nice semi posh delicatessen run by middle-aged sisters, Parisian jaded. We arrived at the entrance where Avenue Foch hits the Bois. The lads were laid out on the grass having a coke and a smoke. Their eyebrows arched when they recognised us as being two. But being lads, and in particular English lads, they didn't cause a fuss.

The Bois is a strange place in October; it's not that visited. But it is still a park in Paris and hence awesome. Most of the call girls and boys were gone home, most of the needles re sheathed, the open spaces all Dumas. Trees designed by nature for secrecy and intrigue, still being used for both. So we wandered into the bois not speaking much, a slight zing of tension in the air. From the fear of our future, from losing Dean and finally from Naya being there.

I gave up worrying about her as we walked. She seemed happy, instinctively walking ahead or behind, picking long blades of grass and whatever leaves there were left, rolling them in her fingers and letting them fall. There was coolness in the air besides our own and each of us was smarting a little bit.

Peter had had a hard time getting out of the apartment he shared with Monique, his girlfriend. She'd made an itinerary for them, as it was seldom he had a Saturday off. But a day off walking the crass aisles of DIY shops was not his destiny that day. She had taken it badly. Mostly I suspect because he had not warned her he had something on. I make her sound like a git, but she was sweet and kind, traits rarely found anywhere in this pointy sharp world. Peter loved her and they were strong enough to keep moving. So Peter was a bit tired and a tiny bit raw.

James was just hung over, a sweaty horse who'd overindulged the previous night at the trough. Feeling slightly giddy yet from the liquor. After we'd left the Bug he had gone on to one of those nightclubs in Paris with prices so frightening, so outrageous you needed to pay in gold ducats. He looked as ragged as he ever looked, which was scruffy spiv banker.

Empathy is my one decent human trait. I could sense the lads were brittle on the Naya issue. They were letting it go out of politeness. We got to what looked like a perfect duelling clearing. Very long, tree encircled, decent width. Naya took all the food and told us to get practicing. I had brought her a book, Beware of Pity, which I wanted her to read. So once she had itinerised the food, she lay back on the rug, dressed like a ski instructor and half read, half dozed, half spied.

James was always a dab hand at making things, so using some branches he constructed what appeared to be a bird table onto which we pinned a balloon.

We'd brought around fifty stones each.

It was obvious from the beginning we had all been practicing. Peter in particular, he burst the target balloon five times, to my three and James's four; out of ten throws each.

That was not going to cut it though. And as we began to include more movement the accuracy faded again. Walking a minimum of thirty metres from the target slightly away from it. One stone only. Throwing mostly wrist high and shot arching was causing us some problems. We practiced and practiced, for what else were we supposed to do?

Naya announced lunch and we moped over and slid down. Was it because there was a girl there we all felt the need to go into ourselves? To act out and burrow in. Not sure we would have allowed ourselves the indulgence of it otherwise. Idiots the lot of us at times, most times.

The food was a banquet and we vanquished it quietly alone with our own worries. Life knocking its fists against each of our private window panes.

Saffron yellow roast chicken, chalky white brie, Blue d'Auvergne, green golden Kro, young pink ham, mottled red salami, some angry brown ribs, sprung green lettuce, a glistening tomato with vinaigrette, perfect mayo mustard, an oily pasta salad and three different types of baguette was our repas that day, my mouth remembers it so perfectly.

Even Naya seemed lost inside, the significance of the balloons and the stones and her being there, making everything spoil a little. The food though, as always happens, generated in all of us the fortification to go on. It consolidated our lives; kept us pinned to the rotation. Peter rang Monique. Invited her down. What was I going to say about that?

James downed two beers and supped a third opening up his capillaries and his smiles again.

Monique arrived quickly. She had been on her way there, to apologise apparently. How many warning bells did I ignore? A cacophony.

Irishness, laziness, desire for reconciliation and smoothness. Five of us now picking and overeating. The Bois egging us on. On a wind whispered whim I'd got up, taken the target down and hidden it in some bushes before Monique arrived. Two groups had traipsed through our Venn earlier and looked slightly askance at it. Although none saw us throw, I'd felt a little uneasy. But French people look at everything askance, they are weird like that.

Naya lay back into me and Monique put on the radio she'd brought, as presumably a pass into the group. Monique was all loved up due to the confluence of the phone call and her being nearby; her and Peter fit together real nice, brains and bodies. Lone wolf James told us about the night before and a humorous version of the girl he'd pulled. The girls feeling included, each of us secretly thinking we should maybe just leave the the stone throwing altogether.

I had packed a few tennis balls to give us something innocent to throw. So between the five of us we played around laughing and joking. Flirting with the various versions of our futures. The clouds in the skies, long quills of white. The trees old, serious and never asked, they pretended to be friendly, but they didn't want us there. The bounce of life in all of us. And this is what I wanted to ruin?

Yeah I did want to ruin it, although I feel I must say it was a false dichotomy. Even then I knew I was going to go ahead with it, on my own if necessary. The others' intentions were still in the wind, blustering around inside them, their own motivations and reasons hazy to me.

I can explain. Mercury rivulets of nonfulfillment flowed through me. I could never again stand to have constructed something only to leave it behind incomplete. Action had to happen or else I would merge softly with the absent night. The creative energy of living, once more manifested as something I was considering walking away from. No. Where would I walk away to? Walking away towards a mirror, to where I had already been?

My mind creaked and yawed. I needed to run something new through it before it ground itself down to pulp. I walked amongst people who knew me better than I knew myself, for they could not see, nor were distracted by, the imagined person so falsely actualised internally. They saw me as I was. The sheen of youth had faded leaving me alone with only drab grey feelings and my worn grainy veneer. Outside my internal camouflage revealed me as I was. The only thing it hid me from was my own gaze.

The afternoon drifted then dissipated away into the entire horizon and we walked out together, me apart. I was beginning to feel crushed up against the decision. The only time I could breathe, the only time I could release the angst, was to allow myself to believe this time I would do it. Naya and I split back to mine. The others getting back on the horizontal escalator feeding them towards their own pretend important destinations.

Saturday evening we spent reading and playing at being a couple. I was in a flinty mood. She had concern in her eyes and worry. Those dancing twin flames made me angry. So we didn't speak. Kissing is speaking I suppose. Our lips still fitted perfectly. We slept that night without the porn act. The only night we ever did. I still feel my body's sadness and yearning for those missed touches and lost caresses. Unforgivable. Regret the most eternal and worst of all mistakes.

Chapter 19

Sunday October 13 2002

She left sometime in the night. I was aware of it. I thought of whether or not I should speak. She didn't come over to me. Slipped out whispering something I missed. The night air grasping her whisper out of my earshot allowing me only hear my name.

I awoke early, full of vim and vigour, piss and vinegar. How do people who don't drink survive all the morning energy? The declining optimism of the day? I was in determined slightly chippy form, one not given to having others around me. Better alone. Always better alone. I made more sense.

I dawdled my way to the duelling clearing. Set up Mr Balloon. I practiced for a couple of hours then James arrived. He greeted me amicably.

"Answer your fucking phone mate. Pissing me off."

"It's over there. Never thought to look at it. What's up?"

"Nothing, just wanted to find out if you were up for a few throws."

"Good work lad. Let's get to it."

And so we threw for hours. Boring at the beginning, one having to collect as the other threw. But after midday something inevitably clicked and we began to connect and the needle slipped into the groove. We enjoyed ourselves, relishing simplicity and task. By late afternoon I was starving and hollow. So we hopped on James's bike and went down to St. Germaine, which was actually nowhere near where we'd been. We went to a famous place on a corner, decent if overpriced. I was not thinking about Naya. Maybe she was not thinking about me either?

Maybe she had the sense to be forgetting about me. I told myself that I would prefer that.

James gave me a file. On it his target's picture, a French left wing politician he had a thing for, and the location of the throw. In French they call them Gauche Caviar, in English Champagne Socialist. This guy was nicknamed Legolas by the French political scene, and possibly even more annoying. But equally as irritatingly earnest. James had words to say, I burnt the pic as he spoke,

"Listen I feel this thing is getting away from us. I just want to tell you I am in. You throw Monday week, I've him down for Tuesday. He's addressing a meeting of foreign dignitaries by the Bourse. I've already got the time off. It's near my office. The throw only takes a millisecond and then we're out of there."

"Yeah I see what you mean, right in your area, aren't you. I'm up tomorrow week. Yeah mulling my one over a little bit more every day. You OK picking me up? Two days out of the office, will that not be noticed?

"Nah mate, Monday I am going to go in late, mostly dealing with the States at the moment, so with the time difference no one gives a shit."

I looked away at the traffic towards Odéon, and the hundreds and thousands of tourists, all dressed for a hiking trip. Pity.

"Yeah I know what you mean. I do feel it's getting away from us. We've to keep at it. I want it. Badly. I have not talked to Naya about it. That's weakening me. Should I justify it to her? What if she wants me to not do it? What if she wants to do it? These're all things hammering away at me. But my resolve is absolute. It won't change."

"We need to talk to Dean. And give Peter a call. I feel better talking to you. He'll feel the same. As for Naya, up to you. You have only just met her, is all I would say. Can you trust her?"

"Might be a bit late for all that compadre, might be a bit late. Dean is a problem. But what do you, Peter or I suggest? The strength of keeping him as a friend, thus applying that pressure on him, is our best hope."

"Physical intimidation will probably not work. And once we do that then it's past a point of no return. Let's go and see him later, bring him for a beer? See what he says."

"Alright. Fuck later. Let's go see him now?"

Off we went. Can never get away from enjoying Paris by motorbike. James drove the way he thought. Haphazard and with his chaotic intelligence. He understood numbers and drove according to computations designed to bring us as close to danger as possible. Numbers attached to everything, dialling up and down according to our proximity and speed and various other physical properties.

Chapter 20

Sunday October 13 2002

The open Boulevard Montparnasse held a lot of memories for me. In the early years of Dean and Geneviève's relationship I used to spend a lot of time hanging out with them. They were a lovely couple then. Their garden balcony big enough to have a party on. Wondrous. I knew the code so we buzzed ourselves in. Slightly forward, but on another day it would have been thought nothing of. Geneviève answered the buzzer and, after a slight pause, she buzzed us up. Elevators, nice. Unlike my own. Fifth floor. The door was ajar as we entered the huge open plan apartment. Turn of the century, maybe older. Very salon-y.

Dean came out of the kitchen looking vaguely harried. He greeted us both with a cursory bear hug if that is possible. Geneviève shouted she would be out in a minute. I sensed they were both about to have a shower or something. Maybe coitus interruptus, although it struck me more likely they had been having a serious conversation.

"So lads, to what do I owe this pleasure?"

Now Dean was not born yesterday, but admitting what it was he sensed would have increased the feeling, so like myself and James, he chose to ignore it.

James spoke,

"Just thought we would knock in say hello before you head off into the sunset. Hope that's OK?"

"Yeah awesome, you guys want a beer or something? Coffee, tea?"

And for a moment everything was OK as we all looked at each other aghast.

"Tea, coffee, where are we Seattle? Fucking Darjeeling?" I laughed relaxing.

"Alright settle down. Relax. Two beers? Cool, go out on the balcony. We can smoke and talk there." Dean blinked his eyes and a year or two fell off him as he made some computation in his head.

We set ourselves up with beers and smokes; put our feet up on the ledge. Tour Montparnasse to the right, looking like the Death Star. Black and red, futuristic and beautiful. It was a peach of a spot, really.

We didn't speak for about five minutes and the air thawed a little, the tension fading. James was in the middle and he started to prattle on about the football we were missing at that very moment. As each year went by we appreciated sport an iota less. We were still its slave, but missing it used to be unthinkable. Sad and good at the same time. Geneviève stuck her head out and said hello, her eyes slightly hooded. She didn't come outside fully and I suppose that meant something. But it could have meant she was busy or distracted. It did not have to mean all the things that spun through my lunatic head. I do remember that day was the last time I ever saw her, and that I didn't get a final bisous. You think you understand, but life is not that, it is not x's and o's; it's not even chess. Chess is a laugh a minute in comparison.

So we should all remember that nothing was obvious then. Or rather, what was obvious was not real.

Once we were alone again Dean began,

"You guys are worried about me?"

I answered, "Yeah we are worried. Not that we think that you're weak. But now you are out of the group you have no onus to keep quiet."

"No onus except for our friendship" Dean said hurt, his eyes flashing deep and mirthless. "No onus except that when I come back......"

James cut across him: "Not sure you've thought that one through mate. When you come back things'll be different. Not sure how, but it'll be different. We could be inside. And if we are they will come for you. Your name'll be on their list. Think about it, they'll want to talk, at the absolute very fucking least."

We all took a slug of beer, a slug equals three swigs. I intervened,

"We should talk about what you're going to say. It works both ways. We keep you out of it. You're only known as our friend. There's no evidence real or otherwise of your involvement with any of it. You'll also have a perfect alibi. But depending on how they frame it, they could come down on you hard. Conspiracy is a real easy dragnet term, a catch all, literally."

James again, whispering aggression totale, "Have you told your missus?"

"Are you joking? She would flip. We're going away to give ourselves one last decent shot. She knows something is afoot. But she doesn't know a damn thing. Swear on my life." Dean.

"Swearing on one's life is bullshit. Just saying." I replied, everyone swearing on each other's lives did my head in so false was it.

"So what do you want from me? What do you need? Nothing I can do except prove it when the time comes. Right?" Dean said with flat matter of factness.

I stopped, and then almost like I hadn't stopped, I continued, "Yeah I think we just need you to think about what you're going to do. And to cease contact with us for a while. I think the main thing in our favour is we are not on anyone's radar. So if they do get on our trail it'll be cold. No way are they expecting this from a group of middle class twats like us. No way. They don't have us infiltrated. They have nothing on us. So you play it straight. Deny, deny, deny. All the way down the line. What ye reckon?"

"How long? How long do you want me to cease contact?"

"For six months minimum. Think about it as a mutual thing. It's too risky. We cannot expose ourselves on the inside. I'll get back in contact with you when the time is right."

James, "Also Geneviève's no mug, she'll suspect something if you let her. So breathe deep and forget about us. She's nothing if not pragmatic. She'll keep schtum, so long as you do not activate her familial defences."

Dean. "Fuck lads, shit. This sucks." He said as he shook his head and the shadow of decision floated over his face. He looked at us both wryly "But what can I say? OK. So it's good bye and you are dust, forgotten to me." With that he slapped his hands together in an extremely Latin gesture.

James and I stood. We all gave each other a proper hug this time. Me especially, I knew Dean longer than I knew the other two. I'd been his best man. I loved him, but I had to move him on or at least aside. We had to start acting like serious men. Like Stonethrowers.

Geneviève was nowhere to be seen. We stood at the door embarrassed now all of us. But then what did we expect? We had culled one of our own for the greater good. Total crap, even if needed. I felt kind of ornery as we traipsed out onto the street. Asking James to drop me home, all I could think of was that I needed to read a 70's thriller to take my mind off all the fucking emoting.

Chapter 21

Sunday October 13 2002

Monday October 14 2002

That night I did not let my mind land on anything. One week later was the first throw and my stomach was sick thinking about it. I read a book about a CIA Special Forces operative. He needed to go rogue to remove an Al-Qaeda cell from the State Department. It made me feel a little bit better. A touch. Was the culture war imagined? Everything we read or saw was a little tick tock of propaganda. Where was our propaganda, where was the propaganda for people who didn't buy it? Fuck Al-Qaeda and fuck the CIA mirror dancing through our lives, interdependent, inter-reliant, cross-pollinated with each other's doctrines. Doctrines honed through being allowed to live alongside each other. If Al-Qaeda was the master franchise, why were there so many willing franchisees?

"They hate our way of life." A more facetious, self-pitying stroke self-congratulatory piece of shit would be hard to find.

I lay there in my pit. Letting all the thoughts come to me. Letting anything that wanted in, in. Twirling and spiralling round and round. Naya, mixed with Dean, with stones, and balloons, digital and analogue, up and down. I fell asleep eventually I presume, afraid, shoulders crouched and curved.

Monday, one week to go, one week to go till the point of no return. I yearned for it now. Kind of sick for it. In work that Monday I worked cleanly and expertly. Sober is a way of life for some people and I could see why. No lurking anxiety, no pithiness, no imagining randy scenarios everywhere. So I did my job. Not sullen, more serene. I would need to be out of it soon, I thought. I'd found work was using up part of me I could no longer spare. Not sure why, it was not difficult, more the opposite. I regarded advertising as Satan's Cinema. I sold print ads, there is no point in lying about it. I used to tell people I worked in publishing. Ha. Might as well have been selling lighters at the Tour.

So that day I was efficient and absent, and as often happens when you are inside yourself and wondering whether anyone will notice, nobody does, because they all have their own problems.

Relax nobody cares.

My mantra soothed my jagged mind.

I wanted to ring Naya. But say what? Probably best to say hello and take it from there? Non? There was more to this than anyone else believed. Not sure what that last sentence meant.

Yeah I know, get on with it. And then suddenly I did.

I rang her as I left. She answered before the completion of the second ring. What to make of that? I was a kind of post-futuristic superstitious moron. Too late to change my roaming maniacal mind.

"Johnny, great to hear from you. I was wondering would you call. How are things?"

I was about to say, I was wondering whether or not you were going to call me, but at the last minute I remembered it was not the television, this was it. No dress rehearsal. I had to try to stay away from myself. I was the one causing all these things to happen. People were all crashing off me; without my actions they would have remained static and secure.

"Can we meet?"

"Sounds serious but we won't mention the seriousness. Yeah I am at my place. My place not le Squat. In the 13th, I'll text you the info. Come up and I will make you something to eat, ça marche?"

Strength and apophasis. I could have cried then on my own in the Métro, like any other time I let something in. I could have gone to the end of the line and walked away off, into the simple distance, like I've always dreamed of doing. But each time I'd tried, my people kept pulling me back. Why was I ignoring these things and creating stories to explain and defend my darling solitude?

Chapter 22

Monday October 14 2002

The Bibliothèque Francois Mitterrand, the Bibliothèque Nationale de France commanded the view from her terrace. A pretty and practical studio apartment. If I looked diagonally downwards there was a school. We were able to sit on the step looking out and we did. She was so nice, so soft to me when I came in. We sat there, Naya linking her arm through mine. Keeping me grounded, stopping me from meandering off into the territories of the mind, where I spent most of my time and created most of my illusions.

I did not know what to say, so fortunately, I said nothing. And that turned out to be the right thing to say that night. She left me there and brought me a glass of beer, some bread and pâté forestier. Slick. She had a steak and we halved it. What girl in the world has a steak lying around? Had she been going to eat it on her own? The only thing I said while she cooked and I lay back on the terrace looking into the old sky, was that we could talk about it tomorrow. That was enough. She nodded.

So we borrowed some more time in the beautiful limbo of compartmentalised existence. Decontextualised. I sat up at the table and we looked each other over as we ate the salad, steak, potatoes and bread. We watched each other, checking the other was still who we thought. She looked normal and beautiful. Her every day unasked for clothing and her strewn hair made her look so grounded and ethereal simultaneously I once again picked up my subliminal things and moved my whole being closer to her.

We may have spoken about the looming problems in the world. The growing American anger with the French, but I doubt it; we were tight during the meal. We circled each other as we ate. Caressing and smoothing without touch.

The meal over, I stood and tidied. Enjoying the motion and the attainability of the result. I cleaned the place, folded away the table and joined her as she sat looking outside. It was hard not to look. Whatever it was about that apartment I was never in another, in all my time in Paris, where there was so much big sky.

"Big sky" I said.

She smiled and kissed me. Giving me kudos for noticing I reckon. Her lips were wet with the wine. She had fat lips, succulent, and I never could get enough of them. I could have chewed them all day and I still planned to. We lay on the bed watching as the darkness came down from above, and up from below.

Naya was thinking about what? How the fuck should I know? We lay beside each other and held hands like long term lovers. I was gasping for her. A crooked slant on my vision. A symmetry of crossed eyes. Searching for poetry in the ceiling I found those cracks that mean nothing except wear and tear. So then they do mean something right? Right?

No need to go into more embarrassing detail, suffice to say. Suffice should be enough. I didn't sleep though and I didn't care one way or another, I was moving towards something else. It was evolving, or in the last convulsion of ending and beginning, as most things are.

I'd only known her a week, so what exactly was I so worried about?

Answer: losing her. Easy enough when you put it like that. Simple.

Once I gathered my thoughts, I got up and went over to the open terrace window and sat there with a depth I did not possess. Looked at the BNF and the stars which were probably planes. And I tried to figure out if I was sad. She skulked over beside me and sat down wordless, lay her head on my back. The two of us were movie like twee. But I liked it that way. I liked the constant touching. I felt it was important.

Being alone all the time, the two things I always missed were the touching and the restaurant ally.

I would say it was around five, we started to talk, well whisper to each other. I wanted so bad to not have to start off on a lie. I wanted so bad to take her with me out of here into the past when I had the time, when I could have loved her enough. Instead I told her the whole plan. It was not a complicated plan. She probably knew it already. She'd probably guessed most of it. But she listened with her eyes closed, softly startling me every couple of minutes by opening them when something caught or snagged as she listened. Then I would see her black eyes, gamine eyes, as I mentioned. Impudence and emotion behind them. Something short of pity.

I told her about the group, the club. And what exactly, I at least, was going to do.

She then started to ask questions. Good questions that made me stop and not speak in my usual, so fast I am intelligent, way.

I lit cigarettes for both of us, made tea, as I prepared an answer for the first question.

"Why?"

No need to pretend the reasons tripped off my tongue. Explaining them to a girl they seemed thin, real thin. I eventually got round to the main reasons. Revenge. Boredom. Searching for substance. Searching for absolutely anything. Desire to hurt these people. To strike a blow for the little guy.

"But you are not the little guy." Naya pointed out.

"Maybe but absolutely nobody else ever does anything. Ever. A manif?"

The French called demonstrations manifestations, they loved to go on them. I admired them, but I also wondered whether or not they had as much power as everybody said. Inequality in France present and ignored much like anywhere else. The marches seemed powerful enough to maintain the status quo but rarely to alter it. The teachers who'd marched a few times that year were paid as badly as American teachers.

"I've thought about this. We all have. You're right, we're not the little guy, the peasant. But I'm talking about what's going to happen in Iraq and is going on already in Afghanistan. I'm talking about things everyone has given up on. I'm not being naive, we'll change nothing. But we'll cause them to pause just a millisecond in their beautiful ornate lives every time they walk out into the open. That's all we want. I ask for nothing in return. The opportunity to be myself." I left out one other reason, or I think I left it out, we wanted to goad them into a mistake, a rash judgement, goad them into opening up a debate or a war.

"Jesus Christ Jon, this is a fucking serious thing. Not playing. Not hide and search, seek. The police will find you."

"Not necessarily Naya. If they don't catch us doing it, they'll have a hard job proving it. Only one stone and what are they going to charge us with?"

"Attempted murder Johnny, get a grip. School is finished."

"Right it's finished and it's time to play. To play with these bastards. Every one of them will deserve it. Pure guilty the fucking lot of them."

We talked on until around seven. She was no happier, but by the time we stopped talking, we were talking about it in terms of what we would do when the trouble started. She offered me the use of her place. I said I would think about it. Come seven she snuck back into bed, I showered and went to go to work. Dealing with things was forward motion. I was hanging on a little. Letting her sleep, I went to slip out but she called goodbye to me as I snuck past her. We went on and did what we did best. That time the amour was like a continuation of the conversation, as if we were trying to convince each other of something, the other was listening but both wanted the last word. Nervous as I continued to feel, it had ended well. I left there strong and light.

Chapter 23

Saturday November 9 2002

Where the hell was Naya? I swam along in my panic.

There were now medical and kill soldiers dropping down over the wall with stretchers, guns and kit. Some stood guard, others fanned out around us towards the squat. One approached me. My gut was twisting inside. What was I going to do if he asked me who I was? What would I say? Why was I worried? Soldiers don't care, and he didn't. He asked us "Are there more inside?" I gestured towards Tom, told the soldier that Tom knew better than I did.

Tom stood there and as he spoke he started to hyperventilate, hands on his knees, dirty tears. I wished I'd thought of that. But I had other things to do. I needed time alone with Tom to ask where Naya could have gone. Or if she had been there at all. I put my arm around Tom pretending to know him. He needed it though, and through the burgeoning sobs, he explained to the soldier he didn't know of anyone else inside. He said he was not sure about the basement, as they were a separate crowd and Tom knew nothing about them. He waved his hand slowly over the three bodies, two of which were now being attended to feverishly, as if excusing his lack of knowledge. Tom had saved two of those three people, although one was dead and another was close, it had not been in vain. Whatever the opposite of in vain was, it was in that.

The basement idea was news to me, but in his defence, not as if we'd been chewing the fat, shooting the breeze. I'd tensed on hearing this news. The swarthy soldier shouted some military stuff at his men, they moved down the slope and round the squat to the back entrance. I needed to have a look as well so I walked down with him, both of us scuttling through the dust in that weird way we all do moving down anything steep.

The captain began talking to me, telling me to get back. I looked at him and told him that my missus was missing, maybe inside. That I would stay out of the way. I looked at Tom again, he was still gently weeping, spent, exhausted and covered in dust like a beige panda, but he was alright. I looked worse. He looked up at me. He was sitting on the ground hands in the grey sand, and mouthed thanks. I shouted Naya to him, I was still shouting at everyone, my arms open eyebrows raised, in the form of an Italian question. He shook his head in some annoying way. I felt like breaking it for him but then I relaxed. Losing my temper was not going to help anyone. I followed the soldier down the slope and round. He didn't seem too interested in me anymore.

The back of the building was worse, like a face without skin. The soldiers were working trying to break through the collapsed entrance. To my eyes, one of the bombs must have dropped just outside the door. There was the unmistakable sound of people inside. Not sure what they were doing. Singing? Definitely sounded like singing.

Yeah they were singing the Marseillaise. Fair play, always worth a belt. Soldiers looked less than impressed. As we stood there evaluating the scene, the first floor to the left, above our heads, in a gradual considered motion, slowly at first, dropped straight down, we all stepped back in a chorus line and the anthem singing stopped. Briefly the sound of the falling rubble and the dust rendered us each alone, but there was no time really for anything except quick personal confusion, so glad of my hard hat. The soldiers increased their pace. I wasn't convinced they'd be able to budge the huge pieces of rubble. I walked around them ignoring their shouts to stand back.

My last visit I was sure I'd seen a little cellar window at ground height. The window had been right where the mounds of wood and debris now where. I began pulling them back. The swarthy commander saw me, and with one order there were three of us. Five minutes later, as more and more debris began to cascade around us, we sighted the basement window. The two soldiers shouted to their commander and used a small shovel to put the window in. The smaller of my two helpers slid down and in the window, his partner holding his leg. I grabbed his other leg unsure of what it was exactly he wanted to do.

We lowered him as far as we could. There were voices and then he shouted back to let him go. He slid through easily enough, he must have been alright as, next thing, his head appeared. He signalled to the guy beside me who told his commander and then they were pushing me aside and the soldier in the basement was handing people out to the rest in a chain. I stood aside. The commander grabbed my arm and told me seriously but kindly to stand back.

He told me, "If she is in there we will find her."

I somehow knew then she was not in there. Why would she be? She had nothing to do with that group in the basement, but I had to be *sure. My mind was still thawing. I stepped back as they brought out eight artists, a gallery of artists. All eight looked delighted. The soldiers bristled at their levity, but they were just kids. They started to sing the national anthem again. This had been a trait of the build up to the bombing. People from all sides of the political spectrum singing the anthem any time they could. I was not of that ilk, but if you are going to sing an anthem, none better than La Marseilllaise.*

The commander told them to shut up and after a few more protest bars they did.

No Naya.

As I walked back around, giving the building a wide berth, the commander was talking to the singers. They were now looking less choral, more like kids who'd been through hell. Their facades having fallen off they started to drop down in the dirt, sobbing, tears wound their way down their dirty cheeks clearing little paths. The soldiers each took one and ferried them round the front.

Tom was up lying on a wall on his front, smoking like a good thing, a paramedic treating his wound, letting him get on with the smoking. He also had a coffee. There was another paramedic trying to cajole him towards an ambulance. I approached him, he handed me a coffee and a smoke. The single most generous act of my life. I lit the smoke. Nothing makes you want to smoke more than smoke, I can tell you that. Smoke and danger.

I could have laid down myself and got a quick kip, but that was not my destiny.

"Tom, you have any idea where Naya is? She's not answering her phone. Was she here earlier??"

"I saw her yesterday but not today. Sorry, thanks, thank you."

"No worries mate. If you see her, tell her I'm looking for her. And if anyone else asks tell them you don't know me. Cool?"

"Cool."

"Bon courage." I kissed him then to tell him what I could not say. He got it though.

Where to next? Fucked if I knew.

Wailings sirens, burning books, rotating blades, crying kids, shouting soldiers, blustering smoke, thudding explosions, booming loudspeakers, collapsing walls, rumbling trucks.

Where was she?

Chapter 24

Tuesday October 15 2002

I needed more practice. I rang my boss at nine and told her the washing machine repair man was coming to my flooded apartment and I would be delayed until after lunch. She was still home and knowing I'd matters in hand she told me not to worry. So I didn't. Next I rang Peter. He normally had Tuesdays off. Lying in bed, he told me,

"Drop over and we'll go out to the Bois in the motor?"

"Sound" I said.

I'd considered quitting work but did not want to draw even the slightest bit of attention towards myself. Leave nothing they could hang their hats on later.

Peter lived out in Clichy. When you mention Clichy to a lot of Parisians they go into paroxysms, it had become bourgeois dog whistle for danger. I liked it a lot though. It felt like a theme park danger rather than the real thing. Most people who lived in Clichy worked so there was not that much messing. I got the Métro, twenty minutes later was at Peter's door waiting for him to get his car. I felt free that morning, as if I was on the mitch from school.

Peter must have felt it as well as he arrived to pick me up in his little Alfa, all happy, chirpy looking.

"Enjoying your day off mate?" I asked.

"Loving it. Why you out and about?"

"Morning off. Washing machine problems. You know the score."

"Everybody knows the score."

And we didn't talk anymore. The traffic swallowed us. Peter enjoying encouraging the Alfa in and out of the city traffic; we skirted the Périphérique round to the Bois.

The clearing was where we left it and we settled into a nice rigorous stone throwing workout.

I was getting better, I needed to be. I'd only six days left and I was worried I'd miss. Missing was something that had been preying on my mind the last few days, gnawing on my neurals. If I missed cleanly then it might go unnoticed. This was perhaps the best scenario. The other scenarios were dire.

After three hours we drove to a restaurant near enough to my work. It was a Japanese place. We loved the buzz and the grub. We got a decent table and, with time to burn, we launched into it. Starting with Dean's withdrawal and then onto Naya and more general logistical issues. Peter, as per his magical power, saw things with alacrity and clarity. Extremely useful both as I struggled to possess either. Peter came at the issues sadly, like a sad, very polite house robot. There was a touch of the end of an era about the whole thing. Peter had a life that was the envy of the rest of us. Monique, a stunning person, worked part time with kids in an orphanage or something incredible. She also worked full time at being the best girlfriend ever, at making herself and Peter perform as a type of power couple. He was bulletproof. So much so he could allow himself to relax around the many women who threw themselves at him. Relax and not cheat. In the rambunctious world of the Paris expat scene, that was a minor miracle. So I listened as he broke it down for me.

"We have double exposure due to Dean and Naya. Dean is further weakened by Geneviève being likely to cop the whole thing once the news breaks. Then the pressure will begin to build on him. We can't expect him to hold out. It's unreasonable and unlikely."

Peter deferentially explained,

"You guys made probably a tactical, if not a strategic error in going to see Dean."

I countered by saying,

"There was little to no chance James was going to leave well enough alone. So I needed to control the situation best I could."

"Well, we need to impress upon James that more contact only weakens any chance we have of stopping them speaking to the police."

"I half agree. If the police do not approach them they'll keep their council. If the police do approach them, then all bets are off. Her family will protect them, but they'll have to give the police something. And that something will be our names."

"That gives me an idea. Why don't the three of us represent three cells, with three separate cut outs between us? I could tell Dean to only give them my name. Then I would insist it was only me. Like the media do. Pretend it was an isolated incident or that I acted alone." Peter said.

I replied suddenly excited, this was what I had been waiting for.

"Better than that. Give him my name. I've the least purchase in this city and like the movie says, there's nothing in my life I could not walk away from in thirty seconds." Guilt tried to invade me then and there. But fuck guilt.

"Liar liar. Written all over your face. More than that though. You've told her what the plan is? Right?"

"Naya knows. But, but I'm not sure they'll be able to connect her to me. I've been with her a week. Granted I am fully in. But I can still walk away. I don't feel like I can live more like this. What's the point? This was and is the point. The stones mean more to me than anything. I no longer believe in any of this. I yearn for closure."

Peter said,

"Dangerous way to talk my friend. Sounds like you are looking to be caught? I don't want to be caught. Remember that, right? I like my life. I'm doing this, well, best as I can explain it, because I want the action, the juice. I miss all those things. I feel I'm being drawn towards that dull night light over there. I want it with Monique, I do, but I want this last thing. I want it for the memories. To punctuate the bridge into the next life."

"A minute ago you wanted to be the cut out? Now you don't want to be caught. I'll be the first cut out. You call over to Dean, try and make it look normal, tell him the plan. He'll not like it, predicated as it is on him talking to the cops, but lay it out for him. No trail, face to face. Watch Geneviève, we cannot rely on her not knowing anything any longer."

"Consider it done. What to do about Naya? I can't tell you. I wish I could. This time last year I would have told you to hug her close and never leave her. Ever. But those days are gone. She has a bit of the bandit in her, so maybe she fancies the idea a little bit. No way is she with you otherwise. So going all For Whom the Bell Tolls might work.

She is from the South after all and they regard anything police related as Paris trying to stick its nose in. Your shout."

Peter continued shaking his head slowly as if he knew it was a bad idea. It was a bad idea. But he continued on anyway.

"I have my hands full with Monique who thinks I'm thinking about cheating on her. Not sure where she got that idea from, but she knows me, and my mind is not on her like it should be. So she's half right. She trusts me and believes me when I tell her there is nobody, but she's not fooled by the truthful specific denial. Not fooled at all. She keeps saying things like, 'I believe you, but there is something?'"

I said, "Yeah the whole thing is much more complicated than I had anticipated. Who knew absolutely anyone cared about us? Leaving the life is not the clean break I'd thought it would be."

Chapter 25

Wednesday October 16 2002

to

Sunday October 20 2002

I can remember the next few days like I remember twenty years ago. The difference between a good ad and a good movie. Those days were ads. Work and practice. Work and practice. The most amount of time off I'd ever taken.

Everyone in the office was naturally delighted, seeing as how I would no longer be able to make them feel guilty about making the bridge. Making the bridge: a French trick when the bank holidays fall on Thursdays, as they often do, they make the bridge over the working Friday and don't come back until Monday. I'd never said a word to anyone about the bloody bridge, not one single word. But I was their mirror. And they often didn't like what they saw. I was disconnected from this thought. Utterly.

Our research was complete; all the files burnt once confirmed. James knew where to be and at what time. I was totally completely terrified and that made the blood flow through every part of me that much smoother. Terror thinned blood, streaming around my warm corpse.

Sunday we spent the day throwing in the Bois. Our routine well established with a look out, catcher and collector. I was not half bad. I reckon I had around an eighty twenty chance, success failure. I arrived home at eight. Naya was sitting outside my apartment leaning against her bike. I'd been avoiding her, it had been relatively easy, she'd not pushed it. Presumably content to let me wreck my own life. But she was there then. I'd only noticed as I came up right upon her. I stopped and looked pretend aghast, as a mask to hide how aghast I really was. I needed this like I needed a hole in the head.

I wanted a pick and mix life. I wanted a buffet, choosing only the shiny sweet things and maybe some prawns. As that was not possible, I was exiting. This made me a coward in my own eyes. I could feel that. I could understand that nobody else understood it yet. They would in time. My character would soon be raked over and spat on, trampled and kicked. I needed that. Maybe then I could feel the catharsis I wanted.

"Naya, how are you? You look well."

I was a total dick. This is what I normally did. Normal her to death. Pretend go through the motions. Click through the gears. But not go anywhere.

She was astonishingly wide to that.

"Ta gueule. I look well. I look alone is how I look, because my new boyfriend has been hiding away throwing stones." She even called me her boyfriend. I exhaled three lungs full.

"Alright let's go upstairs and we can kill each other up there. Although I am not going to kill you." I attempted to placate.

Upstairs she started in on me again as I got together some food. I handed her a glass of vin blanc. Sancerre. Great name, great place.

"Johnny, where've you been? I have been looking in the Bug for you every night of the week. Don't tell me you've stopped drinking? Don't tell me anything actually. Because I would not believe it."

So much for her being cool about us not seeing each other.

It had always been difficult for me to understand what it was a girl wants. Because whatever it was I gave them never seemed to be it. And I was content with that until I met Naya and I understood she wanted me, all of me, the whole lot. She did not want me to keep anything to myself. This was further complicated by us only having met, and me embarking on some barking mad journey towards western people's guilt alleviation.

"I know I am bad. But I think you'd be better off without me at the moment. I'm trouble."

Jesus Christ if I'd told her I had slept with ten women and ten men she couldn't have possibly flipped more.

"Aaagh. I'll tell you who I am better off with or without. I make my own decisions. Not you." She spat this at me along with full on alpha finger pointing.

"OK OK OK. OK. I got it."

I could not help but get angry myself in the face of her onslaught. She'd me in full fight or flight. So I replied,

"Maybe I think I would be better off without you?"

I had a terrible habit of resorting to hurting the other person very early in any confrontation. She was having none of it. Calmly replying,

"Maybe you do? I do not suppose to know if you would be better off with or without me. That is your decision. You are free to make it. I have made mine. I only ask you to make the decision quickly."

She stood tall. Walked over to me, with a hand on my face soft as love, she kissed me and walked out the front door.

"Triple double fuck. Could I not just concentrate on one thing?" I spoke the words although I was alone. "I am all set to hit the head of the European Central Bank tomorrow. And now I have the worm of love burrowing through my brain, into whatever it is scientists have decided a soul is. Joy."

I went and lay down on my bed. I lay only on the flat part and let my feet sit up over the end. I lay there for angst filled epochs.

I had to get my mind right. If my mind was a box and I was concentrating on keeping the inside free to concentrate on the throw, then she was pressing in on each side. Forcing me to be aware of her, despite not allowing thoughts to settle onto her.

I must have dozed off for a while, waking to one of the tramps on the road shouting at her fella. There was no way to ignore it and I listened to them for a while. Back and forth much like any of us, no beauty in it. Just anger and misunderstanding. She seemed to want him to go somewhere with her. I walked over to the balcony and stood for a while watching the street, smoking. She was beating him now and he acted like he deserved it, like some men do, anything for a quiet life. Then he eventually lost the rag with her and they had to be pulled apart. Like two dirty squabbling pigeons. She was crying then, sliding on down the road sobbing. Then shouting back over her shoulder at him as she went to walk away. He pretended he was going to let her walk away; she pretended she was going to walk away. Soon enough, they were back kissing dirty muck kisses. Spit and booze. I had always wanted to spend a few weeks as a tramp, the unmitigated drinking definitely an attraction. Inside the tramp cocoon.

I'd spent a few full days of my life drinking liquor and I'd enjoyed it more than being sober. I've tried to analyse why that is. Why I enjoy being drunk more than sober. I cannot grasp it exactly. Less so now as the hangover prevents the same wild abandon. People will tell you a lot of hokum about escapism. I've never truthfully had anything to escape from. Escape from myself. OK but it's a little bit lightweight as an explanation. The tramps were now back in love. And they returned to their nightly perch right below my window. Another night of bellowing and crying. That was fine with me though. They were as much my people as anyone else.

Chapter 26

Sunday October 20 2002

Monday October 21 2002

I slept solidly that night once I drifted off. It must have been three when I did, but that was OK. Sleep has never appealed to me. Sleep when you are dead. Glib as that is I have lived by it. Never underestimate glib. It has a strange power, a solidity that belies its definition. I woke at seven. The throw was between nine twenty and nine thirty. The conference kicked off at ten and Bernd Schuster was the morning's keynote speaker. He was talking about the fallacy of central banking in a deregulated bandit industry. Was he fuck. But he was head of the ECB and I wanted him hit.

Paris as usual did not care what I was doing and people remained mesmerised by their own misfortunes. I went to my local Berber Bar and had a sandwich, a coffee and a Perrier. My throat was like carpet; I had to add a coke to the mix. Managed half the sandwich. My stomach thought about it for a while, then decided on second thoughts, no. So I traipsed into the toilet and released it.

Back at the bar the drinks went down with the four cigarettes I smoked. Each quicker than and overlapping the other. The bar man noticed but said nothing. He understood a man sometimes is afraid and coffee and cigarettes are all he's got. So he never asked. I needed to pull myself physically together. My organs were going to fall out of my stomach and my heart had relocated to just behind my tongue.

I'd warned the lads to keep mobile silence. Any kind of trail at all could be found eventually. I felt fluid, my bowels were not tight despite the fact they had next to nothing in them.

I got on the Métro. Although I'd warned myself not to be early as any type of loitering in that district would draw attention, I was on course to have time to kill. The Métro calmed me. I got a seat and read a few pages of the Fountainhead; it never failed to divert me. I've never been able to decide whether it's batshit crazy or devastatingly good. The respite allowed me time to make a good decision.

I went past where I was going, onto Ranelagh where I got off and walked over to the other side of the tracks. It was eight fifty. Thirty minutes before my moment of no return. The fear had amped up so high now I was immersed in a watery bubble. I knew my only ally was calmness. I tried to loll back into a calm pool, I tried.

My phone rang. I looked at the screen through the lingering tear. It was Naya. Who? At that moment the name meant nothing to me. For those minutes I was only myself without another life. Alone. As I had sought to be.

The clock, my first enemy to overcome. Time had decided to slow by half; I knew this was due to me. I did not try to speed it up. I closed one eye and watched the world through the other, alternating. I went over the street plan in my head. I had memorised it. Over the past two days we had attempted to recreate the shot in the woods. A train arrived. I nearly got in but forced myself to wait.

The next train was mine. The carriage was full, suited me fine. I was only going the one stop. Getting off at La Muette I walked quickly, purposefully towards the exit not waiting for anyone. I was up, out and into the zone. I knew the route and walked it. I was sweating, my suit not helping, nor the suddenly warm October weather. I walked a measured pace, trying my best to amble; my steps a rhythm pounding inside me. I lit a cigarette and went steadily down the Rue de Franqueville. The throw was to take place on Rue Henri de Bornier and I was suddenly all business. No extra police I could see. The Indian Embassy was somewhere around here but there was nothing special laid on apparently. I walked down de Bornier once; there were some press and a decent throng of people.

I didn't walk to my position. I reckoned I'd five more minutes; walked back the way I came, then stood and put on the replica badge I had made. I lit another cigarette. My blood was roaring through my veins, my heart exploding. Cars were pulling up outside and I strode to my starting point. I was already moving as his giant Mercedes arrived, security was blasé thus far.

The driver and the front passenger got out. The front passenger opened the back door. I rotated the stone once in my clear plastic gloved hand and started moving. Schuster got out, I was strolling away from him, my back to him, the distance was about thirty metres. I looked away to my escape route. I imagined how I looked in slow motion. I looked back once, nearly catching the eye of the driver, but at the final split he was distracted. I threw.

Noiseless.

It arched high at first, then flat and smooth, and I was around the corner and away.

My heart, which had stopped, beat once, and resettled into its booming rhythm. My legs nearly forgot how to walk but they didn't. I could sense rather than hear some commotion, I was not sure.

I kept going making two more turns then onto Henri Martin. James sat there, spare helmet on the seat behind him. The fear now unleashed and untethered tore through me, driving me down deep into madness. I put on the helmet, tapped James twice on the shoulder, as per arrangement, and we were gone. Onto the Périphérique and speeding along. I wanted to fall off the bike and rag doll through the axels of a truck as we passed by. I wanted to but I settled for imagining it. There were definite sirens now as we rose up onto the ring road. I was in work in the guts of twenty minutes. I ignored the eyebrows, more cocked at my suit than at the time, and sat down.

People treated me like any other day and I smiled and was helpful. I tried to get involved in as many humble distractions as I could. I did not go for lunch knowing full well I was unstable. Around about four I felt incredible tiredness, secret private lethargy. I made some sales calls; more staying in touch with clients who I knew liked our product and were not about to cancel any ads.

We'd arranged to meet in the Bug. Peter was working. I trudged over not feeling any elation, more extreme relief and so much tiredness. I was served a large Jameson and a pint. I skulled the whiskey. It quieted the rampant anxiety. Peter looked at me and smiled. He had the news on. Hitherto I'd avoided it. There was no sound and nobody much else in the bar as it was only six. Peter put on the sound. I sat there for once allowing the world to happen without me.

The standoff between Bush and Chirac was now into a territory which was hard to gauge. Was Bush really threatening France with attack if it did not comply? This was most of the news. The third story began with a picture of Bernd being bundled inside the OECD grasping his head. I began to see the Bush Chirac thing was going to be bigger and scarier than anything we did. As I suspected all along: Who the fuck are you?

Motto to live by.

James arrived rakish and suave. Calm and collected. He'd been perfect earlier and I told him so. He hugged me, we spoke in an Irish English bullshit code indecipherable to anyone unfamiliar with our countries' shared idiocies.

James had been paying attention all day. He gave it to us as a bulletin,

"Today the head of the European Central Bank was hit with a stone, narrowly missing his eye. The unprovoked attack occurred at around about nine twenty five this morning. The banker was not seriously hurt although he did go to hospital for observation and minor treatment. He received a couple of stitches. The police have not commented beyond confirming what is already known. There are no suspects at the moment, they have appealed for witnesses. One person has come forward and is helping the police with their enquiries."

My being froze at this last point. James put a hand on my shoulder and told me to relax. Is there anything on earth less relaxing than being told to relax? I politely removed his hand and asked him to continue his report. There was not much else save some footage James had seen of the actual incident. They had the moment the stone hit Schuster on video. James surmised that the camera man or one of the journalists was the one person helping the police with their investigation.

The French police are nay joke and they play hard. My organs which had barely recovered from earlier, tensed back up under my ribcage. I nodded towards the empty whiskey glass and ordered one for James as well. James was up tomorrow at lunch time. Peter was going with him. The logic being two guys chatting in the Bourse area was less conspicuous. The challenge round by the Bourse was all to do with the crowds. Legolas, the French politician, would be well guarded, but this was an extremely busy area. They had worked on a two man solution, Peter walking slightly in front and to the right allowing James to throw without the oncoming pedestrians seeing his hand.

I put my hand in my jacket pocket to look for a light and recoiled as I felt the glove. I took it out and gave it to Peter, who with a look of utter boredom, put it inside a spent can of Red Bull and then into the bin. The whiskey had delivered the alcohol and although I was leaving early I felt stronger. I wished the guys good luck. They smiled, both outwardly calmer than I was.

James "Where you going? Be careful. Be very fucking careful. But good luck as well. There may be another game in town at the moment, but it won't last."

Peter "Who knows?"

Chapter 27

Monday October 21 2002

Naya was on my mind. The fog had lifted, or altered, into a light mist. I was giddy. Glad to be finished with it for the week. The trouble would begin again for me when I needed to organise my next throw. My hatred of all things was quiet that night. I was lovesick. I needed my girl to soothe the pain of living. I needed Naya.

I saw her bike where she liked to keep it; I paused and tried to establish some sort of right from wrong. I was unable. I was not even sure those were the lines along which this thing was organised. I went up to the intercom and buzzed. I could, of course, have rung ahead. But I hadn't wanted to give her an opportunity to refuse me, the gutless wonder.

She didn't answer but I was buzzed in. I took the lonely elevator up to her fifth floor, the door was ajar. I entered and the studio was empty. The shower was running. It was another beautiful war like evening. Sun setting on the old battlefields of Paris. I sat on the step out to the balcony, lit a cigarette and lay back; ashtray on my chest.

I was transfixed by thoughts of the Paris sky and who had looked upon it; Communes and German armies through the years. I watched the old sky with its clouds, snapshots of the past, reflected on the BNF glass. You could almost see into hundreds of apartments. Each apartment with almost the exact same things outside on their balcony; sad little basins, drying towels and cleaning equipment. Not sure how it had come to this for the inhabitants of the greatest city on earth. Nor were they I warrant.

I heard the shower turn off.

I must have fallen asleep despite being arched over the saddle of the balcony door. I awoke to the bathroom door opening and Naya emerging wearing a white top and jeans with boots. Was she going out? I felt jealous of nothing I knew, jealous of her future. I rolled over onto my front and with one eye closed looked at her trying to gauge her.

Inscrutable and opaque behind the smile. I was hoping for some anger. Anger far easier to deal with than indifference or melancholy.

"I am going out for a while." Was what I got.

"Alright. Can I stay here?"

This surprised her a little, I think. It may even have pleased her.

"OK. There is a beer in the fridge and stuff for a sandwich. I'll probably be a bit late."

"Cool. Have a good time."

And she was gone. Whatever waltz we were doing, I could not stop it. I made the sandwich; ham and pickle in a piece of baguette. Drank the beer. Tried to absorb the view into my inner self.

The lads were up tomorrow. Infinitely more dangerous. After tomorrow the cat would be out of le sac. I'd used a stone from a garden in the 16th. James was using one he had found under foliage in the Bois. Each stone had been marked with a code known only to us.

I listened to the news at midnight as I was getting into bed.

Bush's drumbeat of war had increased in tempo, he was whacking it now and he'd lost the beat. His warning to Chirac had been slightly tempered by Blair in his usual creepy obsequious way. The world's weirdo uncle, war monger to the stars.

Simply put we had re-arrived at a stage in the West where everything was done for the good of the elite. Don't doubt it. Corporations, the millionaires and billionaires. 1905. Fuck WW1, fuck WW2, they were wastes of time. Everything those wars achieved rolled back now that those soldiers were no longer watching; next up concentration camps, you wait. They will call them something else, but don't be fooled.

The news began with Bush saying,

"The people of France need to tell their President, they need to tell President Chirac, that they will not support tyrants." Many French may have had no love for Chirac, but there wasn't a person in the whole country that would piss on Bush if he was on fire. Bush again alluded to Chirac arming Iraq, "putting guns into the hands of a madman". And people say Bush did not understand irony. The French were due to address the UN on Friday. The Foreign Minister, James's man Legolas, was the keynote speaker. There would then be a pointless vote on whether or not sanctions should be imposed on France. As a veto-wielding permanent Security Council member, France was untouchable. That is why the whole thing was so strange. I could not see where Bush was going with this.

Chirac had angered Bush immensely by saying America was lying about the WMD. Funny that because, besides the Wests co-opted journalists, every man and his dog knew the Yanks were lying their balls off.

I was worried though. What was Bush talking about when he said "America would be forced to take action?" The French security experts stressed he was only referring to economic action, but I was not so sure. Even Bush could not be bothered invading France, surely? Could he?

The second item, after ten minutes of bloviating bull from idiot experts, was Schuster. There was an interview with Schuster in which he said he was OK, that he was damned if any childish prank, his words not mine, was going to get in the way of progress. What progress? The progress of the neo-liberal doom, so beloved of everyone who went to the capitalist madrasas of Yale, Harvard, Sciences Po and ENA. The continued liquidation of all our self-respect and our state assets. A side note, anyone who utters the word progress should be shot. Me included.

The presenter mentioned the police were continuing with their investigation. I could still walk away. I was not too far gone yet.

Not that I would, but the thought did give me some solace. I fell asleep to French jazz. Empty head and beautiful scented bed. Cool Bliss.

With one sleep cycle complete I heard Naya come in. She sat on the edge of the bed undressing. She smelled of cold and make-up, booze and fags. Delicious. She slid into the bed like a freezing cold assassin. I was half trying not to wake up, my infinite optimism. Her hands and feet all over me ripping the warmth from my core.

"I saw you on the news Johnny." She said this with her face right beside mine, I could hear her smiling.

"O yeah. What did you think?"

"I think you are an idiot. But I still like you." We kissed. Lots of men in this world do not like it when their girl is drunk. Personally I love it.

"I like you too. There is another one tomorrow. Not me. You know you can never tell anyone?"

"I know. What do you fucking take me for? Traditionally in war the women are the last to talk. Unlike the weak men."

"Great, just remember that you can't talk because you do not know anything. That is your defence. Say I was acting weird. But that was why you liked me. Because I was different."

She giggled at that.

"That is why I like you, my weird boy." I laughed too.

God the smell of her, the feel of her, as she was pressed right up against me with every part of her uncovered skin touching mine. I was having a lust crazed turn. She whispered into my ear what she wanted me to do. I figured I owed her for being so cool and Mediterranean about everything. So I obliged, enjoying her sexy combativeness. By the end of it, she had to pull my mouth off her shoulder as I was about to break the skin.

"Jesus Christ. My little maniac." and she laughed again. We descended to the next level of love. We went to sleep masticated to each other. The night was cold enough with clear skies, I slept hard until seven.

I woke up in the traditional position beloved by the movies, with her in under my arm. I lay there for five minutes then slipped into her bathroom and showered my grimy life away. I thought I saw a dark movement, then she was in the shower with me. It was all kind of funny as she wore a shower cap. But the rest of her was uncovered and I lifted her up and then after some heavy panting, on. I was still half crazed from the day before, Naya encouraged the release of all that emotion and fear.

We both finished together, although she may have just been being sound about it, as it was very quick. I felt so electric. I washed her down like I was an Egyptian slave. She then returned the favour. Again with the wet kissing. I liked the taste of her mouth more than anything I had ever tasted. I needed to calm down, although she said she wanted me to calm up.

We were both laughing as we got out and dried each other.

"Maybe we should just go and live in Costa Rica? That would solve all our problems."

"After you go to jail? Oui? You think I am going to wait? I need sex too much to wait."

"Jesus Naya. Actually Jesus Naya nothing. I like it when you talk like that. Straight and raw."

"Thanks honey, have a good day at work."

She was back in bed and asleep before I left. Sweet.

Chapter 28

Tuesday October 22 2002

I walked out into the outstretched arms of Paris, the mother who does not love anyone except herself. Too many children to care about and not one iota to spare. The way we all like it.

The day was colder and slightly drizzly. I was feeling deliciously feverish and wonderfully passive aggressive. Took the electric line 14 to Châtelet, the biggest underground station in the world, the belly of the beast. Emerging onto Rivoli was always a delight. Rivoli tricks you into believing that you have something to do with it. It seduces you into believing you have a stake in the luxurious republic, that you're involved.

France was no different to the States on many levels. Same elite disconnect. Powerful power brokers strolling around where we couldn't see or hear them. But now when they emerged they were going to have to think about getting hit by a stone. Right on the noggin. Tough shit.

Work was fantastic that day. I worked hard and clean. Not a drip anywhere. I had a meeting with a big client I'd been trying to nail for months. The representative was a hardnosed lawyer. She'd pushed me hard on price, despite them being the third biggest employment law firm in France. They wanted to develop an international presence; I had convinced them our magazine was a great place to start. It was, I was not lying. I was lying that I really cared. But the genius of capitalism was I-cared at all. I liked my colleagues and could glean enough out of that to get through the day.

The client had hair made from cosmic straw, her eyes shone life's reflections, she was somehow from Argentina and she was dead sound. By the end of the meeting, due to my lack of flirting, and extremely robust defence of our pricing and product, we were getting on very well. She asked me to go for a celebratory drink. Why not? Times were a wasting. She was not Naya, that did not matter; this was not a French movie, just a drink. There is something about human interaction which can retrace your soul and add a few points to your courage.

We went to a place on Rue Washington off the Champs, I had been there before, back when I was a wooden boy. I texted the lads where I was. Peter was off. Turned out she was half Argentinian, half French; boringly married to some French guy who worked in the automotive industry. Triple yawn. She wanted to buy the first round. But I was having none of it. I ordered a bottle of Saint-Émilion Grand Cru and a plate of meats and cheese. I was starving.

We were well on it when the lads arrived. I'd prepared her for this eventuality. Not that she would have cared, she was having a good laugh. James in particular got on with her. He knew her firm well and he was happy to have a girl to flirt with. Outwardly he seemed OK. When I was next at the bar, Peter left them and slid in beside me, ordering two demi Kro. He had a way with bar men the city over. They fawned over him and responded to his every whim. The beers were on the house for some reason I could not fathom. Peter nodded in thanks.

"So how did it go?" I asked.

"Alright. There's been nothing on the news, well besides Schuster. I think he missed. If we do not hear anything by the end of today, we'll have to assume he missed."

"Maybe. Or they could be controlling the story. Legolas has a big speech this Friday; maybe he told them to keep a lid on it. I couldn't tell whether or not I'd hit my guy either. I didn't wait around to see what happened. It's a problem. But, but the benefits of not waiting around, well, you get it."

"I do, I do. I am ready for tomorrow. I've got a date with the head of big pharma, have had to jettison SocGen, ho hum, my guy is sponsoring a ball at the Crillon."

"What time? You want some help?"

"Absolutely not. There'll be just enough tourists there to give me the cover I need."

"Alright, time?"

"He is due there at five. I heard the staff talk about it the other night."

"You not worried about the security round the embassies and the Élysée?"

"Suppose I am wary of it, but not worried. I'd say the amount of security'll mean everyone is relaxed, rather than the other way around. The escape itself has got me frightened. The last two times I walked it the scenario I envisaged was they would swarm the place within five minutes. But then I thought they cannot really risk that. They can't abandon the king to save a rook, or whichever fucking way you want to look at it. I'll cut back behind the hotel, up round along; I'll be in the Bug in 'bout five minutes."

He looked at me once without life's glaze and I saw the fear. I put my hand on his arm above the elbow. Much better than words. He nodded.

"Alright, be careful will ye, I'll be in to see you. Good luck."

We went back down to the table. Argentina was saying goodbye and we all got the bisous. I told her I'd be in touch. Told her I'd forward her a draft of the ad tomorrow as it would appear on the page. She was a nice lady; we said nothing for a minute, all of us content to chill. Eventually I asked James.

"Well?"

"Well, I got her card." he smiled that matinee idol smile.

"Firstly, leave her alone, she's an important married client. Secondly, that's not what I was talking about, as you well fucking know."

"Yeah o'right. Has Pete filled you in? We're in the dark. My feeling's that I got him. I don't want to put out any feelers. I feel paralysed and pinned."

"Agreed. Well done anyway. I was bricking it, you?"

"Same. I was OK up until about half an hour before, then I lost my lunch and my wits. Peter calmed me and I contem'fucking plated leaving it. The angles were not what I'd planned. I had to throw much more over my shoulder and behind than I'd wanted to. But I still think I got him. Using light coloured stones was genius, I don't think they can see them against the autumn sky. We were around the corner milliseconds after I took the throw. No concrete proof."

"Well if you think you got him then we have to operate under the assumption that you did. Escape and evasion need to be elevated to priority status. Even over the throw."

"O look who's found a reason to live. Go and see Naya last night did we?"

"Yeah I did. She went out but I stayed over anyway. So yeah, let's try and not get caught."

"I am going tomorrow no matter what you two geniuses say. Let's meet Saturday to see if we want to even go to phase two. OK?"

I remembered how I was before my throw, that urgent tightness in my forearms, electro charges flinging themselves all over.

Both myself and James agreed and we drank to our deranged lives.

Chapter 29

Saturday November 9 2002

I needed somewhere to go. I was momentarily debilitated. I decided to use the phone. Fuck it if they catch me now. I was focussed only on her. What else was I worried about, myself? Why survive without her? Finally, some fucking clarity. I needed some transport. I needed a motorbike? James had one. I rang him.

I was using a prepaid unregistered mobile but he answered immediately. God at that moment I welled up. I loved that fucking English prick.

"Johnny?"

"Yeah, James you o'right?"I kind of blubbed.

"Am I o'right? Am I o'right? Fuck me. I am not the one who's been missing for the last three days.

Are you alright?

Where are you?

Are you OK?" James kept asking me and asking me.

Eventually, "Steady mate, steady mate. Give me a second. I am fine. Freaking the fuck out. Was right near that whole thing, watched the bombers lay out their lush carpet of industrial carnage. But I couldn't give a shit about any of it, never mind me. All I am worried about is

Naya. I was at her place, no sign. I thought she would come back there. She doesn't have this number. I left her a note and snuck out three days ago, I think. We fought over me going away without her. I am losing it. Give me something? Anything man, I am dissolving."

"Alright relax. They only bombed two places. The BNF and Pigalle. They've reached some sort of compromise.

Le rapprochement."

We both snorted. There was still hope.

"People have been told to stay out of those areas until advised otherwise. Official advice is to wait until seven this evening before they begin to come back to the city. Trains will be back on at seven." James mollified.

He continued "My guess is she goes to your place. They've that place under guard though. They could've picked her up. Or even more likely they leave her there as bait. You've made a fool of them. One man doing all that? Not sure how I allowed you to talk me into the one man theory. But we can go over that another time."

"I need your bike. I'm at the squat."

"I'm over by Bercy. Stay there I'll come get."

Five minutes and there James was, grinning and slightly posing in his usual ironic fashion. When he saw me he burst out laughing. I was close to feeling normal again but far from looking that way. I took the bike. He wanted to drive me. But it was a trap, most likely, and I had enough to worry about.

The fact the other two lads were getting away with it made me feel infinitely better. I kissed him and hugged him, despite him grimacing. I went to speak and tears welled up. I could not believe the ducts were *still working. James never looked more beautiful than he did that day. The giant burning books in the background, the sparking levelled cinema, soldiers and emergency services everywhere, James stood in front of all that, as if preparing to be photographed for a postcard movie still. James wore a yellow shirt and a denim jacket would you believe, and he was pulling it off.*

James wiped his eye once quickly; he was not of my ilk, he looked at me properly and sniffed graciously; "Take care of yourself. Dean is back in the country we think. Pete says hello and would you answer his texts. We both thought you'd been lifted or killed, or worse, had left Paris. Where did you spend the last few days? They have been swarming all over the city looking for you. Peter and I both spent all day Thursday and Friday being questioned. That lawyer eventually got us out. They semi bought our story, but they were convinced we knew where you were. Lucky we didn't, because I was ready to crack. There is something going on that we cannot see. They asked as many questions about Dean as they did about you. Not fucking happy. I hate feeling stupid. Where the fuck where you?"

"I've been around. Thanks for keeping your mouth shut. I'll tell you the story when we have a drink together. I figured making myself scarce was the best option for all of us." I looked around into the direction I needed to go, peering ahead to see if I could see what was coming. I couldn't.

"Go then. Go get her. Where will you go then? We may not be able to see each other for a while?"

"No, let's meet tonight before we leave Paris. As you say this may be the last opportunity for a long time. Use today's confusion as our cloak."

James gave me another hug. I gunned the engine and sped away through the rubble and around the slow arriving troop carriers. The noise and the dust evaporated into the past, I flew through beautiful zombie Paris. The odd person peered at me, dormouse like, curved noses around corners, sniffing the air for danger. The city stank of it.

One or two old people, too wise to bother with our silly games, had their chairs on the pavements and sat smoking and drinking pastis. They watched the trucks, allowing themselves to be reminded of different times. For a lot of them this was merely what they'd always expected. So they were not surprised, except perhaps by how long it had taken.

Chapter 30

Wednesday October 23 2002

Wednesday, for myself and James the hump, for Peter the first day of the rest of his life. I found myself slightly over-following the news, checking it on the hour, even in between. Not that anyone would have noticed. I was a news junkie no doubt. No word at all on Legolas, although my gut told me there was something the media was not telling us. Like an idiot with a secret, they all looked guilty. I also noticed they had no new footage of him in regards to his speech on Friday.

Around five I could not stand it anymore. I got out of there and headed to the Bug. Naya was meeting me there. Whatever that meant? I was looking forward to seeing her like I had been away at war. This was not going to end well. I was drinking less, fucking more. I was involved in some half-baked, middle class, score-settling, stone-throwing action.

I had never been so happy.

I was worried about Peter though; for all his debonair calm he would be on his own over there. I decided to take a stroll over to the Crillon to see what the story was. A really stupid, lunatic idea. Thankfully the French police had already closed most of the streets in and around the hotel. I was prevented from going to get my face seen. The fevered sirens announced to Place de la Concorde that something was afoot.

The Bug as usual before six was an oasis of tranquil glinting liquor. Peter saw me and I caught a glimpse of the burden he'd been carrying in his hooded eyes. Two glasses, two whiskeys. We shot them, I gagged a little as I gulped wrong, providing a soupçon of levity. Peter was still slightly shaking. I raised my eyebrows in question, he nodded once. Alright. Pandemonium was outside the door. But they never expected someone working right round the corner. Strange the way these things worked. Counter-intuitive was a wonderful way to live. The Ministry for the Interior was across the road; their main objective seemed to be locking that down, along with the Élysée behind. As far as I knew though, neither was at home. But security forces the world over love to go nuts.

A few French toffs came in scarfed up to the nines. The indoor scarf; as worn only in France. They asked what was going on outside, Peter struggled to get it out. I politely suggested the news. TF1 news was live outside the Crillon, where Sébastien Froid, head of NovaChem Pharmax, had been hit by a stone to the temple. Froid had been taken away to the hospital, although he was not seriously hurt.

Peter had disappeared, presumably to relieve himself of his stomach. He returned looking suitably chastised but with more colour.

The reporter described the incident,

"Sébastien Froid Head of NovaChem Pharmax, French/Belgian Pharmaceutical Giant had been getting out of his car to attend the annual Froid Ball in aid of the Froid Foundation, when what was thought to be a stone came over the car. Despite the presence of his bodyguard, the stone hit him in the head and knocked him to the ground.

Mr Froid said afterwards it was "the surprise rather than the pain."

How touching and poetic.

The police were to hold a press conference soon. The press's interest now more heightened. The media again alluding to a spate of attacks rather than saying a number. They replayed the Schuster strike. It really was a peach of a throw. They had a blurry shot of Froid being hit, nothing great. There was no doubting the terror afterwards as people rushed in every direction. NovaChem was one of those lively companies with its dirty fingers in so many strange chemical pies.

Naya arrived in a green dress, her leather jacket, boots and her helmet under arm. And, of course, the Helen of Troy smile. Boom. Like looking into a thirties camera flash. Momentarily stunning. She glanced at the news, was about to say something, then didn't. The cloud of worry passed over her face, then was scattered by our hot and heavy kissing.

"Get a room. Seriously, some of us want to eat." James shouted across the bar pushing through the growing throng.

I stayed attached for a couple more minutes, grinning. I was slightly slipping into an erotic haze.

Was there a room we could get? I thought to myself. Somewhere we could go?

Thankfully Naya had a touch more sense. We detached and welcomed James to our table. Sitting apart enabled us to speak and eat like normal human beings.

I let the other two chat, kept an eye on Peter. He was shaking less, as the night ticked along further away from his crime, and the place began to heave and bellow with the fools, he pulled away from it. We ate hearty burgers, lots of chips and lots of pints. Pints make you messy and Naya and James were up dancing by nine. Early even by our low standards. I dragged her ass out of there by ten, back to my place. I had finally found something I liked doing as much, if not more, than drinking. Naya.

We cabbed it, her bike safe enough in the 8th. We had to go through two checkpoints but they waved us through. Naya's legs the only items of interest in the car. Things were definitely heating up. Tightening. That was why all activity was to cease until next week. Let the authorities do their favourite trick; isolated incident, increased security yielding results. Cock and Bull. Then begin the onslaught on three new skulls.

I was exhilarated by the whole experience and I felt more serious and more involved. I was also calmer during the day. Naya and I were spending every night we could together. I was a light sleeper and she was twenty three, so we slept little. We had a thousand private conversations cramming as much information as we could in with little lovers' whispers. We were doing a crash course on each other. We'd both taken to speaking sotto vocce when we were alone together, it was weirdly enjoyable.

As I got to know her more I figured out what type of jokes made her laugh. So I spent a lot of our time together trying to make her spit out her drink with laughter. Despite this mirth, sometimes the strange French blanket of malaise would gently fall upon us, inexplicable and curiously unavoidable. I would fight it. But in Europe, especially on the border of Mitteleuropa, there is something to be said for the culturally imbued weight of existence; gravity and history mulched together; not much to be said granted, but something. Every time it draped itself over us I'd struggle against it with everything I had. But the clock ticking down was unstoppable and it was that more than anything which cast the shadow we sometimes found ourselves in. Expecting death.

Chapter 31

Thursday October 26 2002

Friday October 27 2002

Rumour and innuendo ruled Paris over the next few days. Nowhere did it better. Everything was building up to the big Legolas UN speech on Friday. The President's court, the media, rabbited on about the expected tone and content of the speech. Conciliatory was the view most expressed and hoped for by the various geniuses trotted out to bay and nay.

Where was Legolas though? This was the intriguing aspect to the story. He had not been seen in public since Monday. The stories flying around were the most interesting part of it. He was missing, kidnapped, shacked up, held captive against his will, in negotiations with the Americans. All ideas trotted out for us to chew over.

It took the media until Thursday to start suggesting that Legolas may have been hit by a stone and keeping a low profile. They knew fine well this was exactly what had happened, but they had to use the old tactic of some foreign gaijan breaking the story. Toadies is too kind for them. Lickspittles more accurate. Cozy. Half the French journalists either slept or drank with the leading politicians. Definitely second or third against the wall.

But when they were finally let off the leash on the Stonethrowing angle, they went bat shit.

The foreign press also loved it.

"The three stones heard around the world?"

Pictures of two of the victims with the headline 'Stoned'. All looking suitably dazed.

There was something about the story that appealed to everyone. It had nearly overtaken the UN speech as the main story in France by the end of Thursday. Nobody seemed to know anything about why. This further heightened the interest as speculation was rife. The media kept wanting to know was it terrorism? Was it a protest? The Foreign Minister, a Big Pharma CEO and the head of the ECB. At one stage or another they tried to tell us that these men were a diplomat, a pharmacist and a banker.

That angle did not have strong enough walls though. It could not contain the idea that these venal establishment millionaires were men of the people. The minute they tried to vox pop it on the streets, the French public told them to cop themselves on. When they asked the man or woman on the street,

"Are you worried?

Are you frightened?"

"Non", the sudden expulsion of air "pfffff", followed by a look normally only given to processed food. They could not find a single taker on the boulevards. French people understood this was a minor attack on the gods on top of Olympus. They knew it had nothing to say to them about their own lives. The French, sometimes they are simply the best.

Up until last night the media had been clamouring for something or other. Going on like the whole of France was in a state of terror. Dream on. The whole of France was not born yesterday. We'd hit the Foreign Minister, the head of the ECB and the head of Big Pharma. The whole of France knew full well they were not next. Listening myself, I would have said the mood was approval, with a soupçon of disapproval, as nothing can be felt in France without some misgiving or other.

Bush and Blair, the soufflé of moron and Judas tried to tie it to the upcoming War in Iraq 2 "This time it is personal."

They claimed "This was exactly the kind of thing we were trying to avoid. The immorality we are trying to root out is beginning to spread across borders and cultures." I still have no idea what they were getting at with that one.

"We have to be open to the idea that this is an Iraqi terrorist cell." Blair schmoozed at us. Insouciance and smarm had never been such easy bed fellows. If only we could have hit those two fucking pricks.

Some wag cartoonist in the newspapers made an allusion to the stones being the weapons of mass destruction the Americans were looking for. The picture showed a weapons inspector standing in front of a pile of stones, telling people that there was "nothing to see here." Someone asked Blair did he think that maybe Saddam had a really really big catapult and was launching them from Baghdad. Blair nearly smirked that time, nearly acted human, but he caught himself just in time and said something or other about "jokes not being welcome, in fact being dangerous, providing succour to the enemy, in times like this." Gobshite.

Looking back it is easy to see the media was overdoing it and should have been focussing more on the speech. Nobody expected what was to come. Nobody. Legolas was to address the United Nations General Council. The whole lot of them. Each one of those men and women ultimately smeared and besmirched by being humanities' representative. Each soiled by their country's own particular brand of corruption.

What message Legolas would bring was a mystery. Bush had clearly warned France a fortnight ago that continued trading with Iraq would amount to a breach of the sanctions and that France would have to bear responsibility for its actions. What responsibility meant was difficult to gauge. Iraq had definitely retooled, but this was the Middle East here. Firstly, had Bush the first ever really un-tooled them? Secondly, this was the Middle East where guns fell from the sky. They make guns out of wine. They are the most heavily armed people in the world.

Christ knows they need to be.

So we were at an impasse.

In box set speak; Preferably 'merican, Sam Spade type.

"Bush and Wolfowitz and all those other galloshes wanted to go in and finish Saddam.

Problem was they had no probable cause.

Problem was they needed an excuse and that excuse was the WMD see?

Problem was there was nobody alive on this fucking spinning ball of oxygen who believed that crock."

Strangest of all was, if France had wanted to go into Iraq, they would just have done it. That is one of the ironies of the situation. UN resolution my ass.

Friday morning early the news cycle changed, there was something new to churn. They had footage of Legolas getting off a jet in Louisiana on Thursday evening. This gave pretty much all of us an uneasy feeling. Was he going to give them the money back? Legolas had spent the Thursday night at some ball in Baton Rouge.

Incredible, rolling back the clock. Some historians came out and suggested that the Yanks still owed the French the money and therefore France might be about to reclaim Louisiana. This was more drivel in a world already swimming in it. I would digress if this whole thing was not mired in the West's 21st century geo-political digression.

The Baton Rouge Ball seemed to be some debutante, old-southern, French thing that strangely suited who Legolas was. Legolas was sired into a family with holdings. Great. He wrote poetry and was known to be a decent singer in the old Baroque French style. He was slightly removed from the average French person's life, being as he was from the gilded moon. Not even the present day moon, the moon of three hundred years ago. His real name meant friend of the emperor, his family home was somewhere close to Fontainebleau and most of Martinique. The word was he was merely letting the locals use his island out of some altruistic bent. His children were international lesbians and cocaine hoovers. But he had a hard on for the Yanks, so a lot of us gave him a pass on all the other stuff.

The speech was due that evening and the whole of France was leaving work early to get to a TV. The country had been side-lined a lot lately. The Yanks were pretending the Brits were their best friends. The French had found themselves without enough colonial action of their own. They needed colonial military peace-keeping war-making as much as the next imperialist country. They had interests.

Chapter 32

Friday October 25 2002

Legolas sombrely but assuredly stepped out into the UN General Assembly to be greeted by, what I would have to say, was a warm welcome. He had elected to speak in French, but we all suspected he would do his own English translation, thus enabling himself to repeat his message.

Legolas was a beautiful man. Standing up there in front of the world he looked in many ways like a man on trial for his beauty. His hair alone put many in Europe and Asia to shame. Recognising this, many looked away from his locks, unable to view him head on. He began with a quote from a French poet, probably a relation. The quote talked about the necessity in nature for division to enable understanding and create strength; how this very division progressed the mutuality of our political and cultural conscience. It was a great quote.

France watched rapt. He went on to explain "France has long felt a strong cultural kinship to Mesopotamia."

This was the first red flag, as no one in their right mind wanted to invade Mesopotamia, try selling that one to the voters.

Legolas continued, "We should not be so quick to provoke war. I am a French man and as a French man I understand the undesirability of war."

"Some people understand war to be something ideological. But France knows that war is destruction first and ideology second. People believe differently because they think of war only through the simplistic prism of their favourite war. World War 2. La version de Hollywood."

"Even World War 2," he explained, "caused the world fifty years of pain. Even the greatest, most heroic and straightforward of all wars did not end with us all as friends. It left us with fifty years of poison, countries like open wounds. Poison that has only recently been lanced for good." His English was brilliant. Lanced, nice job. He paused here as he surveyed the world, letting the delegates listen to their stuttering translators deal with that one.

He then went on to rhyme off a few crap wars, "Vietnam, Algeria, Korea and Afghanistan. All they have left behind is the festering sore of violence, the earth's destruction and the loss of decades of progress. Not one of those wars has resulted in anything worthwhile or good."

I thought to myself unless you are Vietnamese or Algerian. But that is, of course, utterly irrelevant.

It was a good speech and the country was quiet. Outside the traffic had slowed to enable France listen to Legolas regaining its supposedly lost place on the world stage.

Towards the end of the speech he spoke about how France believed,

"That through difference would come strength. That France believed, like the United States (he lightly pounded the podium with the palm of his hand for this) that trade is a means of liberation. That trade with the

Iraqi people is the only way for them to untether themselves from the yoke of tyranny. That trade was the foundation on which the modern world of 2002 was built."

He urged the Assembly to listen, to understand that "it is not France against the UN or the US versus Iraq, it is the United Nations community, the world community together solving a very modern crisis with all the peaceful tools it has. France is trading, (pause) trading for peace."

With that he kind of saluted, although who he was saluting was anyone's guess.

Maybe the salute was an unconscious thing. Maybe he wanted to touch his bandage. The bandage he wore that added gravitas. The bandage he wore to cover up the gash on his head. The gash on his head that the Stonethrowers had given him.

The bandage looked great. The speech ended poorly because, try as he might, selling Iraq weapons was not a great idea. Especially as it only encouraged more death. And, at the end of the day, the whole speech could be summed up as "Non".

The assembly rose as one, some even touching their own non-existent bandage. They then gave him a round of applause, and a standing ovation. All round the hall these men (mostly) touched their own foreheads in salute, to this coiffed balladeer of yore. Standing up on his golden high horse to denounce another set of gods similar but ever so slightly different to his own.

In the Bug everyone stood and touched their hand to their own mock bandages. I dared not look at the lads.

I reckoned I heard Bush throw his "non-alcoholic" beer against the White House wall though.

Chapter 33

Friday October 25 2002

Saturday October 26 2002

After the Stonethrowing of the first half of the week I spent the next few days knee deep in love. Spinning and revolving my life around Naya. I was at work and it went well but I was outside looking in. Seeing the place as mere distraction from the glamorous, slapping, riding sessions. We had decided to try and get some air while we were having sex, which was our new evenings' activity. Snatched bouts of fucking under the many bridges of Paris. Hand jobs, blow jobs, lick jobs, odd jobs; in restaurants and bars.

After the Legolas speech we got caught in a restaurant bathroom over by Les Halles, in flagrante as they say in Monte Carlo. We were escorted out mid meal. I was a bit sore about that, as I had not had my main course. But the restaurant, to their eternal credit, did not charge us for our terrine starters. Naya was a bit embarrassed about that one; hiding under her coat as they saw us to the door. I felt the opposite and looked over at each diner, making eye contact with anyone who wanted. A few were appalled, a few envious, all watching us. I bowed once as we met the door. There was a spatter of applause. I felt we deserved a full round.

Friday evening after the speech you could feel France had regained some of its strut. Paris had rediscovered some of its verve. Some of its Gallic shrug. It was a heady night, cars beeping like they had won another sporting tournament. The clips of the speech were repeated ad nauseam especially the salutes at the end. For the Stonethrowers it was all mana. The country was suddenly distracted and that suited us fine. I was due to throw the following Wednesday. James would throw Monday and Peter Tuesday. We had arranged to meet in the Bois de Vincennes on Saturday. We were training early, the girls joining us mid-afternoon.

I had settled on the head of a Paris based think tank, the Centre for the Advancement of Strategic Studies. French Lord Haw Haw. Jaw jawing about upcoming wars. He was the kind of sideline cheering, faux fence sitting prick I really hated. John Paul Laurent was the chief guy and his office was round by the Jardin des Plantes. A quaint Potemkin façade on a building with a hint of a garden round the back. It faced onto the river and was well back from the road. I'd had my eye on him for months. I'd sat near him a couple of times on the terrace of a local resto, just to get a feel for the security even before I knew what I wanted to do with him. There was none. Why would a guy who spent his entire life advocating military action not have any security?

What kind of world had we created?

The restaurant staff all knew him. I had watched them all fussing and appeasing him. He was a regular. I would take a risk. If he was not there

I'd have to fall back on my Plan B. Which as of Saturday morning was non-existent.

The lads showed up suitably fresh for a Saturday morning practice. All of us had been drinking less; easier to deal with the anxiety when you didn't have a hangover. Grand when you were drunk obviously, but being hungover meant that everyone was a foe when you were a Stonethrower. We all looked better for it.

Vincennes was bigger and allowed us more room and more privacy. The Stonethrowers were big news now, second only to the two fuckwits Chirac and Bush and, after Friday night, Legolas and his cretinous bandage.

"Legolas Heals the World."

"Legolas Bandages World's Injuries."

"World Salutes Wounded France."

"France Bandage UN"

"International Triage."

"Legolas Salutes Freedom."

"Iraqi people watch horrified as two guys, who have never been to Iraq, decide its future." This was the one I wanted to see, but didn't.

The caricaturists of the French press had never had it so good. The best was Legolas running, blonde locks flowing, with a rugby ball marked "peace", through an American Football Team, into the scoring area marked Iraq. Grim granted, but mildly amusing.

A light drizzle and the cold prevented us from being disturbed as we ran through our recently developed throwing drills. One of us was a look out circling our enclosure, one thrower and one collector. We moved through and around a wide space. The biggest lesson of the last few days was that throwing in motion, with no discernible change of body shape was tough for anyone to spot. The morning and early afternoon evaporated into the locally made air.

We cajoled and mocked our way to meet the girls, three tough guys. A triple date I suppose. We all sat with our partners. James had managed to convince one of his recent conquests to join up with us. Clare was decent, pretty and English. We let the day get away from us. The lads all starving due to our secret exertion. The food was a delightful Gallic mix of deli treats. Hot Toulouse sausage, pâté de foie, baguette à l'ancienne, brie, blue d'Auvergne, avocado, warm vol au vents, and eight different types of patisserie.

We'd discussed our next targets earlier. I'd not alluded to the precarious nature of mine. Peter had chosen another left-wing politician, Alain de Jordan, who had a penchant for whores. I never got Peter's fixation with this guy but it wasn't for me to say. Peter reckoned he'd him clocked coming out of his mistress' house Tuesday morning, before Paris really woke up. Peter was gagging to give this guy a splitting headache, and seemed to be operating in the name of chivalry, foolhardy I suspected. His call though, his throw.

James was going after the head of a missile building firm that went under the guise of The Aeronautical European Space Company. Alex Petran was an Anglo French douche who developed missile technology with taxpayer money. Whatever about him, James had his eye on him. This was a seriously ambitious target but James had scouted the target area twice during the week; Petran was due to open a new exhibition at the Louvre on Monday, something to do with the cultural intersection of art and aeronautics. James would be there amongst the tourists, the mob, and weapons manufacturers disguised as humble scientists.

All seemed in order.

We did not breathe a word of this to the girls. Why waste their time? Monique twice brought up the Stonethrowers in conversation, as we all lay on top of our respective others. But no one bit. Not sure any of us could have spoken on the topic without letting on. I stilled Naya both times. She was in ebullient form and was halfway to being friends with Monique.

Everybody was more interested in Legolas. The French morning papers had full page pictures of him saluting the world. I was not sure where this was going. None of us were. But we all agreed we were awake again. Bush was busy working on his ranch for the weekend and was next due to speak to the American media on Wednesday. Skin and hair flying was what was expected I think. Bush had never ever ever had anyone say 'No' to him before, like the Saudi Princes he loved so much, he had grown up without boundaries. It was his move. And he was soon to overturn the whole board.

Chapter 34

Saturday November 9 2002

Pigalle of course, so obvious. Bomb the books and the sex district, the two things Bush and his toe rags loathed the most. Pigalle was a kip though. I'm not sure even I could have argued against that one. As I glided up the serene streets, I experienced fear so strong I thought I was going to have to crash the bike to release myself from it. Hard to shake the feeling I'd have to kill myself to relax the clench. Thankfully the wailing started again, a distracting sound I had grown accustomed to. It was so loud you couldn't but devote some brain to it.

Pigalle was an infinitely messier proposition than the Library. People lived there. Pigalle, a normal Paris residential district interspersed with sex shops, sex shows and bars. That evening it was a lurid pink and red flashing inferno when I first saw it, X's and S's falling and hanging on for life. Why had they left the lights on? I wondered had anyone ever even had cause to turn them off before. There must have been people inside those places as well. Coded warning or no, poor people have to go to work. Cleaners and the like. Dead.

I found out afterwards many died in the Pigalle fires. One hundred and sixty bodies were pulled out of the rubble and ruin over the next few days. But who cares, right? That's not the point, right? The bombs had made the place look even more dystopian. The building tops excavated and decapitated like steaming black boiled eggs, some fronts still flashing XXX or SEX or GAY. Not sure if Pigalle is our finest hour or the opposite. Helicopters were above there also, but it wasn't as easy. The flames and the smoke meant visibility was worse. Even on the street it was hard to see what was going on. The central section of the Boulevard de Clichy was just French fire trucks. Pompiers; a semi paramilitary firefighting force with hard to believe silver helmets. Elite. The whole street burned like a Vietnam, Agent Orange tree line. Vietnam, the war Bush hid drinking under his father's apron.

The noise was too loud to hear. It comforted me.

'Why did I not go round the back? Only carnage and chaos here.' The thought barged its way into my head. I turned around as one of the recently disembarked soldiers suddenly took notice of me. I went in a loop away from Pigalle up behind my area and in and around onto my street. The bottom of the street was a busy West African market normally. That afternoon it was quieter, although by no means empty. It wasn't an area of Paris that mattered; not an area of Paris they would have tried very hard to evacuate. They sold bananas there the size of your arm. Tall stern women walked around with bundles atop their heads showing off. I stopped the bike at the bottom of my road.

The road and everything on it was where it was supposed to be. Maybe there was an unlikely van half way up?

It was around dinner time. The French are weakest at lunch and dinner. No matter what the scenario, someone would have to go and get something. Breakfast does not enter the equation. French breakfast is really a next day dessert with coffee; without cigarettes it is pointless.

I propped the bike against the outside of the bar and asked the barman could I put it in the side alley. He was not my biggest fan; Peter and I had been a bit loud in there a few weeks back and he still hadn't forgiven me. We were definitely the only young white guys who ever went in there, so pretty easy to remember. We hadn't been rude, just silly. Neither of us mean drunk. Laughing-our-asses-off-drunk.

In France there exists amongst most foreigners a code of camaraderie that activates once it's clear we are all operating against the French state. When he saw I wanted to hide the bike, he waved his hand to go on ahead. I had to wheel it through the bar out the side entrance into the alley which connected all the way up through the backyards. I had a quick coffee. Being seen to rush in France is unforgivable, even more so to these African French lads. They'd have thought I was a fucking eejit. I paid the man, downed the coffee and went and stood in a doorway about ten doors down from my place.

I mused. Why do I not have her fucking number? Although what use would that be? Especially if they had a tail on her. Better this way.

The next thing I see is a young guy about my age leaving the apartment building opposite mine. Wearing a bomber jacket, open necked white cotton shirt and jeans. He had keys in his hands. Cop, flic; the dinner boy. OK at least I knew they were there. I needed to go in the back.

I was exhausted and I knew from the look the lads in the bar had given me I looked pure crazed. My hair was singed, my jeans were ripped and bloody, my shirt looked like a bum's rag. Add to that the last few hours' worth of grime, I again looked like a bum. But then I'd looked like a bum when I'd left the apartment earlier. I'd spent the last couple of days looking like a bum. Walking amongst them unseen and untouched. Looking like a bum had gotten me to where I was.

I needed some adrenalin. I refocused on Naya.

There was a refuge hostel behind me; I pushed through the door. The smell from me and the building made for a delicious wake up. I went through two more doors to get out the back.

The back was small and typical. I was able to get over the wall into the next yard up, six more walls to go. Elbows raw now, the pain again from my knee. All these things jolted me in the reality. I reached my building. The door was locked, before I got down off the wall I quietly put my foot through it above the handle. Knocking the glass down to get my hand in, the door was still locked. What had I expected? Using my beautiful ruined shoulder I pushed through the cheap door. Fuck me the noise it made. Hopefully the cops were still on a break.

I skulked around the bottom bannister and then began up the stairs. What was I skulking for? If they saw me it wouldn't be because I was going too quickly. I crept up the five flights to my place. I opened the thinnest door in Paris very very quietly. I was now sliding along the floor on my stomach. I peered into the sitting room. I could hear the idiot tinny voices coming from humanity's great leveller, the TV. The news blurting blah blah blah, Americans Bombing Paris, blah blah blah. Naya was sitting on the couch watching the television in a fake prim way, dressed in a polo neck. What the....? I'd not realised things were that bad, a polo neck? The only part of her skin uncovered was her face above her chin. She was even wearing gloves. There was a definite nod to sexy mafia widow about the whole ensemble. I slid back around the corner and exhaled. Every single part of me, every single cell in my *body died for one millisecond such was my relief. Then it all rebooted and we were off again.*

Chapter 35

Monday October 28 2002

Tuesday October 29 2002

Wednesday October 30 2002

The Louvre was not an ideal place to throw. James knew that already. But he got away with it. Maybe the police needed to get up earlier. He made the throw at one o'clock Monday. There was no doubt he hit him, it was the lead story. They interrupted the lunchtime bulletin to go live to the Louvre.

The beautiful distant-looking reporter spoke in a cadence and a tone normally reserved for world wars. She looked sombre and stoic, her voice suggested that if we all stick together we will get through this turmoil. Yeah let's all stick together with the millionaire missile makers. Spare me please. Thwack.

James had taken the day off work. As a stock broker he was the least likely to be suspected. We met for lunch and sat together watching people, a beautiful Parisian carousel. We both had the boudin, the French black pudding, brilliant. James gave me his, gorgeous. He had some bread. I think by the end of the meal he was OK. He said he was off to sit in the Place de Vosges. He was done and was trying to get his head around it. The Place was the perfect place to distract yourself.

Tuesday too was smooth. The man of the people politician again unguarded save for his driver who never even got out of the car. Peter popped up at Bercy to throw. The shot was a beautiful arched specimen apparently. It hit him in the back of the head. The guy was probably on a high coming out of his mistress' abode. The last thing he expected was a sixty thousand year old projectile at seven thirty in the morning. Peter said that a few people had seen him hurrying away. The area around Bercy was more open and difficult to find decent throwing cover. Apparently a small crowd had gathered outside the Bar Tabac to get smokes, they gave him a little Gallic cheer. He was chuffed and not worried.

Something happened Tuesday evening to stifle any more chuffed ness. A member of the French internal security wing was in the Bug asking questions about Dean. The RG are the Interior Minister's special group. And like any French security group nobody wanted to mess with them. Peter only spoke briefly to the RG leaving most of it for the other owner, Declan. But we were all a little rattled. I figured though I'd take my throw tomorrow, then reassess what we were going to do. I was keen on doing this last throw. Then maybe we'd leave it for a while.

The media had postponed worrying about what Bush would say; instead they had savagely landed on the Stonethrowers as the headline story. Five targets all hit. The police were coming under unmerciful scrutiny. I felt sorry for them. Compared to real crime, this was nothing, but the media wanted the next chapter, they took it personally. The media obviously cared not a jot for who got hit; they just felt that the story was not moving fast enough. They wanted more narrative.

What next? Tuesday night I spent on my own. Naya and I had decided to give each other the night off. I utterly regretted it as I sat down to a plate of merguez, rice and thinking.

'Where was the heat coming from? Why were they enquiring about Dean? Was there something we do not know about?' Questions I had, answers I didn't.

Peter had tried to find out more from Declan. But there was no detail forthcoming. Declan had been asked by the agents to keep schtum about the whole thing. And he had given his word he would. Peter could have pushed it, but there was no guarantee any of this was connected to us. It was all a bit frightening. Why else would anyone be interested in Dean? Nerves jangled raw and flailing, but there was nothing really for me to do.

I lay in my bed and the world unravelled around me. I missed Naya. I may have slept a little that night, who knows. It did not feel like it.

Work was fleeting. It slurred past me. I felt jagged and strewn all over the place. But I stuck to my tasks. Duty my only excuse, my only protection. The restaurant I stood outside was set alongside the think tank. I walked around the block once. He came out at one o'clock every day, a hardworking man. I watched the door as I walked around. By five past one I was anxious. But I needn't have been. I spotted him leaving, walking along the sandy path out of the grounds, maybe his pen glinting in the sun. He stopped to talk, standing, waiting to cross the road, for the man to turn green. I positioned myself back towards him and I threw. I knew it was perfect as it left my hand. I was around the corner into Austerlitz in less than five minutes; my heart pelting. I took the Métro and changed at Bastille, was back in work before the rest of them.

My nerves now ground to dust. I was lock jaw all day. White knuckle physically and mentally. I avoided anything serious that whole afternoon and then I was out the door and over to Naya's. I felt like she might disappear on me if I was not with her at all times. These feelings had no basis in reality. There were no indications that she was going to go missing. Nonetheless I was starting to worry that maybe she would have a motorcycle accident.

She was expecting me and even though it was only five thirty we went to bed. We made the most sense there. I quickly fell asleep and woke an hour or so later. She was out like a light too. I made us an easy pasta, nourishing at least. And that was all I did. I wanted to talk to the lads, but was not willing to write anything in a text or speak on the phone.

Phones were all I'd worried about all week. Again no basis, other than a life spent watching crap TV. A life spent pretending to be in interesting situations. I did feel a little better. Long as none of us did anything now, we would always be leaving it behind. We would be able to pull clear. That is what I wanted more than anything then, to forget about it.

Not a chance of that happening. The worry consumed me and there was nothing I seemed able to do about it. I lay in bed beside the sleeping dark beauty. Naya had asked me earlier simply

"Is it over?"

I'd answered "I don't know. I hope so."

She had taken this, in that weird war bride-like way she had developed recently. Presumably due to her going out with a certified fuck nut.

About half way through the night I got up and I went to look out her window at the black. The orange glare from the street lamps shone up like cheery hell from below. It illuminated the buildings from underneath allowing one to believe they were being warmed.

I loved the window; it was where I had been looking for. I would see the world end there. I would watch it burn.

Chapter 36

Thursday October 31 Halloween 2002

Thursday broke early for me. I used my hands and mouth to wake Naya up, get her going. Slow and friendly, from behind. I had my eyes closed but I was watching us from an imaginary projected viewpoint in front. She kept turning her head and I met her lips each time. I was slithering my tongue into her ear. This was half tickling her to death and making her squirm, half driving her mad with lust. A combination I think she liked. Again she seemed to like everything I did; I think she just liked me, after that she would go along with anything for the laugh. I got out of bed. Before I could ask her not to, she had turned on the morning news.

There they were, all six faces on the screen, all with their war wounds on display, six cartoon bandaged heads. It was maybe easier to understand the whole thing from a postmodern viewpoint. The bandages had become a reverse badge of honour, if that is possible. Legolas had made the bandages stand for being against the Iraq war. So/donc, these guys, the six targets, had never been more liked. It was a low bar.

The media then did a report on young lads in Les Halles wearing the bandages on Wednesday and Thursday morning instead of baseball caps. 'I am French' they kept saying and saluting like Legolas. The fact that it was Halloween was not enough to explain this. It would be a couple more years before Halloween became popular in France.

Wherever the word flabbergasted came from that is where I went in my head upon seeing this. I lay back on the bed, took Naya's nipple in my mouth. I sucked that nipple in the same way one would have a shot of vodka to help brace yourself against the relentlessly eroding waves of life. I sucked on that nipple for as long as it took until it was just me and that nipple. Fuck Oedipus, fuck the lot of them.

Once my mind was again levelled off I cold showered and went out into a world that had just gone all in on nuts. Little did I know the world, as usual, was not done yet.

I must have done something Thursday. I know I achieved my targets. I know I drank a lot of coffee. I know I went for a drink at lunch with my colleagues. I know I read a lot of stuff about what was going on in the world. I know all those things. But I only know them because I can project my life backwards. I can look back in hindsight and guess what I did from little mental footprints I left.

Really though, in a court of law, I would not be able to provide witness testimony for any of it. My head was so full I was losing things as another thing was added. More was on its way. Arriving into an empty pub, I met Peter and his look of total perplexity and crazed hilarity. Like someone who wanted to laugh their way into jail or straight to death. He looked vaguely like a Jack who had escaped from the box. He nodded at the screen behind him. Already down for the football later. The report was from outside the American Embassy, round the corner from the bar, from this afternoon. There was a gang of young lads all with those ludicrous bandages. Looking like total fools throwing stones at the US Embassy. The CRS, the French riot police, were baton charging them. They were pulling one young lad off the line each charge. Isolating and then bringing them to the side for a shoeing. France had had enough.

There were about fifty young lads all told. Amidst the childish scuffles a journalist was trying to ask them were they responsible for the other six bandages? They said they were. The journalist then asked why had they changed their tactics, they said,

"After the speech we realised who the real enemy was."

I fucking kid you not. Six youths were eventually arrested, charged and taken into custody.

I was apoplectic with wanting to kill those little fools. Seriously? The whole thing was insurmountable. We'd all marked each stone in our own way and there was no way the young lads knew any of this. What were they thinking? It was not pride for me, it was vanity. This was all I'd ever done and I knew it was being turned into graffiti.

Fuck that.

I decided right then I was going to turn myself in. I pretended later this was up for discussion. It never was. It was ordained the moment I saw that report. I was going to isolate myself and give them the lone Stonethrower. The media loved that lone gunman tripe. They always did. Easier to cover, less work. Draw them towards the idea that this was a specific freak event, with no outlier element to it, not indicative of any trend or rising tide. This was just a guy. They would lap it up. I would grant them interviews. I'd always wondered why I'd spent my life fascinated by the lone guy theory, now I knew. I wanted to be the lone guy. I was the lone guy.

James arrived in looking like a dishevelled gentleman cat, which was worrying. He was all caught up. We sidled over to the outer elbow of the bar. We both had drinks and fags. I was not panicking anymore. I was being pulled off the surface of the planet by forces outlandish and preposterous but yet powerful and aimed at me.

"Thoughts?"

"Not sure I have any James. Not sure I have any useful ones at any rate. Rage?"

"Yeah rage and loss of control. I fucking knew we should have released a statement explaining who we are."

I let that one go. Tap dancing up and down the linear narrative, pissing on chronology; that was not something I was prepared to entertain.

"Alright. What I am going to do is ring the media, tell them I threw all the stones, alone. Tell them I am the Stonethrower."

"What?" Peter looked at James who looked at me who looked at Peter.

"Yeah I think that's what I want to do. That is what you are going to help me do. The police must know fine well these guys are jokers? Right?"

"So what if they do? They can say it was copycats?"

"No. No they can't. We each have those codes on the stones that enable only us to have been the throwers." I answered.

"Why only you?"

"Because first and foremost, I am in charge. Second of all, I always said I was the one who would take the blame if the shit hit the fan."

"Fuck that mate. We all go down. One for all?"

"Did you really say that? I know things have been a bit strange for a while, but there's no need for that. I want this. There is no point in all of us taking the blame. Right?"

"Why do you think that? There's every point in us all taking the blame. Spread the blame around. Less for everyone to take?"

"Bullshit. They will just multiply the amount of blame there is to go around. That's a dumb fuck idea. This is not some round table honourable thing. There's no honour in something like this. We knew this when we started, we knew this the whole time. We fucking discussed this." I was exasperated.

"Well let's wait see what happens?" Peter mollified us.

"Agreed. I will wait until Monday. And we can discuss it again. But at the end of the day the decision'll be mine. I'll brook no argument."

"There's fuck all you'll be able to brook about it, mate, brook no argument, ha."

"I am going over to Naya, bring her out for a while. Tomorrow is Bush v Chirac the return leg. Watch it here?"

"Sweet. Talk then. Peace and love."

Chapter 37

Friday November 1 2002

Bush, Bush, Bush. The man was a false construct, it is hard to say anything insightful or new about him. I saw a documentary about his campaign, before he stole the election off Gore. He seemed like a human, after he seemed like a thrill seeking maniac. Saddam should have known better than to rile him though. Bush senior had failed to press home his savage advantage; Junior was furious about the whole thing and could not wait to get in.

They were an oil family so there is nothing you could really say about that. America can pretend all it likes it did not realise what type of men the Bushes were. But they knew fine well. Right-wing oil obsessed war mongers. Big deal. Half of America aspires to be this type of guy. Fuckwits, but right-wing fuckwits. The dad was air force, CIA, vice prez and prez, the Grandad was up to some nefarious shit, Junior was devil spawn. The ranch thing was the funniest; he had about as much to do with ranching as a penguin.

Saying all that, his spat with Chirac was out of the blue. Chirac apparently drank Corona, a Mexican beer, which made him more pro-American than any other French president ever, or so the shtick went. Chirac was not about to give any of this up, but he hated being pushed around, and Bush had done exactly that when he issued France with an ultimatum. Diplomacy was a word Bush neither understood nor, more importantly, believed in. Bush believed in bullying, he elevated it to the status of foreign policy, he further elevated it to the status of ideology.

We sat quietly in the Bug Friday evening. Again all of France, I would say all of Europe, was in front of the idiot box. The media were sitting there live on television, with their hands down their neighbour's trousers, jerking each other off such was their elation at this ratings beater. Expert after besuited expert was trotted out to give us their new material. New material, of course, was really microwaved old material with some sauce, the sauce being syrupy idiocy.

Difficult to know what to make of these men, for they were all men, all a little overweight; it was hard for us to ignore the girth of their ineptitude. Television does add ten pounds of stupidity. Difficult to know what to say about the things they said, so wrong were they. Not one of them thought Bush's speech would amount to anything. Their imagination would not allow it. These fat men could only ever tell you what had happened. They could only ever re-chew the food you had already eaten and tasted. They did not serve the future in any way.

Bush was speaking at some veterans' cake sale. The War Monger-in-Chief, the guy who spent his whole service drink driving and doing coke. Whatever happened to veterans? They used to have a little chutzpah? No?

Bush opened the speech with a joke about there not being enough chicken at the buffet. It may not have been a joke, it may have been a genuine grievance. He seemed pretty angry about it.

Bush then began talking about betrayal. As a lunatic, this was a concept he understood extremely well. His pretend bible upbringing was something he could call on. It was a textbook light and dark, up and down speech. Straight out of his pretend bank of memories. Bush was a character from someone's imagination. The cowboy, the humbleness, all complete bullshit. Millionaire son of head of secret police and President from Connecticut. Connecticut was, as far as I can gather, the most high fluting state in the union, the most pretentious; people bathed in sparkling water in Connecticut so the story goes. Bush squinted his eyes, looked into the eyes of the warriors and continued,

"France, the country who gave us the Statue of Liberty, is now feeding and arming our enemies. France is providing not only trade but also moral sustenance to our most natural foe, tyranny."

Natural foe. Nice line. Bush speech writing; nice work if you can get it. Jibber jabber, bible, good versus evil, maybe a dash of Hitler thrown in.

"Of this there can be no dispute." Of course, pretty much everybody disputed it one way or the other.

By the end of the incredibly short speech it was clear that this thing was on. Bush said France had five days to cease all relations with Iraq. He held up his hand to show he knew five.

Bush went on to say,

"America could no longer sit idly by while Saddam strengthened and prepared a new generation of fighters prepared to fight America."

Not bad. Total and utter drivel, but he had France in somewhat of a bind. They didn't really have another throw of the dice. They'd called his bluff and he had not blinked. France could not really walk away from the massive contracts they had signed with Iraq over the last few years.

French industry had experienced a large boon from this. Word on the street was, they were even building power plants in Iraq.

Bush said,

"France has until Tuesday November 5 to prove that it has ceased entirely and without fail all trade relations with Iraq. If not, France would bear the consequences for its actions and its international treachery."

Ho hum.

Peter whistled and said "international treachery" then whistled again. We all liked the phrase, international anything right? The bar was quiet. Bush had not mentioned what he would do. Had Bush ever even been to France? Strange he should hate it so. But hate it he did. He saw in France everything he was not. The poor guy was wrong about this; France was no intellectual and cultural paragon. Well maybe compared to Bush it was.

Naya sat beside me, arms around me. James was with Clare again, they were orbiting each other more closely. The gun smoke danger in the air had us all holding onto each other more tightly. None of us spoke. There was fuck all to say. The stay of execution had been stayed and we all had our own problems to face. I was not sure what I would do, but I did want to spend the weekend with Naya, especially if I was turning myself in next week. I wanted to spend the weekend in suspended sex animation. I had booked us a weekend out of Paris down in the Dordogne. Would be cold, but there had been more stones thrown earlier that day, this time at the British embassy and a couple of British shops. I could not have cared less for these people but, generally, I was becoming more uneasy.

There had also been more enquiries about Dean. I could not really grasp it properly. The agents had asked Peter some questions this time and had queried if there was anyone else they should speak to, anyone else who knew Dean well. Peter had said he would find out. Peter reckoned they already knew the answer to the questions they were asking. That James and I would be next. So a brief jaunt down to duck and wine country where the English grow on trees seemed in order.

We hopped on the bike that night. Naya drove like a mad woman and we made it there in around three hours. A night bullet. We talked a little leaving Paris, but then there seemed no point. We were both experiencing the same things. We both were sore with the way things were going, neither of us looked like we were going to get what we wanted. She wanted me, I wanted whatever it was that was illusive and unattainable. Well that's what I thought I wanted. Turned out I never really wanted any of it.

Chapter 38

Saturday November 2 2002

Arriving into the place near Riberac in the Dordogne, I knew we would be safe for the weekend. I lit a fire to get the chill out of the small house. There was a kitchen, a dining room under the stairs, a sitting room. Upstairs was a large double bed and the only real bedroom. Naya was knackered and that was fine. She'd driven like a superstar. Like most girls of that era she was probably better than me. I thought about things like that, it was why I often was without a girl. She also did not have the nervous thing some girls have, the instilled fear of things outside, experiences unknown. She was tough, violence never worried her. She carried some despotic weapon in her bag; I would catch her fingering it as we talked and walked. She was so attractive; when we were out in Paris, I thought of violence and fighting for her honour all the time. It wore me down. I was real glad to be out of the city. My soul exhaled.

Once the fire was set and lit, I laid out the pâté and the cheese and the bread with a bottle of local Bordeaux left by the owner. We were famished and the food sated us. We lay on the sofa long into the night, as the fire and the warmth creaked through the small cottage's old veins. Naya listened to me as I talked about growing up in Ireland. It was hard to explain Ireland to someone who had no sense of it. To give people the right impression that, like most places, sometimes it was the best place in the world, at other times it was crap.

I had grown up as an incidental person. Slight and trivial. I'd always veered one way then the other. I would often find myself alone as I did not hold on tight enough to friends. That was OK though. I pretended to be various people, as I changed from group to group, finally alighting on a shallow slim personality people let slip by them without too much chaffing. University was a pointless exercise, but I was wise enough to hang on until the end. I learnt nothing whatsoever. Maybe I learnt University was not for me. University was also the first time I realised I'd accidentally prised open my mind and when I began to realise how disastrous this was. The only thing that helped was drinking.

Drinking in Ireland has been much written about: but I only really started drinking when I came to Paris. Liquor was now something I had most days. At least until I met Naya. That first night in Bordeaux I only had two glasses of wine. We didn't even finish the bottle. The main reason I drank before was if I was not drinking I was thinking or, worse, I was bored and I felt panicked. Now she occupied my mind. Our minds intertwined and colluded.

She talked about growing up and what it was like to be a girl in the south, outside of Marseille. She had brothers and parents who together created a smothering blanket of instruction and prohibition. She pretended to go along with this and then by the age of eighteen had organised an escape to Paris where she'd been living for six years. She'd liked the squat because it was how she imagined Paris would be.

Piercings and spray cans, flayed lives with candle lit souls. Her father had bought her her own place when he realised she wouldn't be back and to help him feel like he was protecting her.

"I hated it at the beginning, but now, well I live there more than the retreat." She said.

"I am not sure what changed. I miss my family. And they've all got wives and children now. When I visit they're not worried about me anymore. Their lives are their families mostly and I enjoy their company more. I've been released into the world and they all know that. They were never that bad, but I missed out on many things when I was younger. Like boys."

And then the glint with the flashbulb smile. She could glint at will. That glint flashed through me, weakened me and fortified me towards her, lent me into her. On Saturday we slept and yawned, licked and pawed our way through the morning like sexy cats. There was no television and the only radio station I could get was some god awful French one, Turbo FM. In France French stations are required to play a certain percentage of French music. Like most protectionist things, this is great in theory but in practice results in French pop music being borderline appalling. Not having to compete results in poor music. Who knew?

Naya went nuts when I complained about it, but there was only so much I could take. Besides the French jingle jangle, it was extremely unusual to have to listen to so many Eagles songs on a Saturday morning, not in the late seventies. They are my only complaints of that day. Casual roll around sex and weird French pop tunes got us through the morning. It was as good as bed can get. When you feel the island safety, that cozy isolation when even reaching things requires maintaining a stretched physical link to the bed. Me rolling over her and laughing. She slept on top of me, which was no mean feat for either of us.

The afternoon. We headed off, I knew the area vaguely and I wanted to bring her to a restaurant. Bringing Naya to a restaurant had become my favourite non-olive skin-licking thing to do.

Like me she appreciated the show. She was never too fatigued or too jaded to enjoy the anticipation, contrastingly never too annoyed if it fell short. The place served local fare and was fantastic. It was run by a couple of gay lads who'd escaped to the countryside and to be left alone.

We had duck and wine. Maybe the best thing to eat in the world. Naya had the magret, I had the confit. The amount of natural grease and juice from mine made me feel immune to everything.

We rode around the country side. I drove; it was only fair, although we nearly had to have a full blown argument about it. And by nearly I mean we did.

Evening meal we decided to pick up something from the local supermarket and barricade ourselves into our lives for a little while longer. We were going to have to discuss it at some stage and that stage was going to be pretty soon. I am not sure why, but I intimated she knew what I wanted to do. She'd already given me both barrels over being the main one to blame. Girls were always at that. They were always wrong about it too. For some reason I could never grasp, they always believed in collaborative responsibility. I didn't. I believed in hierarchical responsibility. I also wanted the lads to do what I told them, or else this whole thing was going to continue becoming more and more farcical.

I'd been the one who'd suggested the signatures on the stones. I felt now with Dean out of it that the whole thing had been my idea. I felt responsible. What's so wrong about that? Fuck sake.

I knew that Naya wasn't going to like it though.

And so it proved. She actually threw a plate at one point, flung it at me. That made me love her even more. Having a plate flung at you is one of those things that might sound fun and cinematic, except it's the opposite, it's in fact terrifying. She flung it like a Frisbee. We'd been talking about me handing myself in for a while. She'd taken this part OK, she had guessed ahead to at least that stage. While we'd been talking about it, Naya was under the false impression the three of us were going to hand ourselves in together.

I eventually explained I intended to do it alone and would not tolerate any other way. That's when I got the plate flung at my eyes. I dodged it and then we got into it. She went to walk out. Where in the name of fuck was she going at midnight, in the middle of English Dordogne, in poxy November? It didn't bear thinking about. I'd anticipated this as the conversation had been warming up, and hidden the bike keys. I was slightly afraid she would go out anyway and we would be traipsing round the countryside arguing with each other, like wandering singing minstrels.

"What kind of a fucking stupid idiot, idiot, man idea was that?" Was I think what she said. Her cursing invective had improved immeasurably.

"Whose idea was that? Was it Peter and James' idea? I don't believe it was, was it? It was your idea wasn't it? This is typical 'you are the one in charge, protect all of us' bullshit you try with me?"

"Yeah the lads think we are still discussing it. But I've made up my mind. Why should three of us take the blame when we can get away with only one? They will take one. I can tell them what was written on the stones, nobody else can. I made this plan before I met you. I am sorry. The only thing I regret about this whole thing is I met you too late to change course. I've never ever felt like this about anyone. I don't feel like this about myself. I'd do anything for you. But not this. Us, me and you, took me totally by surprise."

"Do you even listen to yourself? If you even cared about me at all you'd not do this."

"Do what? I've already done all the things that cannot be undone. I just want to take responsibility for it. I cannot let those idiot young fellas take the fall for me. I won't. And don't even pretend you think that I don't care about you. Don't."

I had her there, it was a ludicrous thing to say. But it also showed I'd spun her around and she was not sure where she was. My immortal shame.

I still could not believe I'd become attached to another person. My own parents had more or less let me slip away. I'd never meant that much to them one way or the other. We called each other once or twice a year. They'd other children that still needed parenting; I'd never liked being looked after. As a child my favourite trick was to simply wander off. Wander off and keep walking. Drove my mum mad, she always thought I was walking away from her, leaving her. She was right, I was. I was always optimistic I'd find somewhere better around the corner. When they shouted at me as a teenager, I knew I was too translucent for their shouts and threats to really hurt. They felt it too. I was never an enjoyable child to raise. I gave no love back. I just took their love and left it behind somewhere.

Naya was the first person to activate this in me. I was finding it made me make decisions without sense or symbol. I'd attained a new persona; the man in love, for that is who I had become. I was already defined by my love for her. But I did not understand this at that point; the roots had not made their way through into my brain yet, but the rest of my corpse was utterly captured and held. Long fictional fibrous vines round me and down through me into my little veins.

She was ahead of me on this, in that she had decided already I was who she wanted. I reckon she loved me, but girls are often somewhat beyond that. The decision is the thing, then it is ours to wreck. We're the ones who need the love. Without the love we would wander off. They need something different, something physical and palpable.

She wanted me, all of me. If I was going out to the shop, she was interested, would often want to come with me. I found this bewildering and it destabilised me. Probably was the aloneness dying. I had prepared myself all my life to be alone and I'd never been saddened or put out by it. Like opening your mind and realising you can reject swallowing the long spoon of mindless fodder, that you can create your own reality and sustenance. Naya had awakened in me the desire to paint and hum and sing my own human future.

"I want to give the information to the media first? What do you think?"

"You know what I think. I think you are an idiot."

She was not about to let this one go. So I suggested we go to bed, were she was at her weakest and most powerful. She was the queen of the bed, no doubt. Worship the queen.

Sunday morning was a startling day of birdsong overtures and light beams piercing through unnoticed cracks in the blinds. The countryside around us at that time of year was quite like Ireland. I told her and she said nothing. Not nothing, silent like, more like will get back to me later. I cleaned up as she readied the bike. We communicated only physically that morning. It is difficult when you both understand each other, but there is nowhere else communication can take you unless one of you moves their position. Rock against rock.

We journeyed back to Paris in mostly silence. I still remember it as being one of the great days of my life though. Not having to drive I was able to enjoy a sun and water sparkling journey through the French country side. Old towns with never open shops, seventies France most of it. Day of the Jackal type fare. I was still with her, which was where I wanted to be from then on.

I really only had one more thing to do. What kind of sentence would I be looking at? I could apologise and beg mercy. First offence, well kind of first six offences. I suspected I would have to go to prison, could not see any way around it. The French state was already in enough bother with all the pressure Bush was putting it under. There was no way they were going to let it slide.

She dropped me to my place and we kissed. I nearly walked away then I turned and asked her,

"Do you seriously want to miss time together? I am probably going to be away for a while no matter what happens. I don't really want to be alone. This decision was made before us. We are strong enough for all this. We are. Come up with me, or go home and come back? This is it. This is love."

This might have slightly budged her. I understood she was sore and angry. She'd not asked for much and I was taking away the only real thing she'd ended up wanting.

"OK I'll be back later." She closed her eyes and shook her head as if by doing this she could shake me out of her life, empty me out of her head.

She did come back, sloped into bed, I hugged her from behind. I let her have the silence though, she couldn't have stood to hear any more of my truth. When I think of that day, the distance and the silence, I know it should make me sad, but we held fast that day and she never once threatened to leave me. It makes me think of marriage and something I'd never known until then I wanted.

Someone else.

Chapter 39

Monday November 4 2002

I needed a strategy. I'd been thinking about my next move all weekend. I rang the media contact. I hated being involved with them, but without telling them, the police could spin it whatever way they wanted. They could keep holding the six bandaged fools even after I'd confessed. I told her we needed to meet that afternoon. I chose a bar nowhere near anywhere I knew in Les Halles. Campesinos, bit of a dive. Brazilian beers and grub, not the worst. I gave her a sliver of what I had, told her the exclusivity was predicated on not being messed around and her coming alone. The place was public enough to ensure she was safe, as well as for me to ensure she was not bringing anybody with her. She agreed.

Campesinos was exactly as I had remembered it. I walked in there all the way to the back and straight out again an hour before the six o'clock meet. Positioned myself outside a bar across the way, under one of those terrace canvases, grubby and not see through from the side. I watched her approach; she'd brought some guy with a camera. She motioned for him to sit over opposite outside the bar where I was. The camera had a decent sized lens.

Funny how around this time in the history of humanity, journalists stock had never been lower; and yet compared to five years later, this was not the nadir we all felt it was, it was the peak. The photographer sat down at the other end of the small terrace and placed his camera on the table facing Campesinos. He looked through the lens, nodded to her, as she sat down in the Campesinos terrace, out in the second row from front. What the fuck? Amateur hour, these two fools. A movie had taught me to arrive early for a clandestine meet. A fucking movie taught me the skills I needed to outsmart these two eejits.

I wrote her two texts. Sent one and then the next quickly after. Put my phone back in my pocket. I lit a cigarette and continued to enjoy reading my paper, watching the local flavour of tourists, maniacs and tracksuits that frequented the area. The first told her she had broken our agreement, any more problems and the story would go to someone else. The second told her the photographer had to leave, or else there would be no meeting, and not to reply. The final line,

"The photographer leaving will be the reply."

She looked around with consternation. I was dressed extremely well that day. Suited and booted, as my English friends would say. I'd a briefcase lying on the table. Elsewhere around me were about a hundred more likely candidates.

Suits are the greatest disguise ever. People believe you incapable of malfeasance, when of course the opposite is true. Ask Wall Street.

She rang the photographer. I could not catch any of it. Nor did I try. He got up and wandered off, but there was no way I trusted her now. I waited another five minutes, she rang me twice and was just getting up, when I stood and walked over to her. I placed one of the numbered stones in her hand and beckoned her to follow. I knew a great Syrian kebab shop with no outside. Much more difficult to take photos. I sat with my back to the door, facing a mirror.

Initially I mistakingly thought she was dull looking. Pretty but dull. Brown hair well attended. Eyes alert and untrustworthy, maybe I was projecting.

I introduced myself as the Stonethrower, she put a Dictaphone on the table, making a big show of how honest she was being. She wore a yellow ribbon, I kid you not. There was some sort of always in fashion, French chic that encouraged some women to dress like air hostesses from the sixties. Was a little bit strange, non? Madeleine Delacroix was her name. She was a Parisian. She was twenty seven and was the next big thing in the French sex appeal, reportage nexus. She was angling for a presenting job. She wanted to be out amongst the poor people's eyes like she wanted a hole in her head, hence the attempt at a drab dull disguise.

"So what do you have for me? Why all the cloak and dagger?" She asked. TEFL teachers have a lot to answer for, cloak and dagger my ass.

"Let's talk deal first. I want you to run the report with my face shaded out, I'll give you written specific details of each throw. Details only I and the police could know. These will be withheld from the report and only used as verification. Once your report has aired I will hand myself into the police. I do not want those young fools taking the blame. That's why I need you to ensure it is clear from the report, that these young guys had nothing to do with it. They are guilty only of the embassy stuff. You should think about interviewing them inside if you can."

"OK. When do you suggest I do this? You told the photographer to go away. I work for the television. Without the visual there is no story."

"That is a total load of bollix. People read stories all the time on the news, pictures of relevant stuff in the background. You frame it how you like. No picture of me until I am sure the story is clear on me being the lone thrower. Clear?" Our food arrived, well my food and her water. I offered her a chip which she obviously accepted. She was still a human female. Chips are one of their few weaknesses; presumably it is in their DNA.

"OK deal. I have to check with my boss, but I think it should be OK. Especially as you are going to hand yourself in as well. Might make things easier."

"Tonight? Later?"

"OK. Will you come to a studio or will I come to your place? Studio would be the best."

"Ha. Would it? Yeah not going to happen. We can shoot it on a bench in the street. I will wear a mask. Not a child's mask, a human face mask. Or better still let's do it near the Pont D'Alma, off Avenue de New York? You be there at eleven, I will meet you there and bring some samples. To give you some of your visuals. If there is anybody there, besides you and the cameraman, I will not show. I'll be watching the place from now until then. I live nearby. "

I stood up, walked to the exit and paid. I didn't wait to see if she followed. No sign of the photographer.

I got home by eight thirty, changed into the special interview outfit I had picked out. Naya was nowhere to be seen, she had her own key and, I suppose, her own life.

I decided to walk down to the interview, it took me the guts of an hour and a half, the mask was inside my overalls. I looked like a mechanic. I figured that was pretty non-descript and I would be able to change out of it and get away if I had to.

Chapter 40

Monday night November 5 2002

Madeleine Delacroix looked aristocratic and covert at the same time, like a dolled up Milady De Winter. I think she was wearing a cape. Fair play, it could end up being her moment. My mask was a master stroke, mainly because only up close was it obvious it was a mask. Only then was it apparent.

She began the interview by introducing me as the man who brought fear to the power brokers of France. She was deluded in this, but I enjoyed the flattery. The camera man moved around me and her non-stop, trying to see behind my mask I presumed.

"Who are you?"

"I am the Stonethrower."

"Please explain. Who is the Stonethrower?"

"I am the man who has hit six men in the head with a different stone over the last two weeks."

"Have you more throws planned?"

"No, all operations ceased once people began to misinterpret what it was I was doing."

"Misinterpret how?"

"People began to see solidarity between what I did and the Bush-Chirac problem."

"Do you side with France?"

"I side with no one. If I side with anyone I side with the people of Iraq, the people of France and the people of America. None of whom have any say in what is going to happen. These are bank, oil and arms wars."

"Why did you choose the targets you chose? What was their relevance?"

"I chose the ECB for the continued and growing failure of the ECB to provide safe and well regulated banking to European citizens. Instead they provide intellectual and supposed economic jargon ist cover for all the bubbles about to pop.

The Foreign Minister was chosen as a representative of the rich and their direct birth line to power. He may have stood up to the Americans recently but in many ways he is the French version of his satanic runt counterpart.

Nobody on this scorched and dirty earth needs me to explain why I hit the head of a pharmaceutical company or an arms manufacturer.

I hit the think tanker because they are the advisors of the war kings and I do not take kindly to their immoral equivocation. Finally, the serial misogynist. That was simply to show that the left love power and might is right, same as everyone else. And because he deserved it, his behaviour is a persistent disgrace, as any lady who has ever met him can attest to."

"What do you think of the people who believe you are the leader of a new movement of revolution? What do you say to your supporters?"

"I have no supporters. I have no followers. This is not a movie. Personal revenge was my only motive. Although I knew none of these men, I know them all too well. We all know them and what they do. I am not trying to make a difference. I am not trying to change anything. I only wanted to hit them with a stone. I only wanted to make them think every single time they walk outside and they catch something out of the corner of their eye, for the rest of their lives. I want them to be terrorised by the shadows of birds.

Each stone carries a number and I will provide you with the numbers to verify that it was me and only me who was involved with these actions."

"When will you hand yourself in?"

"I will hand myself in tomorrow evening after this report has aired, and once the police have agreed those currently being held are not responsible for the six throws. I have never even met any of those in custody, what are they doing there Directeur Général? What? Good night and thank you."

She asked me a question as I walked away. I walked out towards Rivoli, stepped out of my overalls, put them in a plastic bag, took off my mask and waited until I got down into the Métro, then I exhaled.

It was on now, whatever about before. I was going to have to do a few pirouettes to get out of this one. I was right in it, exactly where I had convinced myself I wanted to be.

I got off at a random station and dumped all my stuff as the train stopped. Not a single person noticed. The train gave me enough time to walk to a bin, throw the bag in and get back on the train, all one stop. It turned out later I had narrowly escaped that night. She'd contacted them as soon as the interview had ended, they'd had me and then I slipped through their fingers in Châtelet. They should not blame themselves, Châtelet is impossible to imagine as anything other than infernal. Had he ever encountered it, Dante would have given it its own circle.

I got home; I sat down on my sofa. Naya was inside in the bedroom. I could hear her listening to me, wondering what I'd done, wondering what she was doing with me. I'd pulled the relationship taught. It wouldn't take much more tension or the snap would spring us so far apart we'd never find each other again.

I drank a glass of water. I was changing into someone else. That person was obscured from me. Bush was due to speak tomorrow, which could help me or not. Depended on what insanity he and his merry violent men had come up with.

"Hey," I said to Naya as I sat on the bed and undressed.

"Hey." I slipped inside beside her and rolled up right behind her putting my arms around her. I would not let her escape tonight. I needed her.

She turned into me and we sat there so close that we could not see each other properly. Her gaze was one very long question. I held it. I did not know the answer though. I was about to say I was doing my best, but shame prevented me. She pressed her lips once to my mouth. Just her lips and we kissed for maybe two butterflies, however long that is.

I dreamt of love and plasma.

Chapter 41

Saturday November 9 2002

She had the curtains pulled, but they were flimsy threadbare things and you could still see through them, kind of.

"Naya," I whispered. "Naya?"

"Johnny?" She looked above me.

"Down here, don't get up. Stay where you are. Don't get up. Good to see you. You look weird, are you cold?"

I could see this angered her and pleased her at the same time. Pleased to have me back, angry at the trivialities and that I had gone missing on her.

"I look weird? You look like a clodo. Fuck sake. I think I can smell you, were you on fire? Your head is a little bald. The police are across the street. I put on all the clothes because they're police perverts. But I am still naked under these clothes for you. After you wash." She lifted up her pullover and showed me some olive stomach skin.

It was worth it just to get that taste. My eyes gorged.

"This is not a sex call. We need to get out of here? What do you think? Have the cops been over to talk to you? Can you leave?" I had to insist.

I lay back again. Face up. Suddenly I felt futility and fatigue, talk about the wrong time. I explained to myself this was not the time and I was not going to take a step back.

"So do you think we can get out of here without being seen?" I asked.

"Jesus Johnny. I don't know. They've that thermal device thing. They can probably see you."

"Maybe, although I am lying along the radiator out here. The radiator you have conveniently been running at the temperature of the sun," She ignored this dig and continued.

"Where do you want to go?"

"Where do I want to go? Who the fuck knows? Clermont fucking Ferrand? Is this really the conversation you want to have now? I've James' motorbike down the end of the street. The police are a little distracted eating."

"I'm still angry with you. How do I know you'll not leave me again? How can I trust you?" Naya was really not going to let this one go.

"Seriously? Are you Meg Ryan? This is what you want to talk about now. I came to rescue you."

She smiled and laughed.

"You're right. But I'm still annoyed you decided to go without me."

"Go, go where? All I did was go into hiding for a day or three until the heat died down. I told you all this in the note. I was pretending to be a homeless person; I slept two nights outside your house making sure you were safe."

"You slept outside my house to make sure I was safe? You are a fucking eeeeejit as you would say. You're the one everyone wants. Pictures everywhere. Why did you not come in?"

"Seriously? I'll tell you later. Also there's no way you would have agreed to let me go. No way. You are everything I have ever wanted, but I wanted to keep you safe. I wanted to protect you. I felt me not being there was the best way to keep you safe."

"I fucking hate it when you talk like that. I am me. I am the one who makes these decisions. Can you understand that? It drives me crazy. Equal in everything." She stood, then picked up her coat and ran out the door. I jumped to my feet. And the two of us tore down the stairs leaping every floor, Naya first. By jumping round following the twist in the staircase we flew.

When we hit the bottom I grabbed her arm, swung her round to face the right way, out the back and kissed her quickly, both of us crescendoing our energy upwards into each other's mouths. The police were coming through the door as I followed her over the wall, out the back, towards the bike. She went first over each wall. I hate to say it but I slightly enjoyed pushing her ass over. The adrenaline made all of this seem electric smooth. The cops were right behind us and they had already lost me once. They were probably feeling it was more personal than it was. They had just had their dinner though, probably hadn't even finished. This gave Naya and me the edge. I reckoned they must be coming up the front as well. "Keys" I said to her as she leapt the last wall. I pushed them into her back pocket as she went over first. She gunned the bike as I came down on the other side. The only way to get it onto the road was through the bar. I should never have wheeled it in through the bar. So stupid.

Now when I think about the complete brilliant insanity of the whole thing it is through a different prism, but at the time it was the best thing I had ever done. The lads in the bar were now engaged. The police were shouting at us from behind and what sounded like up, out on the street. Would they shoot? She revved the engine, two of the lads held the doors open. The rest of our allies went out onto the street to create enough of a fuss for us to get away. Naya had the bull stamping its foot by the time I hopped on. The engine jerked, tried for grip, caught, then growled towards the door. We tore out that door nearly killing the spectators. They roared a boom of approval that, even now, makes my hair stand up, reminds me that they saved us that evening.

The spectators waved us through Tour de France style. The police arrived down. Two police cars blocked by the crowd sitting up on their bonnets as the cops tried to nudge their way through them. The guys all laughing at the crazy foreigners. Laughing their asses off and saving our asses. I shouted "Merci". Most of them did exaggerated bows. Some of them saluted Legolas style. I gave them the victory sign and somewhat ridiculously shouted,

"Allez le Bleu."

In my defence it had turned out to be a hell of a day. Our saviours roared it back, still jostling with the police cars to buy us more time.

The streets were still mostly empty so we could hear the two cars behind us with the sirens. I suggested we head up and round to the Sacré-Cœur, for the laugh. Then down the steps for the drama.

She liked the idea, neither of us wearing helmets. So I was easily heard. The elation was now double bombing us all the way through each junction, we corkscrewed up the hill. The cobblestones amped everything, Naya had to slow down a little to allow for how annoying and precarious they were. The sirens seemed everywhere. We lost them way too quick, but they were at a disadvantage in the car. Unlike in the movies they were unable to go down the steps around Sacre Couer. The bike much better, I liked our plan. We needed to get to James' place and get some helmets.

What was I thinking? We just needed some helmets; looting was our credit card. There was a bike shop on the other side of Boulevard Barbés. So that's what we did. I used the crow bar from under the seat of the bike. James had always claimed he needed it for protection. It protected us that day alright. Did well by us.

I nearly broke my hand trying to put in the window. The alarm went off. I laughed for some reason, cackled. I was fucking losing it. I got two helmets; I also robbed the cash out of the drawer, about €55. Mostly change.

There are no degrees of outlaw. Once you are out you might as well stay out.

Chapter 42

Tuesday November 5 2002

When I opened my mind's eye the first thought that squeezed in was Naya. I reached for her but she wasn't there. I sat up then and dragged my sorry ass out of the bed. Feeling sorry for myself had occurred to me. And I thanked my brain for asking for that week off. I had queued everything up for my colleagues and I'd unlikely be missed. I would unlikely be back. I didn't have the heart to tell my boss. We were utterly different but close. I'd never really let her down. This wasn't what she expected. She expected all of us to fail. For some reason this created a very pleasant working environment. We all strove to prove her wrong and she was always delighted when we did. She'd given me the week; I'd cited personal problems. She'd not even realised I had a personal life to have problems with. I think she felt I had confided in her by asking her for the week, the French were sweet like that. They allowed you to have personal problems and personal lives. Good people.

The apartment felt cold and empty. I switched on the heat. Naya hadn't left a note. I was close to blowing the whole thing. I was close but not quite there. Honesty was on my side. The fact I was acting in character provided me with a thin shield against her ending it. Difficult for her to reject me on the grounds of me being the person I said I was.

Reckoned I had a few days. Unless she realised I was ruining her life. Then there would be no coming back.

I switched on the eight o'clock morning news.

Slash, blam, swish, ram, blocks and pyramids spinning through the air colliding and then becoming a word. What was it these people thought about when they designed news openings? Were they all completely deranged?

The broadcast began with the presenter announcing,

"We have an exclusive interview with Le Stonethrower."

Next shot was the six young bandaged martyrs each in a separate square on the screen, reminded me somewhat of a celebrity game show, with each celebrity stacked on top of another. They had taken to calling them French victims of a tragic miscarriage of justice. Well played Madeleine.

After the presenter took us to a shot of Le Stonethrower with the river in the back ground, looking like another Halloween reveller being interviewed. Across the screen came the word Le Stonethrower. They had an excerpt from my interview. The parts where I admitted it was all me, and when I said I was going to turn myself in.

Next up, a shot of a bedraggled police spokesman, refusing to be drawn on whether or not the young lads were going to be released on the back of my confession. He made the salient point that the police do not make decisions based on the media. This was complete blather obviously, but hey, it was that kind of week.

Finally a shot to camera of Madeleine in her cape, river behind her, lights and darkness around her. She announced that her station had a world exclusive interview with Le Stonethrower. I was surprised one of the big fashion houses hadn't wanted to get involved, she looked like a reluctant and beautiful history lesson.

"Proof" she said with relish. She looked way better on the camera than I'd expected. "Proof that this man was the perpetrator of these malicious acts. We have given the proof to the police in order to exonerate these young French men caught up in an international terrorist action." Lashings and lashings of tabloid sauce. The word terrorist had been used more and more as the week had gone on. I thought it was a bit of a stretch myself, in years to come of course every single fucking thing was a terrorist. Everything. Two snails on a path, two mobile terrorist training camps.

I was not complaining. When you dance with the media, they are going to fuck you hard, whether you say yes or not. So there was no point in me acting all coy. I still believed I was unknown at that point, which was when my phone rang.

Peter again. He spoke briefly and with an urgent 'you are going to need to hear this' tone.

"We need to meet. Lunch for two in that Japanese place near Pyramide? Twelve o'clock?"

"Cool. Until then."

After getting off the phone I tried to pull all the strands of my situation together but I was distracted again by the news. They were only showing pieces of the interview. The overall report was relatively thorough for a national media outlet. They were mainly trailing the full interview, which they planned to show on the lunchtime show. The station needed to get their sponsors organised and bidding, the country drooling for some action.

In light of what was to come it is difficult to understand how the Le Stonethrower story could have usurped the Bush story, but that is exactly what it did. Bush's planned speech was not expected to amount to much. Maybe a couple of trade sanctions here and there, but as that would hurt business it was not expected to be that big a deal. Perhaps an expelled ambassador, tit for tat type thing. Nobody saw it coming and the Stonethrower story, so important that morning, was soon to be blown out of the sky.

I knew none of this, nor did I suspect it. I was under the impression that the levers of French State power were all being pulled to capture me.

'What did Peter want?' This returned me to my thoughts. There was something I could not gather going on beyond me, running ahead of me. As I rounded each bend it always remained the same distance ahead, just out of reach and comprehension. There was no reason for us to have to meet unless something had broken. Or worse something had been connected. There was nothing to connect, I thought. Unless it was not a connection to us.

I could not see through the swirl around me with any clarity that day. I was struggling.

I made it down to the Japanese place reassuring myself constantly there was no one following me.

Peter arrived in looking quite dapper and a little drawn. I was wearing a suit as well, so as not to arouse any suspicion.

We ordered a soup each and a decent amount of dumpling like things. Couple of Asahi's, no bother. We both settled back.

"I saw the show this morning."

"Well?"

"I am with James on this, he's furious. I'm not delighted. I understand your maniacal desire to be in charge of all of us and to look after all of us like children. But this is maybe a bridge too far."

"Jesus fuck lads give it a rest. Think of it like this: I believe I'll be punished no more and no less than I would be if all three of us were to come forward. Then the three of us would be going to prison for exactly the same amount of time as I will be? Non?"

"Not sure about that one Geronimo. But you're right, I am not going to stand in your way. It may not make a difference though. The Agents were in again yesterday. Declan spoke to them again. This time the weight of the secret was too much so he blabbed."

Our food arrived. I took a swig of beer, burnt my tongue with my soup and then scalded my throat with a dumpling. I needed the distractions.

"Well come on mother fucker, spill it, blab, dit me?" Suddenly and really, really slowly a new front was about to open up.

"Someone recognised Dean that day we practiced at the squat. They didn't say anything at the time. But they've come forward since. The agents reckon he is still in the country. They're actively looking for him as the main man in this."

"Did the witness say how many of us there were that day?"

"That is not clear. If they saw all of us that's going to weaken your whole only one man shtick. Declan thought they had reports of one man throwing the stones and they think that one person is Dean. They seem to be suggesting he's the head of a cell of some description, perhaps an American CIA cell? Fucking bullshit. I am guessing now, but

I would say that the RGs involvement means they think this is a form of espionage or some such. That could destroy your plan."

"You think? Yeah it will weaken it, but not destroy it. Dean's definitely out of the country. Right? Right? So they can't say it was him. Why have they not caught up with him yet?"

"Apparently they're out in the middle of Canadian nowhere, not in cell coverage. Declan got the impression they'd contacted the Canadian authorities and expected some confirmation today. But, as of last night, Dean was their main suspect."

"You know I went to visit Dean before he left. He knows what to say. He knows to blame me."

"Exactly."

I began to realise this was what this meeting was about. I was about to be exposed as per my orders but not the way I wanted. Just when I thought I was going to move to a cozy TV and duvet life. The real truth was, as the morning had worn on and thoughts of Naya had come into my head, I'd been thinking more and more of not coming forward. I had exonerated the young lads, maybe I should just wait and see?

"Not good. So they may be on to me already?"

"Yeah, you told Dean to finger you so he will. Are you still thinking about handing yourself in later today?"

"About that, I was having second thoughts."

"Naya provoked second thoughts?"

"Yeah, not sure she'll hang around for me. She's not very impressed with me handing myself in on my own. No doubt I'd have to spend some time in prison, right?"

"Absolutely. You need to start thinking clearly. They could be at your place now. Declan said they are looking at myself, you and James as well. But both of us have alibis worked out as you suggested. They'll not look for a negative alibi from you, proving that you were not there for the crime you are admitting. That plays in your favour. They'll believe you were there. They'll believe that you made the throws. Will they believe you acted alone?"

I ignored that last comment and ploughed on.

"What should we say about the squat practice session? Why were there three of us practicing throwing stones?"

"Boredom and booze. They're our best assets here, plus ça change. Plus the fact that out of the six throws, your alibis are only flimsy on two. Any idea who might have reported us? Someone in the squat? Someone Naya knows, someone asking questions?"

"Good point, I will ask her. I don't buy it though. Someone recognising Dean, nah. Sorry they are going to have to do better than that."

Then I saw the second thing that Peter wanted to talk to me about, Naya. Whether or not it was possible Naya could have come forward, in some misdirected loyalty to me, to spread the blame.

I asked, "Do you think she had something to do with this?"

"Well you know her better than any of us. Really I don't know her at all. But there is a glitch in the Matrix somewhere here. I can't see it yet. But I sense something is amiss."

"Alright. Fuck this. You, James and I are one rock, no cracks. At the moment I would die for Naya. Unless she's a fucking genius Mossad sleeper agent, with the most incredible back story, then I think we are safe. And I suppose I should say this too, if she is a fucking genius Mossad sleeper agent then I'm in love with a Mossad agent and I ain't leaving her. You're right though. There is something going on here. They don't get what it is we did. They think it's something different. I cannot see clearly what though, not yet. It's right around the corner but I cannot see it."

We then concentrated on finishing our meals. Food for thought. Not sure how I felt. I was not angry with Peter, which led me to believe that a part of me thought that there was some truth in the matter. No way, she was not that type of person. She had never tried to meddle, she'd never shown any sneakiness whatsoever. She was a straight down the middle arguer. I liked that about her. Then again I didn't know her that well, or more accurately, that long. She was a girl, so chances are I would never know her that well. She would have those reserves of emotion and feelings and thoughts I would never be able to tap into. But if my life depended on it, which it kind of did, I would back her. I was backing her.

My head was melting. I needed a proper drink. Japanese beer was not going to cut it. Sorry guys.

"I need a drink. I'm pretty sure they didn't follow me down here. I changed trains three times and twice I got off at the last moment instead of riding on. Both times the platform was empty. Let's go somewhere random, if that's possible, somewhere away from where we normally go? You working tonight?"

"I swopped it off. We should avoid your place for the moment."

Chapter 43

Tuesday November 5 2002

So we bought a few throw away phones and headed to a grungy student bar up in the 5th. Peter half knew the owner. There was no one else in it. Not sure it was even open. James was there waiting for us. None of us went to work much that week. It was mid-afternoon when we started in on the boozing proper. I couldn't do much else. The booze allowed me to straighten out the edges and compartmentalise.

Could they find me there? No. I was safe until I re-entered my own life, I had a few ideas about that.

The owner, a formally destitute Irish guy, brought us over some chips, some bread and a bottle of whiskey. He spent the rest of the afternoon not listening to our bullshit and rigging up a television for the Bush speech. Bush was speaking at 1800 French time.

We talked around the stones until the owner went off down into the cellar. The front door was locked so no chance of anyone coming in.

James spoke first, it came out in bursts, first he was hurt badly by what I had done. More than any of us he liked the solidarity of the group and regarded us as his family. His own family in England were a splintered group of pop up parents and vagabond children. They had never been over to see him ever, as far as I could remember. I'd betrayed him much like they had, slowly and very softly, always telling him it was for his own benefit.

"How the fuck have I betrayed you? Like seriously?"

Peter "You've left him, like everybody leaves him."

James went to speak but Peter had spoken for him. He merely confirmed it, "Yeah mate, big time."

I was exasperated, "That's total rubbish, get a grip of yourself, we'd all be going to jail. It wouldn't be like the three of us in one jail cell. You do realise that right?" I said this and then drank a lot of whiskey. I was not mad on the jail idea myself. I was pretty sane on it. I got that James wanted us all to go down together. He was a nutcase. Should have let him go down on his own.

Later, after, I think I understood what it was that James was so furious about. He felt I was leaving. Leaving him and the group. Our friendships had been the best family he had ever been a part of. And besides that afternoon he was never angry about it around me again. And he was right.

Peter reiterated he thought I'd acted selfishly, but was more interested in what was going to happen next. I apologised mildly. I explained this had been a team effort. How I was now regretting acting alone. But not in the way they suspected.

"I have changed my mind. I'm not going to hand myself in. They're going to have to catch me. But I'm still the only one of us who's taking responsibility, even if you are picked up. Please lads, do this for me? When they bring you in for questioning, say you thought nothing of the stone throwing, some drunken fun. Tell them nothing else. You have the alibis right? James, the lawyer's set up to arrive the minute you guys get picked up, oui?"

James took it up. He was slightly placated and that was alright.

"I have retained the services of a lawyer, expensive and supposedly the best. Peter has the number. Other than that, we're all set. What made you change your mind? The police are not going to be very happy, not happy at all."

"Naya provoked me into thinking about it properly. Then I realised all I wanted was to get the guys from outside the embassy off. Contrary to what I thought, I don't want the credit and I do not want the prison time."

"Remember we'll know when Dean is contacted. We gave him that phone. The password is Whiskey Chief. It will be sent to all our phones and then he'll destroy it. If we get that message it means he has given them your name Johnny." James explained.

We were drinking whiskey with ice, lots of ice. Getting ice in a bar in France was an ordeal. Unless you knew the owner or you drank in expat bars. Luckily we did both. Peter's friend had left us with an ice bucket, a bucket of ice. We clinked our way towards the speech. Our own problems now at least more straightforward. Whiskey is the best alcohol delivery device. It never fails to ignite then pacify the jolting arbitrariness of urbanity and existence, or at least that is the kind of thing you think when you're drinking it. The whiskey wrapped around me protecting me from thinking about anything much else. Made me live now for the moment and enjoy it. Yer man, the Irish owner, opened the bar.

Le News began with Bush walking to the podium. The little bar was rammed with poor rich communist students; it was around the corner from the Sorbonne. The bar hushed, the speech was to be broadcast live, followed by the delayed headlines. The news station had subtitles organised. Good job.

Bush looked quite well. A dark suit, I hesitate to say evening wear, but it was the nicest suit I ever saw him in. It was clear from the outset he was nervous, nervous due to the fact he had rehearsed this speech a few times. The style he had chosen for the speech was Southern prosecutor summation speech, with a large dollop of cornpone thrown on top. Mathew McConaughey would have played him with something shoved into his mouth to make him gummier. Bush would have been better off wearing the white suit from the KFC guy.

Bush began with an outline of the facts as we knew them on November 5. In the last four years France had begun a trading relationship with Iraq that went against UN sanctions, yadda yadda yadda. They had been asked and warned many times. Bush said plainly that he felt he had gone out of his way, 'to encourage France to comply with the will of the world'. Nice line.

Bush went on to state that,

"The plight of the Iraqi people was not being served nor aided by France feeding the armies of their oppressor, Saddam Hussein.

France was enabling the Dictator in his addiction to power, corruption, tyranny and genocide." Presumably a nod to Bush's own past.

"Without French trade Saddam would have starved to death long ago, both morally and physically."

'Without American arms he would not have built up such a big appetite in the first place,' was the thought that wound through my head.

"America has committed to ridding the world of Saddam and dealing with his allies; France has become his ally. But more than the trade in normal goods, much more than this, France has provided Saddam with the stick to beat his own people. France has given this rogue gunslinger, this outlaw, more guns and better guns, better planes and better missiles. American soldiers, dying from French made weapons is unacceptable, it is unthinkable, and yet that is what is going to happen. France has provided Saddam with weapons for too long. France needs to understand that it cannot act with impunity. That France too like everyone else could and would be held accountable.

I, the Commander in Chief, have instructed my Air Force to prepare a list of five targets in Paris, the capital of France. Five punishment bombings, which will serve as a reminder to France, a brutal and eternal reminder that they cannot and will not be allowed to ignore the international community any longer. Five punishment bombings, which are to take place five days from now. The people of Paris have five days to evacuate the city. We are prepared to negotiate on the targets. We are not prepared to negotiate on the punishment.

The United States urges the people of France, the French People to insist their government stop supplying Saddam with weapons, with food, with medical supplies and with infrastructure. We advise the French President and his ministers to look long and hard at themselves as the punishment is meted out, to realise they have been infected by the Iraqi regime and have themselves become a rogue state. Never say that you were not warned. Never believe that you were not told. You ignored me and made a mockery of international law.

Do not doubt my will on this. Do not doubt my word. Cease all trade with Saddam immediately and begin the evacuation of Paris. France will learn that the Sheriff comes for everyone and that no one is above the law. Thank you. God bless America."

Chapter 44

Tuesday November 5 2002

Fuck.

The bar went silent, then, went mental. The young students, who scarcely knew how to tie their shoelaces, who barely understood how to make a gin and tonic, were now involved in something that was not a fad. You could sense how much this all meant to them, this opportunity to live, this opportunity to die, or at least to know someone else who died. For without the understanding of the risk of death there is no life. This was their Algiers, their Tet, their Ypres, this was their computer game franchise.

They began to sing the Marseillaise. Embarrassed at first but then energised by the booze and the hitherto buried patriotism. They all reached for their phones at once; there was scarce reception through the thick walls of the fifth arrondissement at the best of times, that night in Paris one was lucky to have got three texts off.

Although we could not hear a word through the crazed singing of the anthem the three of us grinned. This might be the distraction we needed. I watched the TV switch back to the studio, to the aristocratic friend of the President, the news presenter. He was without speech, without movement, he was frozen. Only maybe for twenty seconds, but it was how we all felt. Had Bush really just said he was going to bomb five targets in Paris on Saturday night?

Yes, was the only answer. Someone came onto the screen and handed the presenter a piece of paper. Presumably it said 'wake the fuck up'. He jerked alive and we immediately cut to a montage of the speech, this time in French, cut with images of buildings being bombed in various other cities and countries America had sought to chastise over the years. When we got back to the studio the presenter looked as if someone had given him a slap and a drink.

Meanwhile the students from the bar had poured onto the street. Even though their city was about to be bombed, they still were not going to buy more than one drink. I envied them their buzz. I was right back sober again. The next glasses poured were fist hard, up to the top. The three of us drank to France, to Bush and to the absolute and utter bullshit that went for geopolitics these days.

"Looks like you are no longer Le Top Story Johnny boy," James exclaimed with no small amount of delight.

"Yeah this could be good for us. Evacuation starts tomorrow presumably. A lot would have been going away anyway this weekend, so they'll just make the bridge, faire le pont. Did not see that coming at all."

I went outside where it was like a scene from a pastiche movie about France. Already everybody seemed half drunk. The anthem the predominant sound from all sides. Cars beeped their horns and around me I saw more than a few of those idiotic bandages. I wanted to get Naya. I tried her on the phone. I sent her a couple of texts. I reckoned they would have more chance of getting through. There was really no service down the thick walled lanes of the fifth. I walked around the corner and there was the Panthéon.

The Pantheon housed all the best French people to have ever lived, like Hollywood Boulevard, but better. All the things I'd ever known flew through my head. The vista I was presented with as I walked around the front was the long view into Jardin de Luxembourg, the Tour but most of all was the people, they seemed, I know this is going to sound glib, or trite if you must, but they seemed happy.

Life was back, and right beside it was its brother. Death.

Chapter 45

Tuesday November 5 2002

It began to rain and then lash, then thunder and then more rain. Nature, like the rest of us, had had enough. I was soaked through. I left the lads back in the bar, I needed to find Naya. My phone was acting crazy. I still couldn't get Naya on her phone, it wasn't even ringing. What to do, what to do? I got the Métro up to her area. French gangs of young raptors were everywhere that night. The city and the people were reeling. Reeling round the fountains. I got out and started up her street as the rain stopped. This was a bad idea. She would be implicated. I rang her door bell, there was no answer. It occurred to me the squat would be a better shot. She might be painting in one of the studios under the squat; large dusty spaces, perfect for creation.

God knows she'd enough inspiration she needed to expunge. All that me inside her head, add some Bush and Chirac, coupled with the normal thoughts of a young woman and you would have some painting, some montage. Her style looked gothic only at first glance. Her new paintings were a bit like shallow sand castles on paper. They were 3D and mostly images of what appeared to be some sort of rhythmic imprisonment. The vibrational lines skirted the outside and inside of what were human cities, as if every single person was a city encased inside fences of sound and vibrations.

She'd been working on this theme for a year or so now, was finally making some headway with it. Although I know not of what I speak, I got the impression she was brilliant. I walked to the squat; it was only really around the corner. It was only right where it was supposed to be. I was serene. Paris was booming. Or at least it would be soon.

The squat was lit up and pumping. Musical notes escaped up and out of the windows. I wasn't really known there, which made it the best place I could be. I went around the back, where Naya had mentioned the entrance to the studios was. There was nobody outside. The back of the squat was cool, but not a patch on the front. I stepped down and slowly opened the door. There were a few pretend lunatics living there at that time. Nothing I'd not be able to handle, but a crazy person is dangerous irrespective of where they are from.

I walked along the corridor peering in. Naya was alone at the far end of the second room. She had spread candles out on the ground; the music was light dance, trippy house. She moved with the little skips and beats, allowing the music to activate her puppet strings. I stood in and slowly closed the door behind me. Not sure she had noticed me by then. Not sure she had. I sat on a nice, wooden, pretty table chair in the gloom. All the candles were up the other end of the room. They flickered as the slight gasp of air from the door passed them. I could hear more anthem singing from up above. It went well with the building. I sat and watched her work.

I was guarding her, I suppose; guarding her from escaping, from anyone who wanted to hurt her. It was unlikely anybody was going to hurt her. But that is one of those things. She worked in a strangely beautiful way. Really slowly. Never standing still. Small gentle movements, most too slight to catch without the shadows.

I was able to relax for the first time in years, right at that moment. All the trouble had been caused and there was more to come. At least it had started. At least Bush had kicked it off in style. Fair play to the maniac.

After about an hour, she picked up a candle and walked towards the door. I had assumed she had seen me. But that was not the case. She was oblivious, and from the candle light on her face, also grubbily upset. My tangled web had wrapped around her, cossetting her in cobwebbed threads of failure and disappointment. I was a prick. How I had arrived there, I was not sure. It was not her fault, but she had to have some of the blame, did she? Which part? I blamed myself for around ninety five per cent of it.

I made a slight movement, she looked up at me, slightly wild looking, very alluring. Is it normal to find all the various states of one's girlfriend alluring? Alluringly sad, alluring rage, alluringly bored?

I spoke first. I should have had a lot to say, but I would have more to apologise for soon enough, so there was no point. Do girls even want boys to apologise? Do they believe in it? I am not talking about all girls, I am talking about the girls I like; they always seemed to prefer me to promise not to do it again, then proceed not to. Their faces always scrunched up whenever I said the words "I am sorry" similar to the face a candle makes when you put it out with a wet pinch. So I have not said it in a while.

"Hi Naya."

"How long have you been here? Hi Johnny."

"About an hour. You OK? Where's your phone? I have been trying to call you all night."

"I left it somewhere. I am fed up with the phone, false connections. Better that you come and find me here. Better for me. Are you giving yourself up later?"

"No, I think I've changed my mind. Well you've changed my mind. But there might be a problem with that."

She did not acknowledge the first part of the sentence. She was a veteran of my bullshit at this stage, she merely shrugged, came and sat down in the small pretty wooden table chair beside mine.

"OK, go on." I put my arm around her, and she let me pull her onto my knee.

"Dean the American guy. Well the French RG have been looking for him. Apparently he was seen by someone throwing that first day outside here. We were all seen, but he was recognised. They have been sniffing around the Bug for him, the last week. I think they'll find him today. He is in Canada. We gave him a phone before he went. When he is caught the pressure will be too much for him. It's not fair on him that he should have to bear any of the heat. We told him if he was caught to blame me. So I'm waiting for a text from him with the code word. When I get the text I'll know he's given them my name."

Well she didn't say much then. She just sat on my leg and thought. Or maybe she didn't think, maybe she just sat. There was a lot to take in. She was probably done thinking.

"What made you change your mind? And do not say me. The last time I saw you in the bed, you hadn't changed your mind. When did you change it?"

"I always felt terrible about it. I couldn't let those young lads take the blame."

"The blame or the glory?"

"Either. I wanted both. But I couldn't ignore how it was making me sick. I woke this morning and you weren't there. That's not something I can handle much more of."

"What?"

"You not being there. I am unable to continue without you. Whatever has happened to me? I am weak without you and strong with you. I met Peter and he just made me say it, admit it to myself."

"Admit what?" Jeez she was really dogging it. I might even have seen her slightly smirk but I owed her more than one, and I needed to be careful not to pull the whole thing down around me, any more than I already had anyway.

"Admit that I love you and I cannot survive without you."

"Ha" she said as if she'd caught me out.

"Johnny in love with Naya huh? That is news. Maybe even good news. So what's our plan now?

What genius idea have you come up with, to bring France to its knees?"

I peered over at her, through pretend stalks of grass. "How long have you been down here?"

"Since lunch, I'm starving. Let's go to my place and eat."

"So you've not heard what Bush said?"

"No, help me blow out these candles, tell me as we leave. Was it funny?"

"Well, my beautiful artist, he told the French people that in five days time he is going to bomb five separate targets in Paris as a punishment. He also advises everybody to evacuate Paris, as the Americans are not going to tell us where they're going to bomb."

Naya blew out the last candle on the floor and took my hand as she lit the way with the one in her hand.

She didn't say anything for a brief moment, peering into my eyes to ensure I wasn't talking shit.

"Well Johnny lucky for you, you lucky boy. This is good news for us I think. What do you think?"

"Yeah hopefully it means I'll not be the only thing on the police's mind over the next few days. I'm suddenly starving as well. There's no sign of the text yet so I'm still in the clear. Let's go up to Boutaucaille see what's going on? You up for that?"

"Totally love, totally."

I laughed. We were not clear of it. We were still in the middle of it and that was grand. I could handle all these things as long as I had Naya beside me.

Chapter 46

Tuesday November 5 2002

Wednesday November 6 2002

I should have told her I loved her again, but I didn't, what was the rush? We left the grounds of the squat nearly killing ourselves scaling the wall like absolute eejits. Nice walk out on the streets of Paris with my girl. America was bombing Paris in five days' time. I was wanted for some inane prank. The prank of my life. It was enough to make one go off the deep end. How deep could this famed deep end really be?

Why in the name of god were we going to a restaurant? Well, that's simply what you do in Paris. Paris is restaurants good or bad.

The restaurant was a little pricey; there was a fish tank in there with non-edible fish, always a bad sign one way or the other. Imagine those fishes' lives, having to watch piggy humans munching. Awful. I sat with my back to a tank only to spot there was another one over in the corner. A bigger one. Whatever, fish are cool. I ordered fish. Fuck 'em. I was shivering in my dirty wet clothes for the first minute or two. The place was pretty empty and very dark except for the fish tank light.

We had a lot to talk about. I went through the insanity of the story one more time with Naya and then we had a long argument. I didn't win that argument. Not even close. That was cool though. I really didn't deserve it. In two weeks we'd had the full bullshit gamut, and pretty much all by me. I didn't even really drink so guilty did I feel. Great as that guilt was, it wasn't helping the evening, and she gave me the nod to shake it off. We would hold for the meal at least, being beholden.

Naya had lamb that had grazed near the salty sea, beside the island city Mont St Michel. I liked it alright, but I am from Ireland. We normally know the name of the lamb we are eating, we are so close to the animals we kill.

We went back to her flat and lay on the sofa. Like old people. Hurrah. Of course there was a lot to do, but we didn't do any of it that night. We mostly slept and hugged and had a tiny bit of sex. I was happy, so was Naya I think. Hard to know. She sure felt happy to me. During the night we stayed close to each other. I wondered a couple of times whether she was lying with her eyes open wondering about me. Not sure why I never asked her, hard to countenance my reticence now.

The next morning I stayed put. I reckoned there was a good reason to go back to my flat, to get some clothes and money. I had the beginning of a plan. Nobody was going to like it. There was nothing else I could've done; this was as far as I was thinking. I was stuck behind a plan. I was stuck. I told Naya that I was going to go back to my apartment to get some things. There had been no call from Dean, but I hadn't discounted it. I was aware of it. There was a clock ticking through this whole week. There was of course the clock ticking until the bombing, then there was the strange sense of incremental pressure building, a hissing in the background accompanying everything I did.

"How are you going to go home?" Was the refrain from Naya. She needed to go out. She left me in the bed. I got up and thought about us. I needed to get away from her or else. Or else what? Well I didn't want to draw her into it, that's what I thought. Baffling thing to think, when all the stones had been thrown, and I was after getting up out of her bed. Baffling.

After I wrote her a note trying to explain what I was going to do without actually explaining it, I put on my remarkably dirty clothes. I thought about that. The good from the bad. Dirt from whence we came.

Chapter 47

Wednesday November 6 2002

I walked onto the street, it was fine enough out. There was not much else to be said. I thought about the dirt again and I came up with my plan. I got myself over to my area as quick as I could. The area looked the same, there was nothing funny looking I could see, but the Barbés area of Paris is a busy area, no messing, deliveries coming in from all over the world I went down to the bottom of the street, and then back up to my door. There was really no sign, so I decided to take a chance, it would be worth it. I ran up to my room. There wasn't much to get; passports, bank cards, and some money I had lying around. I packed a ruck sack of clothes and sundries. Next stop was the Gare du Nord, where I left my bag in a locker. I'd put on a pair of long johns under my filthy clothes.

As I came out of the Gare, I saw the bum couple from below my window. They were walking along, mooching off the various people. I said nothing but fell in behind them. Meeting them like this had been the best case scenario. Otherwise I had been prepared to walk around looking for them. When they moved away from the terrace, I approached them and said hello. He looked cartoon confused, bamboozled, she was a little bit better. I told them I'd like to buy them lunch. There was a local discount store nearby and we traipsed ourselves up there. I put on the dirty old anorak I had brought. It'd never been mine, merely left in the apartment gathering dirt. We'd kept it as a joke. Its raucous colours long faded, very much like something I'd have worn when I was a boy, but much much dirtier. My shoes were still a little too good but already I could see people were not really paying any attention to me.

I was carrying all the money I had withdrawn. That made me uneasy. Not that anyone would have guessed. We got some booze, actually we got a lot of booze. Then we went back to my street and settled down. They didn't care for me really, but I was buying the bleach, the beer and the fags, and that was OK. One of the derelict doorways on my street was deeper than the others; there was some old scaffolding around it as well. The building seemed long empty. They sat in one corner of the doorway and I in the other.

I'd been rubbing grime and dust into my face and checking myself in a window before I sat down. I looked good. Good as in not really like me. I tried talking to my two companions, Marie and Donnie, but that was not really a runner. They were happy with lunch, probably do us for the day, but they were not idiots. I was trouble, they could see that I wasn't with them for some altruistic reason, and maybe that was why they let me stay? Mostly they were like two love birds. I can't put it any differently. Theirs was a love lived at speed. They would squabble and squawk, then kiss quite violently, drink long spilly mouthfuls, then cheers, then sleeve wipe. I liked it. I was jealous.

They were helping me. They gave me a hat, understanding I was hiding with them. It was stinking; I put it on. It started to rain and the cold from the old ground came up into us. The three of us had begun with a can of some rank lager from some kip. We got stuck in, started chomping the fags. The rain made everyone on the street go inside. We were half way down Rue Labat just off Barbés, so the Sri Lankan end was on one side of us and the West African end on the other. Everyone went inside for a minute; one minute later they were all back out again, working and hiving. I put my head back and allowed myself to relax

I reckoned I was alright for an hour or two. I needed to see what kind of heat was on me, there was no helpline I could ring. Dean had not been in touch with me which made me more uneasy than anything else. I'd also jettisoned my normal cell, a novel experience, akin to removing an arm.

Rue Labat was stinking dirty and the rain made it all into a soup of sorts. The smell of the various nationalities' cuisine was certainly all embracing. Darkness fell early in Paris, and I was about to go somewhere else for the night when I heard something peculiar, and sure enough, the street was suddenly all cops. Cops and whatever else had come to enjoy the show. RG presumably. We were about five doors up, so maybe around fifteen, twenty metres.

I lay back against the cold door and opened what was labelled as whiskey, but was more like turpentine; I still managed a decent slug of it. The whiskey was a rotgut stomach warmer and I felt good. The cops sort of glanced at us, but with the weather and my friend's ass showing, there was no real reason for them to pay us any mind. Bonnie and Clyde were well oiled by this stage. They were either wrestling or making out; it was difficult to tell. But they served their purpose, enabling me to watch what was going on. No cop wanted to deal with two drink sick lovers.

The rain eased off and there was a lull in the number of police going up and down to my flat. Then as quickly as they all arrived they began to leave. Sorry looking bunch I have to say, no fun. They spent some time pointing at a flat opposite mine and one or two went inside. I was pretty drunk by this stage; it was probably around eight in the evening. I understood that drunkenness was the only way I was going to fall asleep. I also needed to think about getting my sleeping bag. It was in the lock up. Stupid place for it, but I was new to this and hadn't really planned the whole thing well. I was so cold though. I stood up and wavered on my feet allowing the nearest cop to dismiss my relevance quickly. I shuffled off down the street. I was also pretty hungry. I went to a kebab hatch and ordered the dirtiest one I could see. They invited me to sit in rather than take it away in the rain, I accepted their kindness.

Soaking wet by this stage, I munched my frites and meat. The kebab shops on that side of the street mostly say Turk and on the other they say Grec. The kebabs are, far as I can gather, exactly the same. The sauces may be different but I doubt it.

I finished and trekked down to the station and pulled out my sleeping bag. I realise that my actions seem stupid and maybe they were. But where else could I have gone? They were looking for me now, which meant, far as I could deduce, I couldn't go anywhere I had been before, and nowhere they could send a picture of me. With those thoughts in my head, I smeared some more food onto my clothes, and went back to my street, with my state of the art, totally out of place sleeping bag.

The two love birds were fast asleep. I squeezed in beside them. The smell was equivocal. The sleeping bag was a hangover from another time. I had a black bag as an outer layer to take away from the brightness. The wet also did its parts.

I lay back and let nothing come to me. I had two really decent belts of the rotgut and then I was off, cold stone encased sleep. The odd cop came and went, alternating between which side of the street they visited. Presumably they were watching my apartment; they were going to leave it as bait. Smart. Not genius, but smart.

Chapter 48

Thursday November 7 2002

The next morning began early. The previous day television and radio had mostly been explaining the evacuation procedure to everybody. A lot of people had reportedly taken the rest of the week off and gone down to the family home somewhere else in France. Paris was already half empty. Hospitals had been making arrangements to transfer non-criticals to outside the Périphérique. The Yanks had given assurances that hospitals were out of bounds. But then they were not exactly dead eye dicks. They often seemed to miss. They had a propensity for hitting orphanages, weddings and other soft targets. So nobody was taking any of their assurances as gospel. Bush himself was in charge of the country. So again, not comforting.

The sirens and the loudspeakers warned people they had twenty four more hours to get their things together. The whole thing was still new, so people came out onto the streets and shouted at the cars, vans and trucks broadcasting the instructions. I am not sure if they were shouting at the vehicles in anger or support. There were no real anthem singers up this side of town. The other two were still asleep, or passed out, or whatever it was they were. Having woken I realised I was stinking, I had a whiskey straightener. Strange, it put things into perspective. Whiskey perspective, which is not the same as the other type. I grappled up the wall to a standing position. Marie opened her gruesome eyes and squinted at me. I gave her a few squid for the day and told her I might be back, or I might not.

"Bon courage," this was something people often said to you when you were going to work. I gave her a half kiss. She cackled and lay back down.

It was probably seven. The Métro was a nice experience for once as people did not want to sit beside me. I really missed having a book, but books would have snagged the visual prairie and someone might have noticed.

Where was I going? I wanted to go over to Naya's to see what was going on over there. She would be worried about me. They all would; currently there was no way for them to reach me.

It was the only plan I could think of, is what I kept telling myself. I positioned myself across the street, under a tree, in a walled corner, with a good diagonal view of the entrance to Naya's apartment block. Things were more pleasant in this part of town; the 13th a safer and a cleaner quartier than the 18th. This was what I wanted. I still had my bottle of whiskey so I took a few snorts and lay back. The way the wall and the tree were positioned made it a really secluded place to pretend to be homeless. The whiskey lionised me, made me feel famous; I was in a slight nauseous torpor for a while. There was nothing doing in this area. I was near a park. I could hear the kids squawking and squealing, bird-like in their short speedy dramas. As the morning went on more cars packed for holidays appeared outside apartment blocks, children were loaded in, parents got in looking slightly relieved, but still dreading the pretend happy long car journey.

I could hear the now clarion call of the speakers warning people to start leaving the city. One of the cars drove past me once, Le Spectacle American d'Horreur Militaire, The Americans Bombing Paris was their punchline. Saturday. It was like a revival. Please leave your homes. But why not? It was also an excuse to have a holiday of sorts? Most people in France had someone to go and visit.

The old? Well a lot of them had died the summer before in the heat wave, the rest hid out nonchalantly. The poor, well they'd have to make do themselves. There were some giant tents set up outside the Périphérique and they were made welcome there, as long as they had their papers of course. This was not a great result for the sans papier, the homeless or anyone on the run. The loud speakers announced that anyone without a pass on Friday would be arrested. A fucking pass? Incroyable! How did they get a special pass organised so quickly? Never doubt the French bureaucracy. They are no joke.

I kind of dozed. I dozed and drank. I wasn't having the worst time of my life. I'd removed myself momentarily from everything. I stood at the side, watching without being watched. It was consoling in a way. I ached for Naya. But for her to know anything about me was not a good idea. The most important thing I knew to do whilst homeless was to slow everything down, not to multi-task. There is too much time in the day that needs to be wasted. Each drink was a savoured performance. Cigarettes cupped like at the front, sheltered from the wind and prolonged to the very limit, eventually you were just sucking the warm bitter spit out of the butt.

I was toying with going down to the squat when I saw Naya come out of her building. I could see her pretty well. She strolled out onto the street looking perfect. The sunlight played once on the window of the door flashing behind her. She unlocked her bike. I had to grip my drink-loosened tongue to prevent myself from calling out to her. Reckon she felt me, or someone else, observing her. Would they be onto her yet? I wondered. That would be impressive. The lads only know her first name. Surely to god the cops were busy enough as it was. But then again we were not really talking about the police here. 'The RG would have had fuck all else to do.' I mumbled to myself.

She sat on her bike for a minute, did her hair throw thing, which caused the space around her to vibrate, put on the helmet, gunned the engine and sped off past me. At the last minute she looked around but I was back on the ground, hat down, she had no view of my face. Our cerebral shadows had attempted reconciliation. Would be a while yet.

There was not much else for me to do after that, except settle in for the night. I'd not noticed it before, but by late afternoon the streets had become extremely quiet. The only sound was the blind man's crossing signal every now and again. Friday they were scheduled to bring out the thermo heat machines. But that was a joke, really, what did they think was going to happen? How many did they have? Paris had so many pokey streets and so many lanes, layers of buildings feeding into each other. Courtyards into courtyards. Chances were they were going to concentrate on the more prosperous areas. Once they were done there, they would start in on the riff raff.

I did not plan on going far but I did need to eat. Something piping would be necessary. The Chinese area was up around the corner. They'd not love me, but they would take my money surely, if I didn't hang around.

There was a rickety old table outside one restaurant with an ice cream logo on it. Had seen better days, I sat there. The guy came out; I ordered a large soup and some pork and peanut skewers. I paid and ordered a Tsing Tao, Chinese beer, nice and light. All the whiskey drinking had made me parched. The food arrived scalding hot. Jesus fuck, it was exactly what I needed to thaw my bones, heat up my marrow. There was nothing to do but gobble it all down.

My thoughts were simple. Being a wanted man made elusion my only real task. I enjoyed it well enough. After burning the face off myself, I forced the pork down. The beer was quenching and smartened me up. It was tramp bed time and I knew it. Any book I'd ever read about being a tramp always mentioned the boredom. Trying to fill your days with drinking and walking, getting your head kicked in, looking for stuff on the ground, waiting for people to drop things from their pockets, sticking fingers into phone boxes and the fear at night.

I avoided most of those things. Eating and drinking and hiding saved me from it. There was no one around the 13th the nights I slept there, which could have gone either way. The night I slept up by my place there were three of us and that made it OK, or I was lucky.

Walking down the road with my sleeping bag, warm Vietnamese soup in my bones, I felt lucky. Damn lucky. How long could I stay like this? Exigent circumstances. That night in the corner by the tree it lightly drizzled. Naya came back late enough. No one else was about but I decided not to risk any contact. For her sake, I told myself, for her sake; this was probably me lying to myself. What was my motive in lying to myself though? That part had not made itself clear to me. I began to think I should just up and leave. Leave the whole lot of them behind. Then thoughts of Dean came into my head. I sent out a psychic soothe to him.

A dog came sniffing around me and woke me with the dawn. I scooched him over, he lay down beside me, like he had known me all my life. I was not mad for this turn of events but there wasn't much I could do. Fucking dog, what next, a stick? Maybe the universe was telling me the hobo life was my calling.

Naya left early the next morning. Surely she wasn't going to leave Paris like they suggested. That was not her style. I debated going down to the squat but there was nowhere really there to hide besides in the squat itself. I would have been trapped.

I was comfortable where I was. The day rolled out in front of me. I finished the bottle of rotgut. I would need more. The particles detached and bobbed in front of me, time was disintegrating and re-forming. I felt a softening in the air and the gravity weighed heavy upon me. A lot of the blood was just sitting in my veins. The blood in the top half of the veins flowed well enough, underneath it was sludgy mud.

I had seen around three people all day. The dog had gone some time in between the morning and when I got up. I'd kind of untethered my mind. I needed some liquor and maybe some bread. There was a corner store open. I bought some more rotgut; it was the right look, the right price and the right effect. I bought a skanky baguette hard as a truncheon. I bought some wet scummy ham. I bought a bag of flinty crisps. I bought a large can of imperial cats piss lager. I bought Breton full salt butter. I sat on the ground a ways down from the shop and filled the baguette with everything I had bought, using my hands, à la mode.

The sandwich was a world of heart attack but would fortify me. I divided it into three and that was OK. I sat and I ate one third, washing it down with some piss. There were no people about, it was a little Day of the Triffids. I was quite exposed. It was so quiet though; there was no traffic at all. The ground was so very, very cold to sit on all the time, the cold and the hard were co-conspirators. There was a free newspaper stand outside the shop, back up a bit. I sneakily took two newspapers; one to sit on, one to read. Vagrants read old newspapers right?

The first eight pages screamed bloody murder about the Americans bombing Paris. The world had condemned Bush except for the usual lick spittles, Australia, Berlusconi and Poland. This motley crew stood up for the right of the Americans to administer worldwide punishment willy nilly. Poland I understood, they were always getting abuse from both sides, Berlusconi was called Il Buffone even in his own country, so that mitigates somewhat how one views him. But Australia, what the fuck were they doing? Nowadays Australia seems hell bent on becoming some right wing war loving country. Very disappointing.

I read through it, my mind delighted to have once again been called upon to perform some simple tasks. On page nine there was a picture of me, an old picture certainly, a grainy shot of me living the dream somewhere in the west of Ireland. They had my name below the picture, alongside the shot of me masked in the interview. Also below my photo was a pretty shot of Madeleine Delacroix looking very debutante. Which, I suppose, was what she was going for. The headline, "Le Stonethrower", was designed to annoy pretty much anyone. They had some cursory information about my life. It read like the bio of a flim flam man.

I was wanted; there was a number if anyone had any information. There was no reward. Did the French even do rewards? They were now saying I was a terrorist trying to destabilise the French state, the fifth Republic. A couple of days ago this would have meant something to me. But I was eating my sandwich. I was then going to wander down home. I stored what I had read away for later. There was no point in wasting any of it, there was no point in even wasting the worry or the anxiety, one thing at a time, Zen as a motherfucker.

I wondered how I felt. I ate my sandwich and wondered. I wandered back down to my corner. I had some black bags. Got into the sleeping bag and then I got into the black bags. I settled down with my back against the wall. I wondered again how I felt and what this meant. There was nothing there at all, there was only the cold and the day; the brick of sandwich in my belly. I took some ambitious glugs of whiskey, gagging on each, then I washed it down with a dry smoky smoke. When my brain felt suitably chastised, I once again allowed it to go over my current status.

"Wanted, living on the streets, out of contact, Americans about to bomb Paris. Ho hum." I had begun having full conversations with myself.

"In the plus column, no one knows where I am. I have money. I probably still have a girlfriend, maybe. My sleeping bag is amazingly warm.

So pretty equal there then."

No sign of Naya.

Chapter 49

Saturday November 9 2002

Sleeping rough was definitely wearing a tad thin. I awoke the third morning and I'd had just about enough. My ass and my jocks and my jeans were all one piece. I was gagging for a wash. My mouth felt much like somebody had washed it out with an industrial magnet's runoff. The city now was deathly quiet although the blind man's traffic tune kept on playing. Later on that day the Americans were bombing Paris. I would have to get in off the street for that.

It occurred to me that Naya had not come back during the night, and I had a key for her apartment. I didn't think much about it. I stood up, put the sleeping bag over my left shoulder, pulled off the black bags, leaving them to slide un-poetically to the ground. There was a pleasant drizzle falling. I walked over to the door, entered the code, used the key on the inner door. I was inside in no time. There was no sound whatsoever. I turned on the television very softly. I took off my clothes. I did not have a change, I was not certain the time had come to jettison my bum outfit quite yet. I lay my clothes on the ground like a body and went into the shower, cleaned the filth off me.

I watched the dirt flow around in the bottom of the shower and profundity washed over me. The overall sensation of sleeping rough had deadened and stunned my mind. I was not flitting from one thought to the next, as before. Each thought, like each morsel, was to be savoured and over fingered. I probably stood there for around thirty minutes, slipping in and out of where I was and what I was doing.

I got out and did all the usual, most of the usual. I was not in the humour for everything. Brushing my teeth was, I admit, a pleasure, I was a softie. I put the dirty clothes on the radiator to dry and sat looking out the window, dreaming I was still under my tree watching my friends' lives. I started to cry. I thought about how watching Naya from under that tree was like being dead. Thinking about how my friends would deal with my death often made me weep. So I cried. I thought of my friends' reaction. I thought of my family's reaction, finally I was giving them the opportunity to be real parents. My friends would move on. Paris barely would notice. The media would love it though. A story so easy and sickly poison saccharine they would hardly believe it.

'Young Irish man responsible for spate of stone throwings, found dead under a tree stalking his ex-girlfriend.' Possible shot of Naya looking alluringly stoic and or sad. 'A tragic case of a misguided middle class terrorist, brain washed into thinking that throwing stones at important men was the answer. Johnny Stand the green Taliban. Johnny O' Taliban.'

My mind was going into itself.

The television was wall to wall news as one would expect. There were various reporters stationed around Paris. Madeleine Delacroix was being driven around the city in a jeep, à la military, à la Liberation. She was wearing a red and blue scarf with a hint of gold. It fluttered in the wind, emphasising the difficulty and danger she was facing on behalf of the people of France. Everywhere she went it looked as if she had just liberated it. The scarf was a master stroke.

Madeleine had obviously been promoted after our interview. Interestingly, I was still mentioned every half an hour. I sat with my feet up, sipping mint tea, smoking; the TV a small Parisian thing over to my left; the balcony doors open in front allowing me to see the empty sky I needed so much.

The news explained that many targets had been taken off the table although they only mentioned the Tour and Euro Disney, the yin and the yang. The Americans, as usual, refused to divulge anything else. They did not want the terrorists to know what they were doing, or some such horse shit. Osama had begun to make the Americans act like terrorists, but they couldn't see that yet, nor could anyone else. Although thinking about it now, was Iraq as bad as Vietnam? They killed millions in Cambodia and Laos even though they weren't even warring with them. But then Superpowers be Superpowers. I suppose I prefer the Yanks on balance to a Russian led world, it was just they still really sucked. They loved killing. They loved it so much, most of the time expending ordinance seemed to be the be all and end all of everything.

The television shots of an empty Paris were kind of slick and very post-apocalyptic. The first bombing was due after four, is all we'd been told. The French had fighters in the skies above the city, but no one was clear what they were going to do when they saw the Yankee bombers. The ground defences were also reportedly mobilised, although I didn't really believe a single thing we were being told. The planes had been granted permission by Camemblair, as the French so winningly called him, to take off from his front lawn or some such cloying generosity.

Blair had made another speech yesterday, they replayed it. It may have been the worst thing I ever heard. Blair spoke about politics so disingenuously I struggle to find something to compare it with. The Germans were also involved in negotiations; Schroder had interrupted his job interviews with Gazprom, or as he called it, his "domestic energy policy", in order to try to convince the Americans it wasn't worth it. He wanted them to 'step away from the weapon.'

I dozed off around noon, lazing beautifully through my psych for a couple of hours. When I woke I put on my costume and checked my appearance in the mirror. I looked like a guy dressed up as a tramp. The clean face did not suit the overall look but my clothes were dry, warm and fetid.

I rummaged through my things, came upon a little clarity and found my contact Dean phone. Sure enough the message was on it. Not sure how I had missed that. I'd had so little to do over the last few days. I had checked at some stage on time's river. When exactly? A blurred chronological memory, one long dragged watercolour? Not that it made a difference after the newspaper.

My head was waking up from the granite slumber of the past few days. Suddenness and immediateness had been my enemy before. The message had yesterday as the date. What did that mean? Hard to focus down on where I was and what all those things meant to me. I already knew I was known, didn't I? They had got me without Dean, hadn't they?

Whatever about any of it, my life as I knew it was over. No more. That was definitely the plus side. I could also still hand myself in, although I felt that was a bad idea. I knew the lads' numbers. I didn't have Naya's number anymore. That was a mistake. A stupid fucking mistake.

It was coming up on three o'clock, only an hour or so before the surrealism was to kick off in earnest. I sat back down and watched the sky.

Chapter 50

Saturday November 9 2002

Naya and I were down the road from Pigalle watching hundreds of sirens, most not sounding off, just flashing. There was a low level smoke pervading and inveigling itself into the little cracks and pores and slits that exist in everything. The trees along the boulevard seemed peeved, unsurprising as they had witnessed another day when humans had outdone themselves. Every now and again they would give an impatient gruff rustle.

I kind of, sort of, if you really want to know, drifted off. May have been five minutes, may have been longer. I woke with my head lolling on Naya's right shoulder, drool beginning to appear. Where were we going to go now? Who knows? It was around seven o clock on the ninth of November. Could we go to her house? Probably not.

Surprising, after all this time, they'd never put anyone on Naya's apartment. Maybe they still hadn't got her name. With the squat gone there would be nowhere obvious they could look, but then there were hardly that many Naya's floating around, were there? They surely would find her through the school, although she'd said nobody had the apartment address.

The night felt warm, around about body temperature, and emotional. Naya brought us down to the banks of the Seine opposite the burning library. She parked and locked the bike. We put our coats on the ground. We sat there with our backs to the old wall, watching the four books of the Bibliothèque burn. In front of us was first the Seine, then some boats, a road and then began the steps up to the library. Naya sat between my legs with her back leaning against me. Bar sex, it is impossible to be closer to someone. She seemed oblivious to the odour.

The flames had mostly gone now but the buildings smouldered on. Hundreds of Pompiers milled around, exhausted helicopters brought cauldron after cauldron of water from the Seine to spill languorously down into the atrium of the fire. Below the buildings an excavated square, where all four blocks met together underground. The fire was doing the most damage underground where they had trouble reaching it. The Pompiers were finding it very difficult to get at the underground level. The fire system for the library, which involved pumping water from the Seine, had failed after an hour. They'd obviously not taken into consideration the idea of the Library being bombed. Might let them slide on that one. Although we were constantly being told that the laziest terrorist organisation in the world, Al Qaida, was everywhere. So maybe they should have paid a little bit more attention to the finer details of emergency protocol. Protocol feels good to write. Feels important.

James and Peter arrived down. When I saw them I leapt to my feet and bounded over to hug them. They were happy to see me too and we stood in a blustering circle for a while, waiting for Naya to come over. We then did the group hug thing so beloved of people in those days before we began to repulse each other again.

We sat down facing the fire show, Naya back between my legs. We lay with our backs to the wall, watching the books burn. It was by far the most incredible thing I had ever witnessed in my life. More and more people were coming out of the 'burbs and the catacombs to line the Seine. Anti-American sentiment was running at a higher level than usual. There were dubious effigies being burned.

"Just because you write Bush on a childhood doll does not make it a Bush effigy." I half shouted to no one in particular. Naya turned and kissed me quickly to shut me up, but said nothing, a face full of knowing as only women can pull off. Really soft eyes drawing me in, knowing me.

France had expelled the whole of the American embassy, much to the chagrin of the Yankees. Precious bullies. France had also signed a treaty with Germany in the last few hours, to prevent anything like this happening again. Hindsight geniuses. Nothing ever happens again. Especially war. There is always some kink or other that throws us off. Peter had brought us all sandwiches of rillette and pickle, some crisps and a few beers. He'd also brought me a change of clothes. The surrounding crowd cheered as I went starkers to rid myself of the vagrant disguise. So we sat there like happy fools, munching and scrunching. There was not much to say beyond what was the most important thing.

I had to leave Paris. Ireland somewhat beckoned. Beckoned me to what though? Going back to the ephemeral hue of home. If I was bringing Naya back to Ireland, it would not be for a while. Besides the fact I'd been identified as Irish, the rain alone would kill her.

Ireland was loaded at that time. They say money magnifies character and so it was with Ireland. Our corruption, our laziness, our paedophilia, our poor craftsmanship all worsened by the laser gaze of money. House prices in Ireland were higher than Paris or London or New York. We were later told that this was a bubble. Who blew that bubble? Apparently we did. Little did we know all we had to do was point out that it was a bubble, and hey presto everything would have been OK.

Poor people, will they ever learn?

The full late arrival of velvety darkness helped everyone start to speak again. Up until then, we had mostly been sitting in complete silence. I felt mild elation tonguing its way into my thoughts

Every now and again Naya or I would turn to put a hand on the shoulder of the other. The library burning was so beautiful, so meaningful what with all the French books. But then, does stuff really matter, material things? Symbolic though it all was, there was nothing in there that could not be replaced. Except people. Transpired there'd been twenty people killed. Mostly people with glasses who'd stayed behind to man and woman the library, which needed constant attention. Sightseers started letting off fireworks further up from us. The throng was heaving at this stage.

"Alright gang? Thoughts?"

James went first, he seemed ready to explode. But, before he could get going, along came Dean. I was shocked, James too; Naya had never met him before, so she was neither here nor there on the whole thing. Peter got up and went over and spoke to him; shepherded him into the group. James stood and shook his hand kind of pretend hugging him. I did the same, introduced Naya and then asked him,

"Were you followed?"

Dean "Hello to you too asshole. Don't start all that who dares wins crap with me. I am not in the mood. I spent the last three nights in a cell being questioned on Le Stonethrower. So don't fucking push it."

James "Yeah nightmare, our hearts bleed for you. Boo fucking hoo. Tell us what happened?"

The butting was beginning to grate and Naya turned to me, told me through some secret signal I'd never known existed, told me I needed to intervene.

"Everybody sit back down. Sorry Dean, nerves a tad raw, welcome mate. We've a lot to talk about and not a lot of time. Is Geneviève OK? Was she lifted as well?"

He sat and said "Thanks. Yeah, I will have a beer. Anyone got a choke? Thanks Pete."

And on he went,

"OK so we were coming out of the Yukon, after a brilliant week there off the grid, we were taken, by what seemed to be some intelligence agency. We were driven, without our bags, to an undisclosed location, where we were questioned by both Canadian and French agents. Geneviève is at home now. They weren't that interested in her. That does not mean we won't be getting a divorce though." I wouldn't say he looked sad, resigned perhaps. He continued,

"Anyway, they'd a witness statement from someone, or some people, who'd seen me throwing stones with three other guys on Saturday October 5 2002. They said that date to me a thousand times. They loved this witness because they never backed away from the statement. I remained calm, like these were the Canadians and the French right? Well wrong; me being an American certainly didn't help. They asked me was I working for the Americans. This line appeared at the end of the second day. Are you working for the Americans? I thought they had lost their minds."

We all laughed, although I felt more like screaming. The group budged in closer to itself. We felt more encircled with comrades' love when we realised he'd undergone an ordeal of his own.

"They thought I'd been sent by the Americans to foment trouble and undermine confidence, a Yankee insurgent. The French agent guy looked like a burly pen salesman, someone who'd played way too much rugby when he was young. He claimed to be called Henri. Naturally I didn't believe him. They left me alone once with him and he sort of pretended to rough me up, nothing too heavy, more to see if I would give them anything else."

Naya looked at me and I asked Dean,

"Yeah Dean, what do you mean, how bad?"

"Well what I mean is he gave me a few vicious slaps around the head. He got very intimidating, threatened to not let me back into France, followed by threatening to ruin Geneviève and her whole family."

"Jesus Christ I never saw that angle coming. The one where they thought we were an American terrorist cell. Wow." Peter said it, we all thought it.

I glanced at James who was half man, half scowl.

"If we'd made a statement to the press then this could have been avoided," was all that had been going through his head.

"I know, I know, there is more. I was crying by this stage trying to get them to leave Geneviève out of it. The French guy was a total asshole. I wanted to kill him. Then I gave them your name Johnny, I'm sorry, but I couldn't hold out any longer. As soon as they'd the name, they put us both on a small plane, flew us back to Paris in the same clothes they'd picked us up in. On the flight back there was no food, and obviously no movies. We were in a military plane, I'd say. We didn't talk though, myself and Geneviève, it didn't seem that easy for me to talk to her. Although when I think about it now, I can't understand why not? I wanted to talk to her, but I was frozen. I was afraid of the scene. I was afraid they were listening to us, watching us. She cried most of the way home. I wasn't allowed to touch her; I am not sure she would have let me anyway."

I felt chagrin, "Seriously this is a load of bollix. So they think or thought you're a member of a US backed terrorist stroke anarchist organisation instigating trouble in France in preparation for the bombing? Is that about the size of it?"

There was a ripple of quite small explosions from the Library; it was still omitting a lot of smoke. My question lingered in the smoke, lazily sliding through it, like a lithe fat snake.

Dean looked fucked. We all did. The two lads didn't look or feel great either. Naya looked fine, she couldn't have looked better. Each time I saw her was the best time I ever saw her.

Dean roused himself, he'd been staring at the library as if he just noticed it. He had. We all looked anew through his eyes. Dean needed the distraction.

"Guys I was only gone a couple of weeks, next thing I know they are burning books and blowing up strip clubs. I've to say that whatever faith I ever had in any kind of state organised anything has crumbled to nothing. Americans bombing Paris? There's a nationwide manhunt for my oldest Irish friend, Johnny, who stands accused of being a foreign operative, maybe? Long story short they think you are a foreign operative. That's not good. Can you get the death penalty for that?"

Naya spoke up for the first time. We all looked at her. Hoping she was giving us something that we could attach ourselves to.

"I looked into the death penalty. France is absolutely against the death penalty, has signed and ratified various international treaties accordingly."

"Sounds like a quote?" I asked. She smiled and squeezed my leg and said

"I was worried."

I sensed relief from the group but they didn't know Naya as well as I did. She liked to divide news into good and bad.

"However there is an 'in time of war or imminent threat of war' stipulation that the death penalty could be used to punish a capital crime."

James "There is no capital crime to be punished is there?"

Peter "Not that we know of, no, not that we know of. There was something being mooted earlier that a police officer had been seriously injured in a chase, although to link that would be tenuous. You are a foreigner and there is going to be bedlam over this. Naya may have a point. Would be nice for them to use you as an example. Strange how your enemy lures you into acting like them? Al Qaida, France, America, all mimicking each other round and round."

James laughed and said in as sardonic a voice as has ever been mustered or muttered "So we might all be getting the death penalty. This whole thing has left me unbelievably unsatisfied, where the fuck is my pound of flesh? I thought I'd be eating it by now with shallots. Bollix." With that he stood, thought about his life, where he was, who he was with, where he would go, and sat down again.

Chapter 51

Saturday November 9 2002

"I need to get out of here now." It was really time for me to go.

"Thanks guys for everything. Fucking sorry things did not work out the way we wanted, we ended up being an American terrorist cell who only threw stones. Pathetic in a way. But I would not change any of it. Dean sorry to hear about your marriage, but let's be honest, there is nothing you could have done. Well besides avoid getting her arrested by secret agents, questioned in two different countries. Besides that. There is nothing else you could have done." I gave him what we both needed. The hug of a lifetime. He said nothing, just stared at the buildings.

"Remember what we all discussed, tell the truth we agreed on, do not be tricked by them into admitting their truth. No deviating from this. Remember we have our own truth for the rest of our lives."

I turned to James who was wearing a tank top ensemble and rocking it to the break of dawn, "James you are a legend mate. You have saved me and we have become brothers." I gave him the kiss and the hug I wanted. I used force of hug to try and give him a cracked rib to remember me by.

"Peter you too. Shit this is awful. Until we next see each other. Let me contact you guys first. Peace and love." Peter grabbed me and lifted me and then Naya.

"Naya you staying or coming? Your choice?"

The smoke was still billowing across the Seine, wafting towards us. There was a party atmosphere developing.

"Don't start that shit again. I am coming." Naya remained where she said she would be. Alongside me. She'd never budged.

It was a scene I would play over in my head for a long time, but we needed to get moving.

"I need to get to the Gare to get my stuff. Now would be the best time," I said to her, as we embarked on our life's holiday.

We had the bike. What were we going to do? Go to Spain? Might be the best idea, seeing as there was nothing doing in Paris. She had some family there. The French and Spanish were not on great speaking terms. Not sure why that was, but the Spanish hated the French; they had done something to them perhaps, or they thought they were arrogant? They were not wrong. The French in turn thought Spain a place over run with English, and that the Spanish themselves were half-African; much like the Italians think of the Sicilians.

The streets were pretty full with people despite the smoke and ruin. Paris had taken worse before and survived, so generally people seemed happy, celebratory maybe. I was on the back and as we pulled out onto the street properly, coming around a corner, onto what should have been a busy street, we saw what had been shielded from us by the high wall, we saw them everywhere.

Police.

Chapter 52

Saturday November 5 2007

They told me later after the operations, after the blackness, and once I had stopped screaming, that I had killed her. Thanks, tell me something I don't know.

I remember flying through the air, kind of. I definitely remember the prolonged soft grinding thud of what later transpired to be Naya's chest crushing under me as my body and hers impacted the wall. A perfect violent moment.

One of her brothers came to see me here some years ago, maybe two. I shook his hand. He cried. Since the accident I have something wrong with me, something which means I cannot cry. It is a relief. Her brother knew things about me. Naya had written to him telling him about me, telling him strange things I had forgotten, like how I used to like to make dinner really quickly, how I didn't like her drinking coffee in bars. I only knew her the guts of a month; I don't really understand it. I live mostly in the past now, mostly as in always. Now is nothing anymore, they need to wake me when they want me to deal with now. Luckily there is rarely much to deal with.

I told her brother that I was so very sorry. So sorry I had killed his sister and the love of my life. He accepted my apology, I think; he was very upset. I gather I am upsetting to look at now. That is OK though, I deserve it. I am writing this one handed, although who writes two handed? My other hand is gone, along with my arm up to my elbow, I don't remember them being taken. I miss them quite a lot. Not as much as I miss her though. They had followed Dean, or he had brought them; I have never been able to ask him as nobody has ever seen him since. They watched us, waiting, wanting to see who else would arrive. They arrested James and Peter but they were made release them by James's lawyer. They had no proof. They convicted me using the interview on the bridge overlooking the Seine in absentia.

I find it difficult to see James and Peter looking at me, so I've asked them both to stop visiting. They sometimes write. James is in London, he left soon after it happened. I was still in the darkness. Peter is married; they cannot have children, I am not sure why that means something to me but it does. He is not really Peter now, he is new. I sit in my room, alone and watched. It is hard to know if I am in jail or in hospital. Both probably. The last thing I remember after she gunned the engine, after we sped towards the bridge, before the wheel slid from under the bike, after the first shot, is my arms holding Naya around the waist and squeezing her to let her know. She knew I think. She knew.

The End

I hope you liked the book. If you did please take the time and leave me a review at your favourite retailer. Thanks for reading it.

Acknowledgments and Thanks

I did not write this book on my own goes the familiar refrain, no less true though, no less true. I would like to thank my parents who introduced me to reading. They have thrown me books and love my whole life. My sister Amy for being my No.1 reader and biggest supporter. My brother James for being my biggest fan despite having never read anything I've ever written. My brother in law Robert for cutting me some slack here and there. My friends in Ireland Stephen, Michael, Philip, Roisín and Béibhinn who all read my book when they said they would. Thanks to Claire Giles for all the patience and the cover art. To Atribord for giving me a job in Paris. Finally thanks to the Bug and all the lads, who, despite what anybody may think, are not actually in ABP save as inspiration.

We did live like Musketeers on leave for a few years, we really did. Alex, Martin, Tim, Matt, Ollie and Andy B, thank you all, cheers.

PS. Thanks to Roc and Cassie.

About the Author:

My name is Thomas Bartlett, this is my first novel. I am also a published ghost writer. I was born in Belfast and grew up in Galway. I lived in Paris for four years and Spain for two. Now I live in Dublin. I have been a teacher and a restaurant manager, a waiter and a cook. I have finally alighted on what I was always going to be, a writer. Thanks again for reading the book.

Peace

Thomas

Website: http://thomasbartlettbooks.com/

Twitter: @TomAlicante

Facebook: https://www.facebook.com/tom.alicante

Coming Soon by Thomas Bartlett

Broken Wing

and

All Girl Army

50508969R10160

Made in the USA
Charleston, SC
30 December 2015